PRAISE FOR

THE ABLE ARCHERS

"Occasionally, a work of fiction is best suited to bring little-known but dangerous historical events to life. In the fall of 1983, Soviet leaders apparently became deeply worried that the US was preparing to launch a surprise nuclear attack on the USSR under the cover of a NATO exercise titled 'Able Archer.' Brian Morra's novel *The Able Archers* builds a tension-packed story around those events and paints a cast of heroic figures on both sides who prevent a global catastrophe. While a gripping work of fiction, *The Able Archers* is also a powerful reminder of the value of human judgment—and the continuing peril posed by nuclear-armed powers."

—ROBERT M. GATES (CIA Deputy Director for Intelligence 1982–1986, Director of Central Intelligence 1991–1993, and Secretary of Defense 2006–2011)

"Brian Morra's historical thriller is a fast-paced ride through one of the worst crisis periods of the Cold War. Replete with colorful American and Russian characters, *The Able Archers* is a terrifying yet factual story of how a few people prevented a global nuclear war. It's frighteningly relevant to today's fraught geopolitical scene—one of the must-read novels of 2022!"

—JACK CARR, Former Navy SEAL Sniper, #1 *New York Times* Best-selling Author of *In the Blood*

"A seamless blend of carefully researched history and a fascinating cast of both real and fictional characters create a vivid portrait of the most dangerous days in the Cold War and indeed in human history! In the fall of 1983, the world almost stumbled into Armageddon, and the lessons reverberate into the present tensions between the US, China, and Russia. A brilliant thriller full of practical lessons for policy-makers!"

—ADMIRAL JAMES STAVRIDIS, 16th Supreme Allied Commander at NATO, 12th Dean of the Fletcher School of Law and Diplomacy at Tufts University, and Co-Author of *2034*

"*The Able Archers* is a truly gripping account of one of the most dangerous episodes of the Cold War. Brian Morra's fiction is deeply embedded in historical fact and reveals how near to the brink the Cold War adversaries really came in November 1983."

—TAYLOR DOWNING, Historian, Author of *1983: Reagan, Andropov and a World on the Brink*

"Brilliant and riveting combination of action and suspense, written by one who captures so many details it's easy to imagine the writer might have participated in a similar series of events years ago. Brian Morra's spellbinding tale grips the reader from page one through the twists and turns of spy craft and kinetic military activity to a surprising and satisfying conclusion. First-rate work by a skillful author."

—ADMIRAL TIMOTHY J. KEATING, United States Navy (Retired), Former Commander of Pacific Command and Northern Command

"The publication of *The Able Archers* is exceptionally timely as America faces a return to the Cold War and a possible standoff with our nuclear-capable adversaries. While this is a fictionalized account of a real-world incident that took place during the 1983 NATO exercise Able Archer, it demonstrates the absolutely real possibilities of mismanagement and misjudgment. This would have been an amazing book in 1983, but in 2022 it is much more important. *The Able Archers* is possibly the most important book to be published this year."

—GENERAL BRYAN DOUG BROWN, United States Army (Retired), 7th Commander US Special Operations Command

"Told through characters you really care about, this is a book about one of the least-known and most-important national security crises in our history. And what could possibly be more timely than a tale of US-Russian misunderstanding putting the world at risk? Brian J. Morra knows the Able Archers story because he lived it, and he tells it in vivid, compelling, and frightening detail—with wit and humanity. Bravo!"

—THE HONORABLE JAMES K. GLASSMAN, Former Undersecretary of State, Journalist, and Award-winning Author'

"[Any] curriculum for crisis management planning would be wise to include Brian Morra's insightful novel—*The Able Archers*—which looks at the crisis that brought us close to war in 1983."

—DR. ROBBIN F. LAIRD, Editor of Defense.info.com and SLDinfo.com

"Few know about the inner workings of superpower brinksmanship between the United States and the Soviet Union for over 40 years after World War Two. Miscues and misunderstandings threatened to erupt regularly in outright hostilities. Brian Morra's novel, *The Abler Archers*, addresses a time of particular global danger in 1983, when national leaders failed to understand how political and military actions were misread by the other side. Brian places the reader inside the interaction between dedicated military officers on both sides, who discovered and understood the danger of military confrontation between the major powers, and sought to defuse the situation at great personal risk. Brian's settings, scenes and characters are absolutely authentic and can send shivers up the spines of those who were there and will never forget those events of 40 years ago. His characters are human, and have the best traits of compassion and dedication, that make this book interesting and accessible to a great variety of readers. There is a lesson here for our times, when we seem again to be unable to communicate with our adversaries. Hopefully dedicated professionals will form bonds of trust across national barriers and see us through difficult times."

—**LARRY COX**, Intelligence Officer, Professional Staff Member, House Intelligence Committee, Defense and Intelligence Corporate Executive Technical Entrepreneur

"Brian Morra has crafted a brilliant, fictionalized account of a critical time in global history when the world teetered on the verge of catastrophe. An insider with years of experience, Morra recreates the events happening from September to November 1983, when both Russia and the United States bordered changing the Cold War into an inferno. Thankfully, cooler heads on both sides prevailed. Using an understanding of enemy culture, as well as a desire to not annihilate each other, military from both sides of the fence were able to remove trigger-happy fingers from the button that would effectively end our existence. *The Able Archers* is a book that is not about enemies but rather heroes united with a common goal of saving their loved ones, their country, and each other."

—**CAROLE P. ROMAN**, Award-winning Author of *Spies, Code Breakers, and Secret Agents: A World War II Book for Kids*

"*The Able Archers* is not only exceptionally entertaining and engrossing, but it is a primer and a must-read for the average person to understand what really happens at the nexus of the military, politics, diplomacy, and human drama in complex and sometimes frightening ways."

—JEFFREY "SKUNK" BAXTER, Grammy-winning Guitarist and Double Inductee (Steely Dan and the Doobie Brothers) to the Rock'n Roll Hall of Fame, Leading Consultant to the Defense Department and the Intelligence Community

"There aren't many books that I have read where I cannot stop reading at the end of a chapter. Brian Morra's novel *The Able Archers* is one of the few. I just did not want to stop reading. An amazing book that is skillfully written and a must-read."

—SAMUEL G. TOOMA, Oceanographer and Author

"An intense up-close-and-personal view of the two key players that prevented World War III during NATO's Able Archer 83. Great read."

—NELSON GOMM, Award-winning Author

"It must be really hard to write a thriller when the readers know how the story is going to end; nevertheless, Brian Morra does just that in *The Able Archers*. As compelling as it is informative and as entertaining as it is terrifying, the novel is a great read and highly recommended."

—TOM STRELICH, Award-winning Playwright, Screenwriter, and Novelist

The Able Archers

by Brian J. Morra

© Copyright 2022 Brian J. Morra

ISBN 978-1-64663-562-7

Published by

 köehlerbooks™

3705 Shore Drive
Virginia Beach, VA 23455
800-435-4811
www.koehlerbooks.com

THE
ABLE
ARCHERS

BASED ON REAL EVENTS

BRIAN J. MORRA

VIRGINIA BEACH
CAPE CHARLES

Dedicated to the memory of three men who prevented an escalation to world war in the fall of 1983

General Charles L. Donnelly, Jr., United States Air Force (died 3 July 1994)

Lieutenant Colonel Stanislav Petrov, Air Defense Forces of the Soviet Union (died 17 May 2017)

Lieutenant General Leonard H. Perroots, Sr., United States Air Force (died 29 January 2017)

"Blessed are the peacemakers, for they shall be called the sons of God."

Matthew 5:9

FOREWORD

I n the fall of 1983, the world stood at the brink of nuclear annihilation—and almost no one knew it. Everyone learns in school that the Cuban Missile Crisis of 1962 was the greatest single flashpoint of the Cold War, and it was—until the events of the fall of 1983. It is my firm view that 1983 was the most dangerous year in human history.

The early 1980s were fraught with numerous crises. The east-west détente of the 1970s had fallen apart. The Soviets had deployed new nuclear missiles both in the USSR and in Eastern Europe, and they had conducted a massive invasion of Afghanistan. The Kremlin was sponsoring Communist rebel movements all over the world, including in the Caribbean region—America's front yard. Soviet leadership was engaged in a several-years-long paranoia binge that might have made Josef Stalin blush. Not only were relations strained, the two sides were hardly communicating. Those factors brought us to the brink of global nuclear war in the fall of 1983.

By then, both superpowers—the United States and the USSR—had nuclear arsenals far larger, more lethal, more apocalyptic than those they had maintained in 1962. To make matters worse, the knowledge and understanding that each country had of the others' intentions had deteriorated since the 1962 Cuban crisis. The senior leaders in Moscow and Washington simply were not talking to each other in any meaningful way.

Event after event in 1983 fueled high anxiety in the Kremlin. In the West, particularly in the United States, senior leaders did not comprehend how deeply the Soviets feared the West's intention to launch a nuclear first strike on the USSR. The very notion seemed absurd to Western leaders and, frankly, to most of us in the intelligence business.

The series of near-catastrophes in 1983—and his deep-seated abhorrence of nuclear war—eventually caused President Reagan to reassess his administration's approach to US-Soviet relations. The accession to power of Mikhail Gorbachev in 1985 signaled the rise of a new generation of Soviet leaders, itself chastened by the events of 1983. Working together, Gorbachev and Reagan crafted the Intermediate Nuclear Forces Agreement (INF) to deescalate tensions and limit a class of weapons that played a central role in the 1983 crisis. It's worth noting that the INF treaty was vacated by both Russia and the United States in 2019.

The following pages dramatize how events unfolded in a gradually escalating crisis over the course of 1983, and how the actions of a few—the "Able Archers"—prevented global nuclear doomsday. This is a story of a global Armageddon that didn't happen by the narrowest of margins.

DR. KEVIN CATTANI
Director of National Intelligence,
United States of America
McLean, Virginia
8 November 2023

PRINCIPAL CHARACTERS

The Americans

Lieutenant and later Captain Kevin Cattani: US Air Force intelligence and special operations officer

The "red-haired" major: US Air Force intelligence and special operations officer

Lieutenant and later Captain Sandy Jackson: US Air Force nurse

Master Sergeant David Parent (Pops): US Air Force intelligence senior NCO

Staff Sergeant Jay Weatherby: US Air Force Signals intelligence NCO

Lieutenant Colonel Ben Stroud: US Air Force Signals intelligence officer

Lieutenant General Douglas Flannery (later full general): US Air Force, commander US Forces, Japan, and Fifth Air Force and after promotion to full general, commander-in-chief US Air Forces Europe and Allied Air Forces, Europe

Admiral William Crowe: Commander-in-chief US Pacific Command and later chairman of the Joint Chiefs of Staff

Brigadier General Leonard Palumbo (later lieutenant general): US Air Force, deputy chief of staff for intelligence, US Air Forces Europe and later chief of Air Force intelligence, director of the National Security Agency, and director of the Defense Intelligence Agency

Chief Master Sergeant Charles Jackson: US Air Force intelligence and special operations, senior NCO, US Military Liaison Mission

Major Mark Stablinski: US Air Force intelligence officer, US Military Liaison Mission

Colonel John LaRoche: US Air Force intelligence officer, senior USAF officer, US military liaison mission

Caspar Weinberger: US Secretary of Defense

Brigadier General Colin Powell: US Army, military assistant to Secretary Weinberger and later full general and chairman of the Joint Chiefs of Staff and US Secretary of State

Ronald Reagan: President of the United States

The Soviets

Colonel Ivan Levchenko: GRU Intelligence Officer, Soviet Air Defense Forces

Boyka Levchenka: Musician and Ukrainian wife of Colonel Levchenko

Oxana Koghuta: sister of Boyka Levchenka

Oleksandr Koghut: husband of Oxana and brother-in-law of the Levchenkos

Lieutenant Colonel Stanislav Petrov: Soviet Air Defense Forces, Serpukhov-15

Marshal of Aviation Anatoly Konstantinov: Soviet Air Defense Forces, commander of the Moscow Air Defense District

General Colonel Valeri Kamensky: Soviet Air Defense Forces, commander of the Far East Air Defense District

General Major Anatoly Kornukov: Soviet Air Defense Forces, commander of the Sakhalin Air Defense Zone

Major Gennadi Osipovich: Soviet Air Defense Forces, Sakhalin Air Defense Zone, SU-15 pilot and deputy squadron commander

Lieutenant Colonel Burakovsky: Soviet Air Defense Forces, Sakhalin Air Defense Zone, operations center commander

Chief Marshal of Aviation Koldunov: Soviet Air Defense Forces, commander-in-chief of the Soviet Air Defense Forces

General of the Army Pyotr Ivashutin: Director of the GRU—Soviet military intelligence

Lieutenant Colonel Kirilenko: the senior member of the team Levchenko took with him to the Soviet Far East to investigate the KAL 007 shootdown

Oleg Gordievsky: Senior KGB Officer, USSR Embassy and agent for British intelligence

Marshal of the Soviet Union Ogarkov: Chief of the General Staff of the Armed Forces of the USSR

Yuri Andropov: Former chairman of the KGB, general secretary of the Communist Party of the Soviet Union

MAP 1: The actual and planned flightpaths of KAL 007

Map 2: East and West Germany

EAST
GERMANY

FRENCH
SECTOR

EAST
BERLIN

Brandenburg
Gate

BRITISH
SECTOR

Checkpoint
Charlie

WEST
BERLIN

SOVIET
SECTOR

AMERICAN
SECTOR

Glienicke
Bridge

Potsdam

EAST
GERMANY

——— Berlin Wall

Map 3: East and West Berlin

PART ONE

THE MAN WHO COULD SEE THE FUTURE

" . . . the more experience I had with Soviet leaders . . .
the more I began to realize that many Soviet officials feared us not
only as adversaries but as potential aggressors who might hurl
nuclear weapons at them in a first strike."

President Ronald Reagan, The Reagan Diaries

CHAPTER ONE

THE RED-HAIRED MAJOR

Lieutenant Kevin Cattani, United States Air Force
Tokyo, Japan, and along the Thai-Cambodian border

1979-1980

I hate killing people.

I'm not sure how my boss feels about it. I doubt he even thinks about killing anymore. He's second-in-command of a special activities unit, based out of the US Embassy in Tokyo, Japan. Units like ours handle the nasty sideshows of the Cold War.

During my final year of college, I went through the CIA hiring process and was selected for initial training. Unfortunately, at the final stage, my group of career trainees was told that due to budget cuts, we'd have to wait a full year to enter CIA training. Bad luck for us.

I couldn't wait a year—I had to go to work. I had no interest in returning to my hometown in southern Virginia, and one of the CIA officers recommended that I go into the military and try to become an intelligence officer in one of the services. He explained that after four or five years of military intelligence experience, I'd be able to transition to CIA. This was just a few years after the end of the Vietnam War, and going into the military wasn't exactly a popular career choice for my generation of college students. But I wanted a career in the national security business, and the military seemed like the best way in.

The only service I considered was the Air Force. I don't like the water, so applying to the Navy was out. I couldn't see myself in the Army or Marine Corps—I'm not keen on sleeping outside in the cold rain. Plus, my male relatives were in the Air Force in World War II, and that seemed to mean something to me at the time. So, I joined the Air Force after I graduated from college and went to Officers Training School to earn my commission as a second lieutenant. Then I went to the air intelligence school in Denver. From there I went on to a couple of different courses at the CIA's training center, affectionately known as "the Farm."

I was talking about my boss, wasn't I? He's an Air Force major, but he hasn't worked in the regular Air Force for years. Instead, he's been assigned to covert intelligence units like the one I'm in now.

He's a huge, red-haired guy with massive arms, shoulders, and neck. His personality matches his size—outrageous and larger than life. His eyes light up and glow when he smiles or when something intrigues him. They burn red when something pisses him off, or when he's contemplating violence, which usually happens when something pisses him off.

Irreverent toward almost everyone in a position of authority, he has a bachelor's degree in history from Harvard College. You'd never suspect he's an Ivy Leaguer, and I've learned that he doesn't talk about his time in Cambridge with the patronizing Harvard nonchalance I've encountered in others.

He's fluent in Japanese, Vietnamese, Russian, and God knows what else, and he has a master's degree in Russian studies from Georgetown. He's been an Air Force intelligence officer for twenty-six years and has never been promoted beyond major. That makes him ancient for his rank—he's in his late forties. A major should be in his early-to-mid-thirties.

On my very first day working for him, the red-haired major and I attend a formal luncheon at the Japanese Ministry of Defense. We wear our dress uniforms. I see for the first time that he has as many ribbons as I imagine you'd find on a four-star general. Riding to the luncheon in a staff car, I ask him shyly if that is an Air Force Cross on his chest (this medal is just one level below the Medal of Honor).

Testily, he answers, "Yes, Lieutenant, it is, and don't ever ask me about it again."

The prevailing rumor around the embassy is that my boss's failure to be promoted beyond major is due to a long-ago affair with a colonel's wife. That seems plausible. He's married to an American woman, but he flirts all the time with other women, regardless of their rank or circumstances.

Anyway, he and his wife have been living in Tokyo for about ten years, and she has her own successful business, which gives them a financial incentive to remain in Japan. The fact that the Air Force has permitted him to stay in Japan for years doesn't make any sense. No officer can "homestead" in Japan for the better part of a decade. Yet, somehow, the red-haired major has done just that.

A few weeks after I arrive in Japan, my boss takes me and a small team on what he calls a "field trip." We fly from Japan to Thailand on a C-130 cargo plane with an intermediate stop for fuel at Clarke Air Base in the Philippines. Communist guerrillas shoot at our C-130 as it approaches Clarke—an event that I find rather unnerving. But the red-haired major finds it comical due to the Communists' incompetent shooting and exhilarating because he likes getting shot at without being hit.

Once in Thailand we board an ancient C-7 Caribou airplane, from which we parachute into a terraced field in the easternmost part of Thailand. We land outside of a small village, very near the Cambodian border. It's hot as hell, but we're still in the dry season, so at least we don't have to deal with sideways rain as we make the jump.

While we eat supper that first night in the Thai village's only "restaurant," I notice the red-haired major drinking from a huge canteen he had on him when we jumped. In response to my questions, he tells me the canteen is full of single-malt Scotch. I haven't had the foresight to bring my own booze, so I order a couple of Thai beers, which are laced with formaldehyde, ostensibly to keep the beer "fresh." This ingredient gives the beer a nasty aftertaste that makes you shake your head in a futile attempt to clear the fumes from your brain. It also produces a wicked hangover, even when you don't drink a lot of it. Great stuff! It's easy to understand why the major brings his own booze.

The whiskey has him in an unusually expansive mood, and I decide to risk triggering his anger with a few questions.

"Sir, if you don't mind me asking, how can you still be on active duty? I mean, the Air Force has a strict 'up or out' policy . . ."

Like I said before, his rank of major combined with his twenty-six years of commissioned service just doesn't make sense. He should have been retired involuntarily three or four years ago.

He laughs and says, "Who gives a fuck?" He takes another drink. "Since you want to know, I send a letter each year directly to the secretary of the Air Force asking for special dispensation to be continued on active duty. You see, I have a goddamn Air Force Cross and the Vietnamese National Order of Honor. No secretary of the Air Force is going to fuck around with someone like me. It isn't worth the shitstorm I'd bring to Washington. That's also how I get to stay in Japan as long as I want to."

This exchange and the Scotch loosen him up, and he asks, "Have you been to Thailand before, kid?"

"No, sir."

"Well, this is the shithole part of Thailand for sure, but the beaches down south are great. It's a great place to take some leave." He takes another drink and looks at me like he just thought of something cool.

"You know, Kevin, I haven't been this close to the Cambodian border since 1970—can you believe it? How about you? You been here before?"

"No, sir, I've never been in this part of the world before."

"Well, don't let this crap village fool you. The people here are wonderful—very generous and sincere. Bangkok, on the other hand . . . is full of stealing bastards. Loads of dope, too—the real bad stuff. Of course, back in 1970, I wasn't on this border—I mean here in Thailand. I was on the other side of Cambodia—the Vietnam side. Where were you in 1970? I bet you were marching outside of the Pentagon protesting against the Vietnam War like a fucking pussy."

Does he have any idea how young I am? "Major, I was in junior high school in 1970. I'm from southern Virginia. If people were protesting back home in those days, it was against school desegregation—not the Vietnam War. But I knew about the invasion of Cambodia and the Kent State protest, of course, and Neil Young and his song *Ohio*. I wasn't living in a cave."

The major's eyes flash angrily at me. "Invasion of Cambodia, hah! Son-of-a-fucking-bitch! Did you know that more than half of the goddamn Ho Chi Minh trail was in Cambodia? The NVA (North Vietnamese Army) used Cambodia as a sanctuary for years. They'd stage attacks into South Vietnam and fall back into Cambodia, where we weren't allowed to touch the bastards. Nixon finally let us go after the motherfuckers in 1970 and everybody back home goes batshit crazy. You were probably protesting 'Cambodia' in the streets with the rest of the goddamn hippies."

"Sir, I was thirteen years old. Cambodia wasn't a burning issue in my seventh-grade class."

He warms further to the topic. "And I bet you think the 'domino theory' is a hoax, too! You and your fucking hippie friends. Tell that to the poor bastards living under Communist rule today in Laos and Cambodia. Take this asshole Pol Pot and his goddamn Khmer Rouge. He thinks he's fucking Josef Stalin purging the intelligentsia and the kulaks. Do you know how many of his own Cambodian people he's killed? No? No, you don't, and neither does anyone else, probably not even those Khmer Rouge bastards themselves. The United Nations doesn't know. CIA doesn't know. Jane-fucking-Fonda doesn't know and doesn't give a shit. Nobody fucking knows. And we'll probably get our fucking balls shot off tomorrow when we try to confirm these rumors of genocide. Washington wants confirmatory photos and interviews with survivors, and we have to try to get our asses out of there before the fucking Khmer Rouge holdouts find us and kill us."

He takes a long draw on the canteen, while I contemplate being killed tomorrow by Khmer Rouge dead-enders. I gently ask, "Major, so, were you involved in the Cambodian, um, operation in 1970?"

"Goddamn straight I was *involved!*" He roars like a red-haired wildebeest. "I was assigned to an ARVN [Army of the Republic of Vietnam, or South Vietnam] airborne brigade. I was the only 'round-eye' with them. Unfortunately, the ARVN tanks and heavy weapons that were supposed to support us against the North Vietnamese regulars got bogged down on the shitty roads. This left me and my airborne dudes isolated, with limited firepower. We were on our own when the NVA counterattacked. The NVA hit us with fucking tanks and artillery, and we got slaughtered. It was like Custer's Last Fucking Stand. I'd been in combat before and I'd seen my men get killed, but this was different. Everybody around me was getting hit. The South Vietnamese guys fought hard, but it was hopeless. We were totally outgunned. And the North Vietnamese infantry—those motherfuckers—they executed the wounded. I killed a bunch of those NVA motherfucking bastards myself . . . worst day of my goddamn life. I was shot three times."

Wow.

He pauses, yawns widely, and contemplates his scotch, "So are you a hick from the sticks of Virginia or one of those goddamn Virginia gentlemen? Which are you?"

Me? A Virginia gentleman? "Sir, I'm not a Virginia gentleman."

"Really? Cause you sure as hell look like a goddamn Virginia gentleman. You don't look or talk like a hick. Why do you have a fucking

Italian name if you're from goddamn southern Virginia? You majored in history in college?"

This torrent of questions is the first time he's asked me about myself. "Yes—I concentrated in Russian and East Asian history at William and Mary."

The major raises his eyebrows. "That's a good school—William and Mary. The second oldest college in America after Harvard, isn't it? Well, how's your Russian? Any good?"

"Fair." I don't want to exaggerate my language ability to him.

He raises his eyebrows again. "How was the Farm? How'd you do there? And I don't want to hear about that pussy case officers' course. How did you do in the paramilitary course? Don't lie. I've seen you shoot. My wife shoots better than you."

"I did okay. The other guys in my class were SEALs and green-beret officers who all knew what they were doing. The paramilitary course was just a refresher for them. It was hard for me, but they helped me through it. I could run faster than any of them, so that gave me some credibility."

"Your record says you ran track in college?"

"Yes, and cross country."

The major has another swig of Scotch. "A good runner, eh? Could come in handy when the time comes. How tall are you and how much do you weigh?"

How much do I weigh? Am I a Miss America contestant?

"I'm 6'1" and I weigh about 175 right now."

This elicits a nod and a once-over. "What color is your hair? It ain't red and it ain't brown."

"I don't know—auburn?"

He takes another drink. "You're a good-looking kid. I bet the mama-sans love your ass. You gettin' any in Japan? How old are you?"

"Twenty-three."

"Twenty-three? Well . . . okay. That should be okay . . . twenty-three. That's old enough. Yeah, okay." The red-haired major looks off into the distance and nods to himself.

Old enough for what—to get killed tomorrow?

"Hey, goddamn it, why aren't you growing a beard like I told you to? You can't go into the shit without a beard, my friend."

I'd rather keep talking about the invasion of Cambodia in 1970 than discuss my pathetic attempts to grow a beard.

"Sir, I stopped shaving when you told me, but I just can't grow a goddamn beard."

The major, who is sporting an impressive red beard after only a few days of trying, looks at me like I am an alien being. "What the fuck? What do you mean you can't grow a fucking beard?" His normally sparkling eyes are raging red now.

I repeat myself. "I just can't grow a beard. What can I say? I get sideburns and chin hair, but that's it. Maybe I am too evolved to grow a beard."

The red-haired major looks genuinely shocked. "Jesus fucking Christ. Well, the Khmer Rouge won't care whether you have a beard. They will shoot you whether you have a beard or not. Too *evolved* to grow a beard! Motherfucker. Look, go do a final weapons-check right now, then go get some goddamn sleep. Jesus fucking Christ. Too evolved to grow a beard!"

Someday, I'll say more about our mission in Cambodia. I couldn't sleep the night before we crossed the border, worrying about how I'd respond if we got into a fight with the Khmer Rouge. As it happened, after we'd done what we came into Cambodia to do, we were humping it to our extraction point when a group of Khmer Rouge caught up to us near the border. These were real die-hard bastards taking refuge in western Cambodia after the North Vietnamese kicked them out of power.

We had quite a little battle. The red-haired major killed a lot of Khmer Rouge fighters. Everybody on our team fought hard and killed, but my major was especially good at it. Thank God for that. As for me, I don't like killing people.

After what my boss calls "our little fracas" in Cambodia, he seems increasingly concerned about my mental health and decides it would be a good idea for me to do something different for a while.

After we return to Tokyo, he tells me, "Kid, you need to clear your head for a while. Do you like the ocean? Ever been to sea before?"

Is he telling me to take a beach vacation? "Major, I like the ocean all right. I haven't 'been to sea', however."

He smiles, broadly. "Well, I'll fix that. The salt air will do you good! You'll be a new man after a couple of weeks at sea."

So he sends me to participate in a joint Japanese Navy-U.S. Navy exercise in the Sea of Japan. The exercise is designed to test our ability to defend the western coast of Japan against a Soviet naval and air assault. I'll be on the Japanese Navy command ship *Nemuro*.

On the final day of the week-long exercise, everyone is ready to go home. I've had all the sea air I ever want to breathe. and I'm tired of speaking broken Japanese with Japanese officers who speak broken English. I imagine that the Soviets, who have been observing the exercise by aircraft and ship and probably by submarine, are no doubt anticipating downtime when they get back to Vladivostok tonight.

The sun is going down over a heaving Sea of Japan as I grip the rail outside the bridge house to steady myself. A large Soviet Naval Aviation Tu-16 intelligence collection plane (a converted bomber) makes its final pass right over my ship—so close that I can feel the jet wash from the engines. The big plane dives low over the *Nemuro* and opens its bomb bay to drop the contents of its latrine on the foredeck. A big pile of smelly gunk makes a direct hit. The Soviet pilot rocks his wings in triumph at his successful "fuck-you" bomb run.

As he clears the bow of *Nemuro*, the pilot makes a radical, hard-right turn that causes his starboard wing to dip dangerously close to the sea, which is raging with whitecaps. As he executes the turn, a large swell comes up and catches his starboard wingtip. The big jet shudders and nearly comes to a complete stop in mid-air. I watch in horror as the plane cartwheels like a child's toy across the waves, disintegrating before my eyes. The scene unfolds like an old newsreel or action movie footage—incredible to behold and impossible to register in the moment.

Immediately, alarms sound on the bridge, and the ship's helicopter is launched to search for survivors. There are none. The entire crew of about fifteen has been killed on impact.

In the waning light, Japanese divers manage to find two mutilated corpses and a leg. That's all that is found of the crew. The bloody remains are laid temporarily on the deck for the ship's senior officers, medical officer, and me (as the American witness) to view. I've seen many dead bodies before, but nothing like these. The effect that blunt-force trauma of this type has on the human body is stupefying. I won't shake the image from my mind for several months. Just moments earlier, these crushed Russians had been looking forward to a night of a few beers followed by a sound sleep. Laid out before us is evidence of the imminent danger inherent in enemies operating large, complex war machines so close to each other. Here, too, is the product of unhinged hubris and bravado. Such a waste—it makes me physically ill, and I head below to my cramped stateroom and throw up.

CHAPTER TWO

THE FIGHTING MAJOR

Captain Kevin Cattani, United States Air Force
Tokyo, Japan and Yokota AB, Japan

Spring 1981

The red-haired major still hasn't been promoted and he is pushing fifty now. After almost two years, I know I need a break from working for him, or I'll go fucking nuts. He agrees—too quickly, it seems to me—and he makes sure I am assigned to the intelligence staff at the Headquarters of United States Forces, Japan, in the western suburbs of Tokyo at Yokota Air Base.

I have mixed feelings about the change. Working at the embassy and doing missions with the red-haired major is heady and exciting stuff for a young kid like me. I'm apprehensive that going back to the regular, "blue" Air Force—especially in an office job—will be a big come-down.

The red-haired major worries about that, too. "Look, kid, transitioning into a headquarters job in the 'real Air Force' is gonna feel weird to you. Don't let the headquarters bullshit get you down. You've done things those pissants haven't. You still look like a punk, but you're not. You can call me any time if you get into trouble—okay?"

The red-haired major is right—this transition to an office job is tough. Even though my job as chief of intelligence analysis is a good one, there are days when I want to blow my brains out with a shotgun. The office routine is killing me after the adrenaline-filled days with my crazy major.

Fortunately for me, two positive things happen that help with my transition. First, my new job entails presenting a daily intelligence briefing to the commander of United States Forces, Japan, and his staff. The commander, Lieutenant General Doug Flannery, Jr., is a great guy, and he personally promotes me to captain shortly after my arrival.

Second, I meet a lovely woman. She's the kind of woman I could really fall for, and I think she knows that about me. She's agreed to a third date, which makes me both hopeful and apprehensive about screwing things up.

This past Saturday, while I'm on a long run on the base, a car bumps me on the hip at an intersection. I react instinctively and slap the hood of the car to get the driver's attention. The driver gets pissed off and follows me to the next intersection where he screeches to a halt in front of me, jumps out of his car, and gets into a fighting stance.

I need to control my natural inclination to beat the shit out of him and try to deescalate the situation.

"Look, man, you hit me on the hip with your car and now you want to fight? This is crazy. I don't want to fight you."

The driver remains in his fighting stance. "*You* hit my car, you shithead! You're a pussy if you won't fight." He snickers and tells me to give him my military ID card.

"Only if you give me yours." We exchange ID cards, and I peruse his and see that this guy is a fucking major! What have I gotten myself into now? He writes down my information and asks me where I work. After I tell him, I take off running with a terrible feeling in the pit of my stomach. What if this crazy bastard does something nuts? You never know about guys like this one.

Later that afternoon, I get a call at my quarters from a judge advocate general (JAG) lawyer. He tells me the major wants to press charges against me. The JAG also tells me the base commander has been briefed on the situation and will hold a nonjudicial hearing on the matter next Tuesday morning. What the fuck? A hearing! This asshole hit *me* with his car!

I hang up the phone with the JAG and immediately dial the red-haired major at his apartment in downtown Tokyo. Thank God, he's home, and he answers right away. I describe the situation to him.

The major starts laughing. "You fucking punk! You should have broken that pissant's neck!"

I don't find that particularly helpful. "Major, seriously, what should I do?"

He stops laughing. "You need to wear your dress blues to that hearing and be on your absolutely best behavior. Do your 'Virginia gentleman' thing. Be nice. The base commander is probably an asshole, so kiss his ass. I'm serious about this."

I know he's right. "Yes, sir. I'll be on good behavior."

"Remember . . . Virginia gentleman—pour it on like Southern molasses. Call me only if the hearing goes sideways. Otherwise, I'll know if I don't hear from you that it worked out."

"Yes, sir. I got it."

"Oh, Kevin, one more thing. This is important. Don't forget it. Whatever you do, don't forget this. Are you ready? Ready? *Don't fuck up!!*" He laughs again and hangs up the phone.

The hearing the following Tuesday is the Air Force's version of the Navy's "captain's mast" process. It is a nonjudicial approach to dealing with misconduct or disputes under Article 15 of the Uniform Code of Military Justice.

The hearing convenes in the base commander's office. He is like the mayor of the base, and he also commands the C-130 wing based at Yokota. Even though I am assigned to a higher headquarters, I am a "tenant" on this colonel's base, and therefore, I am subject to his authority. Like the red-haired major advised, I wear my dress uniform to the hearing, which is attended by several senior officers, including a colonel who is the base commander's top lawyer—his senior judge advocate general officer.

The base commander smiles as he reads the "fighting" major's complaint aloud. Why the hell is he smiling? It seems to me that he is signaling his support for the fighting major. I'm still amazed that this asshole major filed charges against me. Why is this fucking colonel smiling? He looks like a grand poohbah sitting behind his big desk. He's a very large man and he makes the enormous desk look tiny.

The colonel finishes reading the major's complaint and asks me to tell my side of the story, which I do in the space of a few minutes. Everyone—especially the fighting major—listens carefully to my testimony.

Once I've concluded, the colonel asks my accuser if my account of the incident is accurate. The major stares at his shoes and a look of profound anguish clouds his face. I actually feel sorry for this dickhead. He tells the colonel that my account of the incident is correct and that he believes he overreacted to the situation, but he also says that I had no business hitting the hood of his car. The room is silent after he finishes. He keeps staring at his shoes.

The JAG officer speaks up. "Major, if the captain's account is accurate, then why did you file charges of assault against him? By his account, you could be the one—or should be the one—to be charged with assault. Do you agree?"

The major's face and neck turn a deep red color. "Sir, I was angry, and I should not have filed these charges. I really . . . I just want this thing to go away." He looks like he wants to crawl out of the office and head straight to the officers' club bar.

The JAG then turns to me. "Captain Cattani, based on your testimony, do you want to file charges against the major—assault charges?"

This is crazy. I don't want to file charges. I just want out of here.

Before I can answer the JAG's question, the base commander interjects. "Look, the major is a highly respected officer in my wing.

He commands our aircraft maintenance squadron and does a helluva job keeping our C-130s flying. He is a good family man. I see no reason to destroy this man's career over something like this. And you, Captain, you have a bad temper, and you are lucky that you *didn't* fight the other day. The major is a competitive martial arts expert, and he would have torn you up."

Uh oh, I feel the rage building in my chest, and I turn to face my accuser. "Major, let me ask you—have you ever been in combat? You may be a great martial-arts fighter, but I take one look at you and I can tell you aren't a killer. Colonel, the major is damn lucky I didn't fight him that day because with the training I've had, I would have killed him in about ten seconds."

It is now the base commander's face that goes deep red. "Captain, you mind your bearing. I want you to accept the major's apology and agree not to bring charges against him. Then I can close this hearing and we can all move on to more important business."

I am seething, and my skin is hot to the touch. I speak very slowly and clearly. "I don't want to file charges against this guy. I don't want to ruin his career."

The base commander smiles his weird smile again. "All right. Good. My ruling is there is fault on both sides. And JAG, it looks like there are no charges to be filed. Major, do you agree to immediately drop your charges against the captain and proffer him an immediate apology?"

The major looks like a man who has gotten a second lease on life. "Yes, Colonel, I agree to drop the charges and I offer a full and sincere apology. I was out of line. I overreacted."

The commander is pleased and is ready to wrap up. "Okay. I also order you two to stay away from each other while you are on my base. Got it?"

The fighting major and I look at each other and turn toward the colonel in unison and nod.

"All right, I want you two to shake hands and get the hell out of my office."

The fighting major and I stand up, face each other, and shake hands. I come to attention, salute the colonel, turn, and leave his office. Christ, what a crock of shit. I am shaking as I leave the base headquarters building.

I go to my quarters about 6:00 PM and pour myself a big glass of Glenlivet. I sit in my most comfortable chair and am starting to nod off when I'm awakened by a knock at my door. Christ, who the hell could that be? Can't everyone just leave me alone?

I open the door to find a woman standing there with a smile on her face that quickly fades to a frown. Sandy Jackson is a first lieutenant—a nurse—at the Yokota hospital, and I have forgotten that we have a date tonight—our third date, which is always the important one, isn't it?

She looks me up and down and frowns. "Why are you still in your uniform? Did you forget we have a date tonight?"

I wave for her to come in and I shut the door. "I can change quickly. I'm really distracted because of today's hearing—I'm sorry. Look, I'll be ready to go in ten. Let me get you a glass of wine."

Sandy looks at my glass of Scotch on the side table. "No thanks, I don't want wine, but I will have one of those."

I like a woman who likes whiskey.

I pour Sandy a big glass of Scotch and go to my bedroom to change. I am such an idiot. How could I forget we were going out to dinner?

Sandy is a very pretty woman with unusual, captivating eyes that give her an exotic look. They're striking blue, shaped like ovals. Those eyes are the first thing one notices about her, but the rest of her is equally gorgeous. On our first date, I complimented Sandy on her amazing eyes. She told me that her mother is descended from the Ainu people native to northern Japan, who are known for their large eyes and pale skin tone.

Sandy's own skin is a light cocoa color and she's one of those people who always seems to be on the verge of smiling.

Her father is Black, a chief master sergeant in the Air Force, the most senior enlisted rank. She's told me that he's stationed in Germany and that her mother prefers living in Germany to the States.

Sandy speaks flawless Japanese and has an ease about her that I find a little unsettling but compelling. I can already sense that I like her more than she likes me, but I guess she likes me well enough to have agreed to a third date.

I drive us the short distance to the base's ersatz Tex-Mex restaurant, where we take seats in a relatively secluded booth. With her typical assertiveness, she orders a pitcher of Corona without asking me what I want to drink. She takes a long sip of beer. "Okay, sir, I want a full briefing on today's hearing."

I smile sheepishly. "There isn't much to say, really. It was a non-event."

Sandy replies with an exasperated gasp. "A non-event? You realize that your hearing is the biggest news on this base in months, don't you? All the nurses at the hospital are waiting to hear what happened. You know this base is like *Peyton Place,* don't you? And your hearing is big news!"

This is a complete surprise to me. "People are aware of the hearing? How? Why would they care?"

She looks at me like I'm an alien being. "Captain Cattani, you are completely oblivious to what goes on in the real world that the rest of us inhabit. Of course, everybody on this base knows about your hearing! All the nurses have a crush on you. Don't you get it?"

Why would anyone care? I don't get it, but I summarize the hearing for Sandy.

She only interrupts me once. "Wait, you told the base commander, with the JAG officer present, that you would have killed the fighting major if the two of you had fought? You didn't actually say that in front of the goddamn lawyer, did you? Christ, Kevin, you are lucky the JAG didn't charge *you* with something. Did you mean to say that? I mean, you said that major had martial arts training"

"Yeah. I shouldn't have said it. But it's true. I'd have killed him, even with his martial-arts bullshit."

Sandy looks at me with a mixture of skepticism and amused horror.

We finish dinner and I drive us back to my apartment.

She is feeling amorous and asks if she can spend the night. She is a beauty and I'm not going to say no.

During the night, I have nightmares.

In my dreams, I'm back in Cambodia and struggling to carry a wounded teammate on my back, trying to get to one of the two helicopters waiting to evacuate us. The red-haired major is right in front of me, yelling at me to get to the chopper. I see two PJs (Air Force para-rescue jumpers) scramble from another chopper. Abruptly, I feel a heavy blow drive me and my passenger face-first into the ground.

I get up on one knee with the wounded man still on my back, and I am trying to scream at my major and one of the PJs. I cannot form words, and I feel a complete state of terrifying, paralyzing panic wash over me. I try harder to scream, but nothing comes out of my mouth. A primal moan is the only thing that escapes my lips. I feel like I'm choking.

Suddenly, Sandy is shaking my shoulder, begging me to wake up. I am still trying to scream. I hear a terrible moan—like the sound of a wounded water buffalo—surround the room. It is coming from me. I wake up and the awful sound stops.

Sandy turns on a light and looks at me with terrified eyes. "Are you okay? Were you having a nightmare? What's wrong?"

I sit up and try to downplay things. "Yeah, I had a bad dream, but I'm okay. Please go back to sleep."

She isn't buying it. "Wait a minute, you had a fucking nightmare. You scared the shit out of me. What is wrong with you?"

I try to smile at her. "Yeah, you're right. I had my granddaddy nightmare."

She recoils. "You fucking name your nightmares? This sounds like a reaction to trauma to me. What is your nightmare about?"

I lie back down on my side to face away from her. "I am trying to get to a helicopter. I am screaming. Nothing comes out of my mouth. I cannot speak. I can't form words. Instead, all that comes out is this horrible moaning sound."

Sandy gets up and gets dressed.

She leans over and kisses my forehead. "You need to talk to somebody. Look, I have a friend, Brad, at the hospital. He is a psychotherapist. You can talk to him. He is really good."

I sigh more deeply than I intended. "Sandy, I can't talk to a shrink. I have security clearances—so many clearances that—well, I can't talk to him. If I talk to a shrink, then I will lose my clearances and I won't be able to do my job."

She glares at me. "Well, that is stupid. Really fucking stupid. You need help. You should talk to Brad."

I hear my front door close gently and Sandy walks out of my life. I'm afraid I will never see her again.

CHAPTER THREE

ALONE, UNARMED, AND UNAFRAID

Captain Kevin Cattani, United States Air Force
Yokota AB, Japan and Kadena AB, Okinawa

Spring 1983

I was right about Sandy. I didn't see her again. Not long after our night together, she departed Japan for an assignment at a large medical center in Germany. She's been gone for almost two years now. Even though we dated just a few times, I miss her like a missing limb. That sounds a little stupid, I know, but it's how I feel.

Today, a team of naval intelligence officers from 7th Fleet headquarters at Yokosuka, Japan, visits our intelligence center at Yokota. The Navy visitors' purpose is to alert us to an upcoming exercise, called FLEETEX 83, that the Pacific Fleet plans to conduct in April. This will be the largest U.S. Navy exercise in the Pacific since the end of World War II, and they call it a "demonstration of American resolve to defend its interests in the North Pacific Ocean." The exercise will involve three carrier task groups, more than forty-five ships, and hundreds of aircraft. The Navy will conduct it under extreme operational and communications security. The Pacific Fleet will sortie its vast armada into the Sea of Okhotsk via the disputed Kurile Island chain (claimed by both Japan and the USSR but occupied by the latter since 1945). The Soviets consider the Sea of Okhotsk their "lake," a virtual inland sea. It is one of the jealously guarded bastions for their nuclear-missile-launching submarine fleet.

The Navy officers warn us, "The fleet will disappear, and we don't want you guys doing any intelligence reporting that might leak and give the Soviets any clues as to where the fleet might be." That's why they're here—not as a courtesy, but to tell us not to fuck up their exercise.

The plan is for the US fleet to reappear at a time and place of its choosing and demonstrate to the Soviets that we can "shapeshift" a huge armada: turn it into a ghost fleet and then make it reappear adjacent to their shores. It is a remarkable plan and a remarkable meeting.

After the naval officers conclude their presentation, my boss, Lieutenant Colonel Ben Stroud, asks them why they are planning an exercise to "punch the Russians in the nose." He is concerned that the Navy's plans are so provocative that the Soviets will react in unpredictable and potentially dangerous ways. The Navy officers smile condescendingly. One retorts that FLEETEX 83 has been approved by the admiral commanding American forces in the Pacific theater, and he is in full support of the plans. They're telling us to "shut up and color."

After they leave, Colonel Stroud pulls me aside and tells me to be extremely vigilant once FLEETEX kicks off in April—"this exercise could start a war out here."

Late in the exercise, the Coral Sea battle group emerges undetected from the wind and rain of the Sea of Okhotsk to appear just off the coast of the Kamchatka Peninsula, not far from the major Soviet Pacific Fleet base at Petropavlovsk. I wish I could have seen the ships emerge from the fog and blackness. It had to be an epic scene, worthy of treatment by a great cinematographer.

On the opposite side of the Sea of Okhotsk, *Enterprise* and *Midway*'s massive battle groups transit silently southward through the Kurile Island chain, on their passage back to the east coast of Japan. They, too, are a ghostly presence on the sea. Shortly thereafter, FLEETEX 83 ends, and I'm pleased to report that it did not cause World War III to erupt.

A couple weeks after FLEETEX, I receive a highly unusual phone call on my direct, unclassified phone line. The caller is a certain Colonel Stone, commander of the strategic reconnaissance wing at Kadena Air Base on the Japanese island of Okinawa. He is curt and orders me to call him back on the secure phone.

Despite the crappy secure phone connection, the colonel's message is clear. He wants to know why his unarmed reconnaissance planes are being intercepted by unusually large numbers of Soviet fighters on every mission. An intercept, also known as a reaction, is an operation where an enemy fighter (more often, a flight of two fighters) races into the sky to find an adversary plane. The actual intercept occurs when the fighters form up next to the adversary plane, or, more provocatively, position behind the adversary as though to prepare to shoot down the plane. Such tactics are meant to intimidate and warn American aircrews to stay well clear of Soviet airspace.

Our Okinawa-based crews are growing anxious since the Soviet fighter reactions are well outside of established peacetime norms both in their numbers and in their provocative nature. What is causing the Soviets to deviate so radically from their normal behavior? That's what Colonel Stone wants me to find out.

Intelligence collection missions are hazardous even when you are not hunted by swarms of Soviet fighters. In March of 1981, an RC-135/

Cobra Ball aircraft (the Cobra Ball version is configured to observe and collect data on ballistic missile launches) crashed in a terrible North Pacific storm. The Cobra Ball pilot had landed just short of the runway on Shemya Island in the Aleutian chain, blinded by the appallingly heavy wind and rain. Six of the twenty-four crewmembers on board were killed.

The unofficial motto of reconnaissance aviators is "alone, unarmed, and unafraid." Colonel Stone's message to me is that the motto still holds, except for the "unafraid" part. Not only are the Soviets reacting to our flights with an unprecedented number of fighter interceptors—as many as fourteen fighters per RC-135 flight—some of the Soviet fighters are arming their air-to-air missiles (essentially "warming up" the missiles' sensors for an imminent attack).

Unsurprisingly, those provocations scare the American crews. They know that the Soviets shot down more than forty American intelligence collection planes during the first decades of the Cold War. While it's been years since such a shootdown, the collective memory of those downed airmen remains a powerful force in the minds of the current crews.

Immediately after hanging up with Colonel Stone, I go to my boss's office. Lieutenant Colonel Ben Stroud is a tall, thin, bespectacled man, about forty years old. Everyone respects him greatly. Even so, the enlisted guys call him "Dennis the Menace's father" behind his back, since Stroud looks almost exactly like the nerdy father of the impish cartoon character. He wears heavy, horn-rimmed glasses and appears spindly and somewhat like a milquetoast—at first glance. Incongruously, given his appearance, he is an extremely tough guy and an inspiring, no-bullshit leader.

After I brief Stroud, I grab my best guy—Sergeant Jay Weatherby—and tell him that he is now to work full-time with me on this Soviet problem. Weatherby has a long hangdog face with almost no chin. He smokes cigarettes constantly and talks slowly in a sleepy Alabama drawl. Most people get the wrong first impression of Weatherby: they think he is somewhat slow if not dimwitted. In Weatherby's case, his appearance belies an incredible mind. Those who know him—his peers and superior officers—recognize him as a fast-rising superstar analyst.

Answering Colonel Stone's question and briefing his crews in Okinawa is now my number one job. The guys who work for me have served as crew members on RC-135s. Most of them flew scores of combat missions during the Vietnam War. They understand viscerally why the crews in Okinawa are scared.

As we begin to piece together the story, I decide I'd better get some help from my old colleagues at the US embassy in Tokyo, and I fly downtown on an Air Force helicopter.

The CIA guys at the embassy tell me that the Soviets issued a formal complaint—a demarche—to the US ambassador in Moscow in mid-April in which they complained about the US Navy's antics during FLEETEX 83. The Soviets asserted that "several" US Navy fighters (from *Enterprise* and/or *Midway)* participating in FLEETEX 83 carried out a mock attack on Soviet military assets on Zeleny Island in the southern Kurile Island chain, just off the coast of Japan. The Navy not only violated Soviet airspace, it conducted practice bomb runs on Soviet facilities! This information hits me like a bombshell. No wonder the Soviets are so pissed off!

Armed with this new data, I can't wait to get back to Yokota and brief Colonel Stroud and my guys. Unfortunately, on the return helicopter flight to Yokota, our helicopter suffers a catastrophic engine failure. It shudders, and the engine next to me bursts into flames, igniting the fuselage. The Air Force copilot gets on the intercom and yells for me to put out the engine fire with the extinguisher under my seat. I manage to get the engine fire somewhat under control, but the helicopter lists frighteningly, and we're going down fast. The pilot yells for everyone to brace and manages to execute a hard landing on the outfield of a suburban high school baseball field. Thank God the Japanese love baseball.

The helicopter is a total loss, and all of us are very banged up—the two pilots and the three passengers. The guy who was sitting next to me has a broken ankle. The second passenger is badly concussed. I have whiplash and a lot of bruises, but otherwise, I am okay. Both pilots have whiplash and probably worse. The Air Force and the Navy send rescue teams on helicopters to pick us up and take us to various hospitals.

I'm taken to Yokota, and I bullshit my way out of the hospital and go back to the office as quickly as possible. I walk gingerly into Colonel Stroud's office.

"Jesus, Kevin, are you all right? I just heard that your chopper went down. Shouldn't you be at the hospital?"

"Colonel, I only have a sore upper back. I'm okay. Really . . . Anyway, I received important information from my guys at the embassy. They tell me that the Soviets issued a formal diplomatic protest and delivered it to the US ambassador in Moscow, claiming that US Navy fighters overflew one of the Soviet bases on the Kuriles during FLEETEX. A US Navy overflight of Soviet territory led to all these crazy Soviet reactions."

My boss takes off his heavy, black glasses and rubs his forehead. "Kevin, you need to review every public report and every piece of intel traffic from the date the Soviets claim this happened and see if you can find anything that corroborates the demarche. Get busy on this. If those Navy cowboys overflew the Kuriles . . . Christ."

A US overflight by combat aircraft of Soviet territory is an act of war

My team contacts the large National Security Agency—NSA— signals intelligence (SIGINT) site at Misawa Air Base, located at the northern tip of the main Japanese island of Honshu. Sergeant Weatherby queries Misawa and confirms that the Soviets tracked several US Navy fighters violating Soviet airspace. The Navy fighters remained over Soviet territory for as long as twenty minutes. Reuters press reports mention the Soviet demarche being delivered to the US Embassy in Moscow.

Given the Soviets' embarrassment over losing the FLEETEX 83 "ghost fleet" in their own backyard, the fighter overflights had to be the last straw for them. When confronted with the Soviets' official diplomatic complaint, we find that the Pacific Fleet command in Hawaii responded that any such overflight would have been due to navigational equipment errors, which were prone to happen in high latitudes!! Perfect! Why didn't I think of that bullshit explanation?

To make matters worse, we learn that the Soviet air defense base in the southern Kurile Islands, which hosts a MiG-23 fighter unit, *failed to launch a single fighter* during the Navy overflights. Later, we will learn that many Soviet officers in the Far East air defense district lost their jobs, and possibly their heads, over this fiasco.

We have the answer. We now know the reason for the Soviets going apeshit about our intelligence collection flights. We had poked the Russians in the eye, and they were poking back.

My team develops a comprehensive briefing and I present it to Lieutenant General Doug Flannery, the senior US military officer in Japan. In his role, General Flannery is dual-hatted as the overall commander of US Forces, Japan, and Fifth Air Force (5AF).

I meet him in his office on a Sunday morning to give him an update on the latest Soviet mischief, and he looks ragged, with a grey pallor to his handsome face.

He smiles sheepishly. "Babes, these official dinners are gonna kill me. The wife and I didn't get home from downtown Tokyo last night until almost 3:00 AM. You know how the Japanese love their sake toasts—kampai!"

"Yes, sir, it's best to let the Japanese 'win' those drinking contests."

"Absolutely right, babes."

I brief him on the reasons for the heightened Soviet activity. When I finish, Flannery asks me, "What's the bottom line?"

I respond, "Any aircraft tracked as a 'border violator' by the

Soviets will be shot down. No Soviet air defense commander can afford to risk letting a border violator get away. His career, if not his life, will be over."

"Good Lord. Okay, what do you and your bosses recommend?"

"Sir, I know that Colonel Stroud would like the national authorities to review the routes of our intelligence collection flights and determine whether to move the flight routes farther from the Soviet coastline. Soviet radars are notoriously imprecise, and they may erroneously track our aircraft as border violators. Under the current circumstances, such an error would lead to a catastrophe."

General Flannery ponders my recommendation. "I see. Go ahead and brief your findings to Colonel Stone's people at Kadena and continue to monitor the Soviets and update me every week, or more often if necessary. I will talk to the right people about the flight routes. I'm not very optimistic they will agree to a change."

I fly to Okinawa the next day and I deliver my briefing at Kadena Air Base in a cavernous, secure hangar, filled with hundreds of crewmembers.

The colonel introduces me and the whole hangar erupts with profane yelling and booing. What the hell? This is a fucked-up way to begin a serious briefing. It is such a rowdy scene that I tell Colonel Stone, who is seated in the front row, that I can't continue until everybody shuts up. To emphasize my point, I leave the stage.

I watch from the wings as Colonel Stone jumps up on the stage and yells, "Everybody shut the hell up and listen. This is an important briefing. General Flannery personally sent this captain here to brief you guys on all this crazy Russian shit we are dealing with. So shut the hell up unless you have real questions. I don't want to hear any more bullshit. Over to you, Captain."

I begin again. After I brief my findings, questions are hurled at me, and I handle them as they come. Most of them are thoughtful—some are nuts.

One guy asks if the standard flight regimes they are flying are still safe—a perfectly reasonable question. I hem and haw with my answer because I don't want to tell them what I really think. I don't think the standard flight paths are safe, however, I have no authority to change them. The crews know immediately that I am hedging, and they start hollering.

Colonel Stone shakes his head and hops up on the stage with me and tells them to shut up. I'm done. He shakes my hand and shouts into my ear that the presentation will reassure the crews that higher headquarters actually gives a shit about what they are facing. I hope so. I feel like the briefing has been a failure, but Colonel Stone reassures me that it was just what the crews needed to hear.

CHAPTER FOUR

IT DOESN'T MATTER
WHAT I THINK

Captain Kevin Cattani, United States Air Force
Yokota Air Base, Tokyo, Japan and Honolulu, Hawaii, USA

July 1983

The Soviet Air Defense Force maintains its incredibly high level of activity well into the summer of 1983, and I keep General Flannery apprised of the situation on a weekly basis. Frankly, we all wonder when the Soviets' resolve will break down. To keep up this intense campaign month after month must be exhausting for their men and debilitating to their equipment.

General Flannery is increasingly concerned, and during one of my morning current intelligence briefings, he tells me to go to Hawaii and brief the new commander-in-chief of Pacific Command (CINCPAC), Admiral William Crowe.

This order makes me uneasy, and I ask, "Sir, should I tell the entire story, including the part about the US Navy fighter overflights of the Kurile Islands?"

I know that this part of the story is radioactive. The Navy has never really acknowledged the overflight occurred, and I am a junior Air Force officer. I won't have any credibility with a Navy admiral. It is highly likely that my conclusions will be dismissed, or worse, General Flannery may be accused of making false accusations.

He pauses and considers the implications of my question, "Yes, but don't berate the Navy. Don't make the overflight the central part of the story. Admiral Crowe needs to know that the Soviets are on a hair-trigger status out here: this business with the Soviets can get out of hand in a hurry. As you've told me, if the Russians think somebody is in their airspace, there will be hell to pay."

I contemplate this for a moment. "Yes, sir, and will you be with me in Hawaii—I hope?"

"Yes, babes. I'll be with you." The general grins and shakes his index finger at me good-naturedly.

A few days later, General Flannery, his executive officer, and I fly to Hickam Air Force Base, Hawaii. Hickam adjoins the Navy base at Pearl Harbor, where the US Pacific Fleet is based. Both Hickam and Pearl were attacked by the Japanese Navy on 7 December 1941, and the Pacific Air Forces (PACAF) headquarters building at Hickam is still peppered with bullet holes from that Sunday morning attack more than forty years ago.

Admiral Crowe's headquarters is located at Camp Smith, on top of a large hill, high above Pearl Harbor. The new commander-in-chief of American forces in the Pacific is a tall, ruddy-faced, somewhat rumpled-looking intellectual, whose career has defied the Navy's standard template for how one rises to the rank of full admiral. He is too, well . . . intellectual? He earned a master's degree from Stanford and a Princeton PhD. Although he is a Naval Academy graduate, he doesn't have a lot of sea duty on his record. Famously, he turned down an opportunity to become one of Admiral Hyman Rickover's nuclear Navy acolytes. Although he has just arrived in Hawaii, having most recently commanded all US Naval forces in Europe, he has a great deal of experience in the Pacific.

In the secure room that abuts the admiral's office, I walk through my briefing, soft-pedaling the US Navy overflight. Admiral Crowe listens with keen attention and asks no questions until I finish the entire briefing. Then he asks me for the bottom line.

I keep my response brief. "Admiral, the Soviets are on a hair trigger in the Far East, and any aircraft that they think is violating their border will be shot down. That said, this massive air defense surge has been underway since mid-April and the Soviets must be dead tired. It must have affected aircraft maintenance standards and personnel performance. Nerves will be frayed, as well."

Crowe nods and asks. "Would they shoot down a civilian aircraft?"

Shit, I never considered that. We were so fixated on the danger to our intelligence collection aircraft that the thought of the Soviets attacking an errant civilian airliner hasn't occurred to any of us. Flannery stares at me.

Crowe waits for my answer for a moment. He's patient but he won't wait forever. "Well, Captain? What do you think?"

"Admiral, if they think a civilian aircraft is a border violator, they will intercept it, identify it, and try to communicate with it. If they cannot identify it or communicate with it, then I think all bets are off. I mean . . . that is, I think that the command structure in the Soviet Far East is so paranoid that the impulse will be to shoot first and ask questions later. Nobody wants to be the colonel who lets another border violator get away."

Crowe smiles. "So you are saying that the US Navy set this in motion? Because of the overflight of the Kurile Islands?"

General Flannery attempts to interject a comment, but Admiral Crowe waves him off.

"I want to hear what this young captain thinks. He's the expert— right?"

I bite my lip. "Admiral, the Soviets believe that our fighters violated their airspace for up to twenty minutes. The Russians issued a demarche stating that our fighters performed simulated bomb runs over one of their military facilities in the Kurile Islands. I can't prove the Navy did so. All I know is that the Soviets think it happened and that they filed an official protest about this incident with the US ambassador in Moscow."

Admiral Crowe looks at Flannery. "General, I'll have my exec call Pearl and ask CINCPACFLT to drive up here immediately."

General Flannery and I lock eyes. This is precisely the outcome we don't want. It looks like we are being set up to have a confrontation with the four-star admiral commanding the Pacific Fleet—one of Crowe's key subordinates. The massive FLEETEX-83 was conducted on his watch and at his direction. I read the Navy's after-action report on the exercise, and it touted FLEETEX as an enormous success. One can't argue with the exceptional skill, daring, and professionalism the Pacific Fleet demonstrated during FLEETEX-83. Who cares if it provoked the Soviets? And if provocation causes them to burn out their air defense forces—then, well . . . fuck those commies, and good for us!

While we await the arrival of the Pacific Fleet commander, Admiral Crowe returns to his office and General Flannery walks to the visiting VIP office to make some phone calls. I'm left in the secure room to fret about the coming confrontation. I feel like I am about to go into combat.

I know this much—the commanding admiral of the Pacific Fleet is a very busy guy. Like Crowe, he is a four-star admiral. Getting a call from his direct boss and being told to drop everything on his schedule and drive up to Camp Smith must be a major pain in his ass. He is unlikely to be in a good mood when he gets here.

With the arrival of the commander of the Pacific Fleet, we reconvene. Admiral Crowe tells me to start the briefing from the top. I don't get far. When I gingerly mention the Navy overflight, the briefing comes to an abrupt halt.

The Pacific Fleet chief's first comment isn't promising. "Admiral Crowe, what can this Air Force captain possibly understand about naval operations at sea? I cannot corroborate his story, which is unsubstantiated speculation. Who knows why the Soviets think we overflew their island? Or why they are behaving the way they have since April? Maybe they are trying to improve the performance of their air defense troops. Or maybe they simply ran out of vodka and are drinking hydraulic fluid again. Admiral, you understand how crazy the Soviets can be. Honestly, I don't have time for this."

Crowe gestures at me to respond. He looks amused. I glance at General Flannery—he does not look at all amused.

Good Lord . . . here goes . . .

"Admiral, we know that the Soviets filed an official protest with the American ambassador in Moscow about a US Navy overflight of their territory, including military facilities on the Kurile Islands. And we have additional intelligence that appears to substantiate the Soviet claim about an overflight. We also know that they replaced senior officers in the Soviet Far East after the incident. We know that they sent two Bison bombers to violate US airspace by overflying Nunivak Island in Alaska just two days after the Navy overflight. The one thing that is clear is that the Soviets think a US Navy overflight occurred and they claim that our fighters spent more than twenty minutes in their airspace."

The Pacific Fleet chief is unmoved. He tells me in a condescending tone, "Captain, do you think you understand the Russians? Do you? The Soviets cannot be trusted to tell the truth. Hell, Stalin signed an alliance with Hitler, and then fought the biggest war in the history of the world against him. Stalin killed how many of his own citizens? These are evil people with a failing form of government. They lie. I don't believe anything they say—or care what they think. Maybe they replaced officers in the Far East because they were drunks or incompetent and they couldn't track us during our fleet exercise. Maybe they are reacting so often because they need the training. You don't know why they are reacting the way they are, and you cannot prove anything, so it doesn't matter what you think."

Crowe's expression changes. He looks at me gravely and motions for me to respond. General Flannery looks at the floor, taking an unusual interest in the pattern of the carpet.

I gather myself. "Admiral, with respect, the Soviets think this happened, and I believe it does matter what *they* think because what *they* think is driving them to change their operations in ways that are potentially dangerous to our reconnaissance aircrews. And sir, you are correct—it doesn't matter what I think. What matters is what the *Soviets* think, and they believe that there was an overflight, and their entire air defense network in the Far East has been on high alert ever since, potentially endangering the lives of our reconnaissance crews, and possibly those of civilians on commercial airliners." My upper body is shaking when I finish. I wonder if I've gone too far with the admiral. This encounter can't be career-enhancing for me or General Flannery.

Admiral Crowe ends the meeting on that point. "Okay, Captain, that's enough. I think you make a crucial point. What matters is what the Soviets think, and I believe you have a good handle on that. Good work. Thank you and General Flannery for coming. You've done some nice work. Very thorough. I understand the situation much better now."

I haven't presented my entire briefing, but I've provoked the conversation with the Pacific Fleet commander that Admiral Crowe wanted. I can only imagine the conversation that the two four-star admirals have after we depart. We drive back to Hickam in silence. I'm worried that General Flannery is angry with me. His approval is very important to me.

As we are getting situated on the general's plane for the return flight to Tokyo, Flannery finally says to me, "It doesn't matter what I think! It only matters what the Soviets think! That's classic and so true, although I don't think the commander-in-chief of the Pacific Fleet will add you to his Christmas card list any time soon. I'd also avoid Navy officers' clubs for a few years if I were you. Great job, babes."

I thank the general and fall asleep. I sleep most of the way back to Tokyo.

CHAPTER FIVE

THE TARGET IS DESTROYED

Captain Kevin Cattani, United States Air Force
Yokota Air Base, Tokyo, Japan

1 September 1983

I schedule myself to give the current intelligence briefing to General Flannery and his staff on Thursday, 1 September 1983. I arrive at my office at 1:00 AM to begin preparing briefing items for the morning. I start to work on a story regarding the Soviet war in Afghanistan, but I struggle to find much new to say about the conflict, which has been raging since December 1979.

Master Sergeant David Parent (Pops to the enlisted guys) is NCO of the watch tonight, and he is working with a second lieutenant named Josh Stafford, fresh out of air intelligence school at Lowry Air Force Base in Denver. Pops is a Black Cajun from somewhere deep in the Louisiana bayou country and is a superb intelligence analyst and leader among the enlisted force.

I'm trying to stay awake and find something interesting to brief when Pops appears at my door. "How's the briefing going, Captain?"

He doesn't wait for me to answer and continues, "Can you come into the watch for a minute? The Soviets are running a weird exercise that I think you should look at."

"Sure, can you tell me what's up?"

He shrugs and says, "I'm not sure. It looks like the Soviets are running an air defense exercise out of Petropavlovsk, which is weird at this time of night. I have never seen anything like this before."

"Well, if you haven't seen anything like this before, then it *must* be unusual."

I follow Pops into the watch, and he takes me to the huge map where he has marked up numerous flight tracks around the Soviets' Kamchatka peninsula. I check the clocks that are fixed to the wall high over the map board and see that it is now 1:50 AM Tokyo time.

The Russian fighter pilots are flying a crazy number of hours per month reacting to our reconnaissance flights and shouldn't require much, if any, training. Certainly, they shouldn't need to train in the middle of the night.

Pops takes me through his analysis. "I have been coordinating and comparing notes with Elmendorf and Misawa [Elmendorf Air Force Base, Alaska, and Misawa Air Base, home to the US military's and the NSA's two big signal intelligence sites covering the North Pacific]. Sir, none of the guys at either site have seen anything like this exercise at this time of night. We were expecting a Soviet ICBM test launch tonight to the reentry area near Kamchatka. Our Cobra Ball was up earlier to monitor the test, but it'll be back home at Shemya by now."

"So, given all that, there doesn't seem to be any reason for this level of air defense activity in the middle of the night. Did the Soviets conduct the ICBM test earlier tonight?"

"No, sir, it doesn't look like they did. Cobra Ball was on station during the launch window, but the launch never happened. The Ball went off-station about 1:00 AM our time and then headed back to Shemya. Take a look at these tracks. These look like routine fighter reactions related to Cobra Ball, which was orbiting right here—you see?"

He points to an area of the North Pacific well off the coast of Kamchatka on the big map board.

I squint for a closer look. "Yeah, that makes sense, but these other fighter reactions don't . . . they don't seem to be anywhere near the Cobra Ball orbit."

Pops nods. "Exactly. I don't understand all this other crazy shit— why would the Soviets be looking way over here?"

"Have you checked in with NSOC?" (The National SIGINT Operations Center, located at NSA headquarters at Fort Meade, Maryland.)

"Yes, sir, and they agree that this is a weird exercise. They don't have an explanation either, so they're not very helpful."

"Well, that's a switch for NSOC," I say sarcastically. "Okay, well keep me apprised. Grab me if you think you need me to look at anything. Hey, wait, I have an idea."

"Sir?"

I address the young watch commander. "Lieutenant Stafford, go down the hall to the CAF and ask them to call the Tokyo Transport Ministry and see if they have any trans-Pacific airliners off course."

Stafford nods and takes off at a trot toward the CAF, the Command Advisory Function.

The CAF is the operational section of our combined intelligence/operations unit. The function is manned 24/7, like the intelligence watch, but it is staffed with officers who are themselves reconnaissance pilots and command and control experts. The big room has five tiered rows of desks and chairs overlooking a huge plexiglass map of Northeast Asia and the North Pacific. It looks like the air operations centers one sees depicted in World War II movies. Frankly, the technology is about the same as it was in World War II. Enlisted technicians plot the routes of American intelligence collection aircraft on the plexiglass, annotating pertinent data by writing backwards from behind the glass. It is a laborious, precise process. The commander of the CAF sits in the center of the tiered rows, providing him a great overview of the entire operation.

A few minutes later, Stafford is back in the watch. He reports that the Tokyo Transport Ministry's air traffic control center is maintaining that all the trans-Pacific airliners are calling in as expected and without incident. The Japanese believe all the airliners flying tonight are on proper course. I can't think of anything else to do at this point and I go back to my desk to continue wrestling with the morning briefing.

After a while, I find I can't concentrate on it, and I go back to the watch for an update. I find Pops perched atop a high ladder that enables him to write on the high reaches of the map board. I look at the clocks again and it's now 2:15 AM Tokyo time. Pops is plotting a track that stretches from Petropavlovsk on the Kamchatka peninsula westward across the Sea of Okhotsk.

I ask Pops, "What track are you plotting?"

He climbs down from the ladder. "Well, sir, it's not a real track. I figured I would do an experiment. I am plotting a ghost track beginning at the point where we saw all that fighter activity around Kamchatka and projecting it west by southwest, which will take it to and possibly over the southern half of Sakhalin Island. I think this is the most logical track for our ghost to take. We know that the Cobra Ball went home quite a while ago now, but what if there *is* something out there? What if the Soviets are looking for a real airplane?"

I respect Pops's creativity here, but I am skeptical. "Like what? The Transport Ministry tells us that all the airliners are checking in nominally—no issues."

Pops replies, "I realize that this could be an exercise, like NSA claims. If they think it's an exercise, it's hard for me to argue with them. After all, not much the Soviets have done since April makes a lot of sense. So why should tonight be any different? Captain, my ghost track may be a complete waste of time, but what if it isn't?"

Indeed. "Sarge, don't get me wrong, I think your ghost track is a brilliant idea. Press on with it. Lieutenant Stafford, have you had the CAF check in with the Transport Ministry again?"

Stafford looks up from his desk. "Yes, sir, and I think that is a dry well. All the planes are checking in on time, and the Transport Ministry has no way of independently confirming where the planes are located. They can't radio them, and they have no radar coverage that far out in the Pacific, so they have to rely on what the airliners transmit."

I decide to press the young officer a bit. "Lieutenant, what do you think we are dealing with tonight?"

He stands up and walks toward me. Standing beside me, he looks up at the big map. "Captain, Misawa is working the problem and they have more resources than we do, and they don't have any answers. Sergeant Parent is postulating a ghost track that is projected from the area where we observed the last fighter reactions. If that ghost track turns out to be a real aircraft and if it is heading west toward Sakhalin Island, then we should see a new round of fighter reactions as it approaches Sakhalin—especially from the Soviet Air Defense bases on the southern end of the island. Based on the sergeant's ghost track projections, the track ought to be approaching Sakhalin at about 0245-0300 local. Maybe we should talk to Wakkanai, sir."

I ponder that suggestion for a moment. "Yes, maybe we should. Let me see what I can do. Good idea."

Wakkanai is an old American SIGINT site at the northern tip of Hokkaido, the northernmost of the Japanese islands. This site has the best chance of seeing any activity around Sakhalin Island, at the western edge of the Sea of Okhotsk. The Americans moved out of Wakkanai a few years ago. It was reoccupied not long ago by Japanese SIGINT specialists. I don't know much about the site, but I have heard that the Japanese are running what amounts to skeleton crews, especially on the overnight shifts. The tricky part is how to communicate with Wakkanai, which is now a Japanese facility. It's possible that the Americans at Misawa can communicate directly with Wakkanai, although I can't. I decide to contact our Japanese counterparts in downtown Tokyo and have Sergeant Parent make inquiries with Misawa.

I get on the teletype that connects us with the intelligence watch at the Japanese Ministry of Defense. When the Japanese respond, I am happy to learn that Lieutenant Colonel Sakai is chief of the watch tonight. He and I have traveled on official business together around Japan and to Hawaii several times. We know each other well, and his English language ability is terrific—far better than my Japanese. He is a rising star in the Japanese Air Force, and he recently received word that he will be promoted to full colonel in 1984. He told me a few months ago that he is studying French because he will be stationed at NATO headquarters in Belgium next year as Japan's senior military liaison to NATO. The last time we had lunch together, he ordered in French, which didn't go over well since we were at a sushi bar in the Ginza district of downtown Tokyo.

Colonel Sakai has little of the reticence one finds in most Japanese officers. He has a natural swagger and confidence about him and a reputation for speaking his mind to senior officers and Ministry of Defense officials. I have seen him dressed down in public more than once by Japanese generals, and he takes it in stride. The tongue-lashings don't change his aggressive behavior. He has the courage of his convictions and I have never known him to be wrong about a professional matter. I contact him via teletype. The teletype is slow and cumbersome; however, it is the most reliable form of secure communication with the Japanese.

"Sakai-san, kombanwa. It is Captain Cattani calling in from Yokota, sir."

"Kombanwa, Cattani-san."

"Sir, we are dealing with a confusing situation tonight. Can you tell me if you are receiving reports from Wakkanai now?"

"Cattani-san, the Wakkanai team is working, and they are reporting. Why?"

"Sir, your team is better able to collect against Sakhalin Island than anyone else, and we may need that tonight. Can you please help by sending me anything Wakkanai collects related to unusual Soviet air defense activity—in and around Sakhalin Island? I know this is an unusual request. However, we have seen Soviet fighter activity around Kamchatka tonight that we can't explain. I wish I could be more specific, but we really don't know what the Soviets are up to. Thank you." God, my message sounds vague. I wish I could be more percise, but I rely on Sakai being smart enough to parse it.

The Japanese colonel quickly responds. "This *is* an unusual request. If I understand correctly what you want, then I will need to ask a higher authority."

"Yes, sir. I will stand by."

About fifteen minutes later I still have no response from Sakai and Pops is back at my desk with a very worried look on his face.

"Captain, that exercise that we saw over Kamchatka earlier, well, it's back. But now it's over Sakhalin."

We hustle to the watch, and I see that Pops has continued plotting his ghost track over the Sea of Okhotsk. It is nearing the east coast of Sakhalin Island. I look again at the clocks over the map board, and it is now 2:50 AM local. He is getting reports of Soviet fighter activity from a base on Sakhalin right about where his ghost track should be—no wonder Pops looks so worried.

I turn to Stafford and say, "Go down to the CAF immediately and brief Colonel Hawk on this development. Also, tell him that I recommend he send one of his senior NCOs to sit down here in the watch with us. Let him know we don't know exactly what we are dealing with, but it may be serious. Okay?"

"Yes, sir."

I go back to the teletype to recontact the Japanese. "Sakai-san, do you have any feedback for me?"

"Not yet, Cattani-san."

I feel powerless. I must be missing something. If Pops's ghost track is a real airplane, then it is headed for Sakhalin, and it will be met by Soviet fighters and surface-to-air missile batteries. What the hell could it be? The CAF checks with the Transport Ministry again and they still have heard nothing unusual from their trans-Pacific airliners and they are growing annoyed by our inquiries. It's tremendously frustrating to be in the dark like this. At least we know we are keeping everybody alert through the night, for whatever that's worth.

I go back to the watch, and Pops is up on the ladder again, adjusting his ghost track. Could Pops's ghost track represent an errant civilian airplane, or is it just a ghost, representing nothing?

I walk back to the teletype and contact Sakai again.

"Cattani-san, I have permission to send you reports. We are watching the situation carefully."

"Thank you, sir. I will be standing by."

I walk to the CAF to give Colonel Hawk, who is commanding the CAF tonight, my perspective on the situation. Stafford and Pops have their hands full dealing with reams of message traffic and keeping up constant communication with Misawa. I am the senior intelligence officer on duty, and I figure the colonel ought to hear from me.

After I brief him, Colonel Hawk, who is a very cool customer— he's an SR-71 pilot—is visibly alarmed that the "exercise" we'd seen over Kamchatka has started again near Sakhalin. He sternly tells his guys to be alert and ready for action.

As I turn to leave the CAF, Hawk casts me a worried look and motions for me to walk back to where he is sitting. "What do you think is really going on, Kevin?"

"Colonel, I wish I could give you something. It's either a complete 'nothing' or there is a real plane out there. If there is an airplane out there, and it violates the Soviet border, well, all bets are off."

Hawk emits a low whistle. "This is like the briefing you did for General Flannery—I mean the warning you gave about border violators. For God's sake, I hope it's not a real airplane."

"Yes, sir—me, too."

Back in the watch, I see it is now 3:15 AM local time. "Guys, what do we know?"

Pops is the first to respond. "Captain, we have fighter activity over Sakhalin, and Misawa is simply going apeshit trying to figure out what the hell is going on! The Misawa guys are telling me that they are so busy they don't have time to talk to us now."

"Did Misawa give you anything on Wakkanai's status?"

"Not really. Reading between the lines, I think they have something going on at Wakkanai but they won't tell me."

Pops and I walk over to the teletype to see if the Japanese have sent us anything. Nothing. I send another message to Colonel Sakai.

He responds right away, "We are getting unusual reports, but it is taking a long time to translate from Russian into English. My guys at Wakkanai are Japanese, you know!"

"Copy that, Colonel Sakai. Domo arigato. You can send the reports to me in Russian, or phonetic Russian, and we will translate them here to save time." I await Sakai's response.

The Japanese colonel gets back to me after a couple of minutes. "Yes, Cattani-san, we will send you the reports in Russian. That will save valuable time."

"Thank you, Colonel."

I turn to face Pops, who is standing beside me. "You go back to the watch and keep an eye on things. I'll stay here with the teletype. If I get anything, I will be in immediately."

"Roger that, Captain."

I check my wristwatch—3:30 AM. I have completely dropped tomorrow morning's current intelligence briefing. It looks like we have a real-world situation, and the morning briefing will be about whatever 'this' is.

We know Soviet fighters are active, but we don't know much else. Nothing comes in from Sakai via the teletype and I go back into the watch.

Pops briefs me. "Sir, I have updated my ghost track. I built two different tracks using two different airspeed factors. The faster speed is what we would expect from a 747 airliner. The slower speed is nominally for a 707—like an RC-135. The faster speed has the 747 just west of Sakhalin. The slower track is just east of the island. Based on the most recent Soviet activity, I think that the faster track makes more sense."

I like Parent's analysis. "So, this is probably a 747—a civilian plane? Should I start waking up guys and getting them in here? Or will it be more of a nuisance for you to bring them up to speed?"

Pops doesn't hesitate. "Sir, get Weatherby in here to help me, please!"

"Will do."

I wake up Weatherby at home. I can overhear him tell his wife he has to go to work immediately. Her response is to curse loudly, with my name prominently mentioned. Weatherby is our most talented analyst, and it will take very little time to get him up to speed. He also is a Russian linguist. He is in the watch by 4:00 AM.

I contemplate calling Lieutenant Colonel Stroud, but I still feel that I don't have any definitive intelligence to justify waking him up.

I contact Sakai again. He tells me to stand by the teletype. This is the same kind of machine that my father's generation used during World War II, and it is reliable—but slow. Suddenly, a message comes rattling over the machine. It's in "pidgin" Russian, very tough to decipher. I run into the watch to get Weatherby to help me.

I yell at Pops. "What are you getting from Misawa?"

It is now 5:00 AM, and we are still in the dark.

"Nothing yet."

We wait and wait, feeling blind and helpless. Weatherby is trying to read a new message in Russian from Colonel Sakai, and we go to my desk to read it as best we can.

Weatherby is sweating and smoking bundles of cigarettes. "Sir, this is a shitload of fighter activity and this ain't like any Russian I know. Can you help me with some of this crazy gibberish?"

I crouch over Weatherby's shoulder. "Well, your Russian is better than mine, but let's give it a go."

My heart is racing, and my head is pounding. I wonder what my blood pressure reading is. I get the same fight, flight, freeze feeling one gets from the anticipation of combat. I glance at my wristwatch and it is 5:30 AM. Suddenly, I worry that all this Soviet activity is just an exercise and I won't have a current intelligence briefing for the general's staff meeting. What if I have been on a wild goose chase all night? I'll look like an idiot.

Then Stafford comes running down from the CAF. It is 5:45 AM.

"Captain, the Transport Ministry just reported to the CAF that one of its trans-Pacific airliners is 'missing.' They believe it is a Korean Air Lines flight en route to Seoul."

Holy shit. Pops's ghost track is real!!

"Make sure the flight commander at Misawa has this new information. I know they aren't talking to us right now, but get it to him one way or the other."

I sprint down the hallway to the CAF to see if they have a flight number for the Korean Air Lines plane and ask if they can get any other information to help us complete the puzzle. They don't have the flight number yet, but they are working to get it.

I run back to the watch. Pops is there, standing by the map board. "Captain, Misawa is still going crazy. I don't know what they are getting, but they're getting something. They're too busy to talk to me."

Time seems to accelerate and decelerate. What did Heisenberg say about that? Einstein also wrote about the relativity of time. Oh, well, I guess it isn't relevant what they thought right now. I gotta keep my head in the game.

I look at my watch and it's now 7:00 AM. Christ, where did the night go? Weatherby hurries in with a new message he's pulled off the teletype from Colonel Sakai. He rolls the paper out on a desk so the two of us can read it.

"Okay, Sergeant, let's see if this tells us anything."

We start deciphering the phonetic Russian as best we can. Weatherby, as usual, is amazingly helpful. I read something of real importance and exclaim, "Holy shit! Look at this section."

Weatherby furrows his brow and translates along with me. "Sir, it sure looks like the Soviets think there is an actual airplane, and they're trying to intercept and identify it. The target changes course.

The fighter tries to identify it. I can't make out what this next section is trying to say. Shit, this looks real. This *is* real."

We look at each other in a state of shock. "Sergeant, call Colonel Stroud and ask him to get in here immediately! Tell him I mean *immediately!* I need to keep working this stuff. And after you call Stroud, ask the watch to update the commander of the CAF. Got it?"

"Copy all, Captain." Weatherby takes off to call Colonel Stroud.

Jesus, what is going on? It looks like the Soviets found a real airplane and are trying to identify it. Due to the latency caused by listening, translating, analyzing, and reporting, everything I am reading now happened hours ago. Whatever happened to this ghost plane has already occurred.

I need to talk to Colonel Sakai.

"Colonel, this appears to be a very urgent situation. What is your assessment?"

"Cattani-san, yes I agree—very urgent and serious."

"Colonel, do you have another message yet from Wakkanai?"

"Yes, and I've called in the senior officers. I will send you the next message."

"Thank you, sir."

I run into the watch. "Guys, what do you have from Misawa?"

Pops responds, "Sir, they are in full panic mode up there, and they can't take any time to talk to us. One of my buddies thinks they may have recorded the Soviets reporting a 'live missile firing.'"

I stare at Pops in disbelief. "Lieutenant Stafford, go to the CAF and ask Colonel Hawk to come down to the watch right now! We need to brief him here—at our map board. He needs to know that we are calling in the seniors. Colonel Stroud will be here soon, too, and I want to brief Stroud and the Hawk at the same time."

"Yes, sir."

"Sergeant Parent, go ahead and execute the senior officer recall list. Tell them that I need them all here for a real-world situation."

"Yes, sir."

Weatherby and I go back to the teletype, which has started to rattle again. We have a go at the new message. "Okay, Sergeant, let's see what we have. This looks like a fighter acknowledging orders from the ground controller. He is getting into a firing position. The pilot then reports something I can't figure out. It looks like here . . . he fires two missiles! Good Lord."

Weatherby has a desolate look. "Holy shit, Captain." He sighs, quietly.

I continue translating. The Soviet pilot's last transmission is, "The target is destroyed."

CHAPTER SIX

PRELUDE TO WAR?

Captain Kevin Cattani, United States Air Force
Yokota Air Base, Tokyo, Japan

Thursday, 1 September 1983—Morning

A CRITICOM (which stands for critical communication), is a message that is sent through the communications network with the highest possible priority. A CRITICOM overrides everything else on the network. A CRITICOM must be delivered to the President of the United States within twenty minutes after the White House receives it, no matter where in the world the President is.

No one wants to issue a CRITICOM based on intelligence that turns out to be wrong. On the other hand, there is an obligation to ensure the President is delivered critical information as quickly as possible. The natural inclination is to act cautiously. The dilemma lies in the tension between the need to act quickly, and the need to get it right. A CRITICOM is too important to be based on speculation. Intelligence officers have to get it right the first time. The President will make decisions and act based on the information contained in a CRITICOM. The information must be accurate.

The news media, on the other hand, has no such obligation. The rush to "scoop" the competition drives them to report information quickly, even if based on speculation or flaky sources. News reporters can always change their story later, no matter how much damage their erroneous early reporting causes. Intelligence officers don't have that luxury—certainly not with an event as momentous as the one at hand, which could be a prelude to war between the world's two superpowers.

I have a major decision to make. "Sergeant Weatherby, ask Lieutenant Stafford to call the flight commander at Misawa and ask him if he has the same information we just got— 'The target is destroyed.' Okay?"

"Yes, sir, on my way. But what does this mean? What target?"

I give Weatherby a withering look.

"Okay, on my way, sir."

I check the teletype to see if there is anything new from Colonel Sakai. Nothing. I contemplate my options and suddenly, Weatherby is back at my side. "Captain, Colonel Stroud and Colonel Hawk are in the watch. And you should know that Misawa doesn't have the info we got from Colonel Sakai."

"Okay, stay here and watch for any new communication from Colonel Sakai. Get me as soon as anything comes over the teletype."

"Yes, sir."

I walk back in the watch to see that Colonel Stroud is firing questions at Pops and Stafford. He sees me and asks, "Kevin, what do you have? The guys have gotten me and Colonel Hawk up to speed with the essentials. Do we have a real airplane in trouble?"

"Colonel, the last message from the Japanese contains the phrase, 'The target is destroyed.' I have to emphasize that this is based on *my* translation of the message."

Stroud's eyes bulge behind his big glasses. "Hold on . . . 'the target is destroyed'? What the hell does that mean? What target?"

"Sir, the CAF has been calling the Transport Ministry all night. Shortly after—hey, Stafford, what time did you tell me about the ministry's missing airplane report?"

"Captain, let me check my log. It was right at 0545 this morning."

That seems like days ago. "Okay, thanks. Colonel, the ministry reports they are missing a Korean Air Lines plane. It may correlate with the ghost track that Sergeant Parent has been plotting here on the map board . . . across the Sea of Okhotsk. Misawa reported a lot of Soviet activity around Sakhalin beginning about 3:00 AM. And it seems the Soviets found a plane, identified it, and destroyed it."

Stroud practically shouts at me. "Captain, if they shot down an airplane, is it the missing Korean airliner? What is Misawa saying? They are the cognizant SIGINT authority out here, not us."

"Sir, Misawa basically stopped communicating with us because they're so busy. We're getting their reports, of course, but they aren't responding to us—to any of our questions."

Colonel Stroud considers his next move for a moment and says, "The best approach would be for us to issue a CRITICOM simultaneously with Misawa, assuming they agree with the reporting. I will call the commander at Misawa. Wrongly issuing a CRITICOM is not a career-enhancing move."

"Yes, sir. Should we contact General Flannery's aide and have the general come in?"

"I think so. Do it. I will call the Misawa commander."

Stroud makes his call to Misawa while I contact General Flannery's office. Flannery will be in the watch shortly, and I need to be prepared to brief him upon his arrival. I look at the wall clock. It is almost 8:00 AM.

Stroud says, "Kevin, Misawa is issuing a CRITICOM. The commander up there told me it is our call if we want to issue one, too. We agreed on common language and I want you to write it up."

"Yes, sir."

The two CRITICOMs hit NSOC at NSA headquarters, Fort Meade, Maryland, almost simultaneously. The senior watch officer at NSOC acknowledges receipt via secure teletype. It is shortly after 7:00 PM on 31 August in the Washington, D.C., area. He also writes that they will need validation prior to sending the CRITICOM to the White House. He opines that since it is becoming apparent that the "target" is probably a civilian aircraft, it is doubtful that this is a national security event and may not warrant passing along to the President. Really?! Not a national security event? What fucking planet is he on?

This perspective, provided from some 6,800 miles away, strikes me as absurdly out of touch with the reality we are confronting. Of course this is a national security event or soon will be.

General Flannery walks into the watch center with the vice commander of 5AF, an Air Force brigadier general.

Flannery looks around the room and glances up at the big map board. "What do you have, gentlemen?"

Stroud responds, "General, Captain Cattani has been here all night and he is the best one to brief you. We have a potentially serious incident over Sakhalin Island. We just sent a CRITICOM to NSA."

The general almost jumps off the ground. "A CRITICOM? Has it been sent to the White House?"

Stroud responds, "Sir, NSOC is holding it, pending validation. They also aren't convinced it is a national security event because it likely relates to a civilian airliner. I am confident it will be sent, but NSA needs to be convinced that the Soviets shooting down a civilian airliner is something the President ought to know."

General Flannery gives Stroud an exasperated look. "The Soviets shot down what? Colonel, is the NSA guy here?"

"General, I am here." The senior NSA civilian representative to the command has just arrived.

General Flannery turns to acknowledge the NSA rep. "Okay, it sounds like we need you to get involved, and we will need your help with the folks at Fort Meade." Then he turns to look right at me. "All right, Kevin, what have you got?"

I report the events of the night as succinctly as I can. In addition to General Flannery, everyone in the watch is listening intently as this is the first time most of them have heard the story from start to its apparent finish. General Flannery sits down on a metal stool a few feet from me and studies me intently as I talk. His demeanor is subdued, yet intense and sober. He asks a few questions, using a softer voice than usual. He never was given to histrionics, and his attitude in the moment is a study in emotional control. He is studying my face as if to discern the truth revealed by my facial expressions. His silent probing makes me nervous about my analysis.

When I conclude, he responds, "All right. I got it. Do you believe this happened? That the Soviets shot down an airplane? A civilian airliner?"

"Sir, we cannot be absolutely certain at this point, but yes. I think the reporting we have tells us that they shot down somebody—most likely the Korean Air Lines plane. I can say that with 99 percent certainty."

"Wow, I don't think I have ever heard an intelligence officer give me 99 percent odds on the sun rising in the east."

I smile for the first time all night and morning and say, "Sir, the Japanese Transport Ministry report concerning a missing KAL flight seems to correlate with our reporting. So I think the Soviets shot down a civilian Korean Air Lines flight tonight. A 747 full of civilians."

The NSA senior man tries to interject something, but General Flannery waves him off. "Relax, everybody, I believe Kevin. Colonel Stroud, what is NSOC saying now?"

"No response yet, General."

"Let me read your CRITICOM message."

Pops hands the general a paper copy of the CRITICOM. Flannery takes his time, carefully reading the text we have just issued. "Kevin, what is the fastest way to get a message to NSOC, so that we can guarantee that they actually read it quickly?"

"General, the most reliable way is to send them a teletype message with FLASH override priority. We can send it from that teletype right over there. The secure phone line is often pretty flaky—the line drops your call more often than not."

"Okay, show me how to use the teletype. I will type the message myself."

I show General Flannery how to send a message. He can approve a FLASH override priority himself, which saves a lot of time and ensures that his message will get through a communications network increasingly clogged on this busy morning. It is a momentous decision for him to send a message like he is about to send to NSA, and he must know it. If he weighs in on a CRITICOM that turns out to be erroneous or exaggerated, he will retire as a lieutenant general. A mistake at a moment like this will mean that he can kiss making his fourth star goodbye.

I stand beside him as he calmly taps out a message to the watch director at NSOC. Strangely, he has a little smile on his face while he types. Essentially, his FLASH message reads, *Immediately convey USFJ CRITICOM to White House. My intelligence team is convinced that we are dealing with a serious national security event as detailed in our CRITICOM." Lt Gen Douglas Flannery, Commander.*

General Flannery smiles. "Well, Kevin, how's that?"

"General, that is a very concise message."

We get a return message from the NSOC watch director indicating that he has sent both CRITICOMs—the one from Misawa and ours—to the White House.

Flannery speaks to everyone assembled in the watch, "Okay, guys, what do you need from me? Let me know if you need my help to get resources—okay? I am going to the CAF now to convene the battle staff. Kevin, I will need you to come down there and brief them. The main thing they will need to understand is the threat environment we may face around Sakhalin Island. Don't sugarcoat it. Understood?"

Every intelligence officer in the room nods.

General Flannery points at the big map. "What is this body of water called—the one between the mainland and Sakhalin Island?"

Several of us respond simultaneously. "The Tatar Strait, sir."

"Okay, so that is where I should send the SAR guys—right?" SAR stands for search and rescue.

Colonel Stroud walks up to the map. "Probably, sir. If an aircraft was exiting Soviet airspace over Sakhalin when it was shot down, then it probably would go down in the Strait, or possibly on the Siberian mainland. It is hard to say, but, yes, that is the right area for SAR."

"Got it. Kevin, come down to brief the battle staff in thirty minutes. Stroud, you come, too."

General Flannery turns to the senior intelligence officers. "Guys, I am sure you will need to call your respective chains of command. Make certain that your agencies understand they need to give you top priority for resources. Okay? I am relying on you guys to keep the intelligence leadership in Hawaii and Washington up to speed—got it? J-2, I want you to call the ambassador downtown and tell him what we are dealing with. And make sure the CIA chief of station is apprised. Okay? We are all going to be very busy, so make sure that you keep each other informed. Remember that this is a team sport. There are no different-colored jerseys here. After we brief the battle staff, I will establish my base of operations in the CAF. Colonel Stroud, make sure your watch brings me any updates as they come in. Kevin, you are going to need to stay here all day to brief my aircrews that will be flying into the Tatar Strait. Have you been here all night?"

"Sir, since 1:00 A.M."

"Okay, well, I need you to stay sharp all day now—got it, babes?"

"Yes, sir."

With that, General Flannery calmly walks out of the watch. He still has a little smile on his face. What is that about? He isn't happy, obviously. He must be worried about a confrontation with the Soviet Union. Nonetheless, I think he welcomes the challenge and the opportunity for his command to be center stage and to show the world what his team can do in a crisis. He always appears in control of his emotions, but his preternatural calm this morning is both comforting and disconcerting. For Christ's sake, he was smiling to himself while sending the most momentous message of his life on the watch teletype! I didn't even know he could type.

Meanwhile, there is a ton of work to do, and everyone is scrambling. At the same time, the day shift is arriving and getting briefed, and all the analysts and NSA people are showing up for work, thinking that this will be a normal working day. They are disabused of that assumption rapidly.

One remarkable report we receive that morning from the Japanese at Wakkanai concerns a conversation between two Russian radar operators on Sakhalin Island. One of the operators is at Sokol Air Base on Sakhalin. He tells his buddy at a distant radar site that he overheard someone talking about the debriefing of the Sokol-based pilot who shot down the mystery aircraft—the fighter pilot thinks he shot down a civilian airliner—a Boeing 747!

His friend responds, "My God, Reagan will start World War III for certain now!"

Soon thereafter, the Japanese media reports that the missing plane is a 747 with 267 passengers and crew on board.

The flight's call sign is KAL 007.

CHAPTER SEVEN

WHITE WOLF

Captain Kevin Cattani, United States Air Force
Yokota Air Base, Tokyo, Japan

Thursday, 1 September 1983—
Saturday, 3 September 1983

The events of the morning begin to blur together. The watch is inundated with message traffic and augmented with additional personnel. One of my most senior analysts tells me that he is feeling like he did in Vietnam and is battling "existential detachment." I tell him to go help the younger guys and keep busy—there is a lot to do, keeping busy shouldn't be a problem and it will help him keep his focus. Existential detachment—Christ!

We get press reports that family members and friends are awaiting the arrival of KAL 007 at Seoul's Kimpo airport. The television news media and wire services are starved for information and resort to reporting rumor and innuendo, such as "the flight had an emergency and landed safely on Sakhalin Island," or "the Soviets forced down the aircraft and it is at an airfield near Vladivostok" or, perhaps "the airplane landed safely at a remote airport on the northernmost Japanese island of Hokkaido."

Worse still, a Korean Air Lines spokesman puts out an official statement asserting that KAL 007 has been forced down by the Soviets and is on the ramp at a Soviet Air Base on Sakhalin. None of this is true, of course, and it gives pitiable and false hope to those awaiting their loved ones at Kimpo Airport.

Washington now sees this episode as a serious international security event. For their part, the leadership in the Kremlin is silent.

My team is reviewing last night's events, and we reach a consensus that the shootdown is a colossal Soviet mistake. It exposes tremendous shortcomings in the Soviets' entire air defense system in the Far East.

This viewpoint is not unanimously shared, to put it mildly. Many voices blame the Soviets for criminally, and intentionally, shooting down a civilian airliner. My protestations to the contrary are largely dismissed as naïve, if not silly.

I'm convinced that the Soviets were confused by the proximity of KAL 007's flight path to the orbit that the RC-135/Cobra Ball was flying last night. Given the months of heightened alert amongst the Far Eastern air defense forces, their radar operators and pilots were operating on fumes. Operator exhaustion, combined with inaccurate radar, created utter confusion.

The Soviet air defense troops and fighter pilots in Petropavlovsk blundered by failing to intercept the border violator over the Kamchatka Peninsula. This blunder was compounded by their failure to follow the mystery aircraft over the Sea of Okhotsk. By the time the intruder was redetected on its approach to Sakhalin Island, it simply had to be intercepted and identified. And if the violator failed to respond to warnings, then it had to be taken down before it left Soviet airspace.

We know from our analysis of the US Navy overflight of the Kurile Islands in April that any Soviet commander who allows a border violator to get away unscathed is risking everything. In my mind, there is little doubt that the Soviets have made a terrible and dangerous error. It's a mistake that may lead to a shooting war between the Soviet Union and the United States.

How could a professional air force commit such a stupid error?

And if they didn't know they were shooting down a civilian airliner and believed that they were shooting down an unarmed American intelligence collection flight—that is somehow supposed to be better? I understand why so many find incompetence combined with exhausted, hair-trigger paranoia to be an unsatisfying explanation. How much more satisfying it is to believe that the Soviets acted with malice of forethought.

As ordered by General Flannery, I brief the battle staff on the situation. They listen attentively, and many officers take careful notes and ponder the actions they will take within their organizations to deal with the crisis. The overall tone is businesslike, and General Flannery lends the proceedings a sense of calm resolve.

We learn that President Reagan has been briefed about the shootdown at his ranch near Santa Barbara. Secretary of State George Shultz is appointed the administration's point man on the incident, and his strident rhetoric blaming the Soviets for a heinous act will set the tone for the entire US government.

One of General Flannery's first actions is to order two C-130 Hercules search-and-rescue planes to fly from Kadena Air Base on Okinawa to Yokota. As soon as the aircrews arrive, they are ushered into the battle-staff conference room. I join General Flannery there. He tells me in a voice loud enough for the crews to hear, "Give them what they need to know about the threat they're going to face. You know the Soviets in this area better than anyone. Remember what I told you earlier—don't sugarcoat it."

I take a deep breath. "Yes, General." I am beginning to feel very fatigued. The adrenaline I've been running on has worn off. I have to rally to keep my focus.

The crews listen somberly to my threat briefing. I see some visibly wince when I talk about the threats posed by Soviet fighters and surface-to-air missiles (SAMs).

As I brief, I notice that the SAR crews contain female nurses and emergency medical technicians. I know it's 1983, but it is still a bit of a shock to see American female servicemembers in flight suits about to fly into harm's way. They will go into an area that is crawling with Soviet fighters, whose pilots, no doubt, are all jazzed up with the events of earlier this morning. And any aircraft, even a rescue aircraft, that is perceived to be a border violator will be shot down.

Among the C-130 crewmembers are PJs—Air Force Special Operations para-rescue jumpers. These guys are highly trained paramedics who can parachute or rappel into crash sites and other dangerous situations to rescue downed airmen or crash victims. PJs like these guys helped save the red-haired major and the rest of our team in Cambodia a few years ago. They'll be needed if any survivors are found in the water—a highly unlikely scenario given the frigid sea and the many hours that have passed since KAL 007 was shot down.

After the briefing, General Flannery dismisses the crews, but he asks the two aircraft commanders to stay behind. Both are highly experienced lieutenant colonels and Vietnam combat veterans. Flying into dangerous airspace is nothing new for them. They ask General Flannery if they will have friendly fighter cover when they fly into the Tatar Strait area.

General Flannery looks them in the eye. "No, you won't. I cannot get fighters up to Misawa until late today at the earliest. I need you to fly up there alone. I know it isn't what you want to hear, but I need you guys to get up there and see what you can find. Alone."

One of them smirks. "General, does this captain know what the hell he is talking about? I mean, this kid looks like he is about sixteen years old, and he has put the fear of God into our crews. Is it really that bad up there?"

Flannery fires back, trying to strike a balance between empathy and firmness. "I know he looks young, but this captain is my expert. He knows his stuff. He is the one who discovered the Russians shot down the Korean airplane. I need you guys to pay attention to what

Kevin told you and lead your crews accordingly. You guys know that the crews will take their cue from you. I promise you that I will get fighters up north as soon as is humanly possible. I'm counting on you. The country is, too."

Somberly, the commanders both say, "Yes, sir." They walk rapidly out of the conference room to catch up to their crews.

Flannery looks at me and shakes his head. "I better get busy getting those fighters I just promised."

Thursday, 1 September 1983—Afternoon

The hours pass by, and my fatigue deepens. I've been up since midnight. The press is reporting that the Korean CIA has stated that the missing plane is "definitely" on the ground at Sakhalin. Worse, the KCIA is claiming that the source of their "definitive" information is the American CIA station in Seoul, South Korea. Colonel Stroud asks me to call the CIA station in Tokyo to find out what the hell is going on with these KCIA reports.

It is afternoon and all the secure phone and teletype lines are jammed up. Junior NCOs are sending "flash override" messages, thinking that what they are reporting is of vital importance (for the most part, it isn't). I finally get through to the CIA guys in Tokyo and they report that their colleagues in the Seoul office completely disavow the KCIA's claim. I'm not surprised. The source is likely some junior guy in the KCIA who wants to inflate his self-importance by telling reporters that he has the "inside scoop."

I'm mentally and physically spent. I ask Colonel Stroud if I can get some sleep. He agrees and tells me to come back at 5:00 AM tomorrow.

Thursday, 1 September 1983—Evening

I go home and collapse on my bed in my uniform. I sleep for a few hours. I wake up in the early evening, take a shower, and put on a fresh uniform. I go back to the watch at about 9:00 PM. It's still 1 September.

Colonel Stroud shakes his head and grins when he sees me walk in. He tells the officer of the watch to update me on the latest developments. There's a massive Soviet search-and-rescue operation underway in the Tatar Strait. The Soviet Navy has several ships in the area and there are numerous aircraft flying over the Strait, including quite a few fighter planes. The Soviets have numerous bases in the area from which to operate. It's relatively easy for them to localize the crash site and surround it with ships and cover it with their own SAR aircraft. If there are any survivors, the Soviets are in the best position to find them. And of course, the Russians want to get to the Korean airliner's black box before we do.

Our two C-130 SAR airplanes from Kadena completed their first sortie and returned safely to their staging base at Misawa. They report a few scary moments courtesy of several Soviet MiG-23 and Su-15 fighters flying mere yards off their wings. Our pilots exercised extreme caution to steer clear of Soviet airspace and remain over international waters. Hope of finding any survivors has vanished.

General Flannery has established himself in the CAF and he's moving additional aircraft to provide airborne surveillance, command and control, and SAR support. He's still working on getting fighters to Misawa. The plan is to deploy Air Force F-15s that are based in Okinawa to Misawa as soon as possible. The problem is that Misawa is some 1,300 miles from Okinawa. Earlier, Flannery asked the US Navy's 7th fleet commander to send Navy F-4s, which are based just outside of Tokyo, northward to Misawa to provide combat air patrols. The three-star admiral commanding 7th Fleet told General Flannery that he wants to comply; however, he must get permission from the commander-in-chief of the Pacific Fleet before he can take any action. The issue is that "chopping" (or lending operational control) of Navy fighters to the temporary control of an Air Force officer is highly controversial in the Navy. Getting the Pacific Fleet to agree to General Flannery's request takes many high-level phone calls and far too many hours.

Friday, 2 September 1983

I go home about midnight and sleep for a few hours so that I can be back on duty by 5:00 AM. By the time I get home and turn on the television news, the truth about the shootdown of KAL 007 is being reported around the world. This is not true within the USSR, of course.

The families waiting for their loved ones at Kimpo airport in South Korea get the tragic word of the fate of KAL 007, and I see their heartbreaking reaction on the television news. Their awful experience is made even worse by the earlier, inaccurate press reports and the false assurance from KAL that misinformed them of the "safe landing" of the Korean airliner in the Soviet Far East.

Dawn on the 2nd of September sees US Navy F-4s flying combat air patrol (CAP) over Hokkaido Island, right over Wakkanai, in fact. They are close enough to the Tatar Strait to respond to potential threats from Soviet fighters, and far enough away so as not to appear provocative. Air Force F-15s from Okinawa are flying to Yokota en route to Misawa, where they will join the Navy fighters in providing CAP support to the unarmed US aircraft flying over the suspected crash area.

A few minutes after I arrive at the office, I walk to the CAF to check in with my intelligence analysts, who are camped out in front of the situation board. General Flannery is also there, sitting at the center of the top tier of the dais. He sees me and motions me to come up to his side.

"Kevin, I want you and your guys to stay on top of every Soviet threat we see today. The CAF has a variety of radios, so we can communicate with every one of our planes—Navy, Air Force, and Coast Guard—including the fighters. If your guys see hostile intent toward any of our planes, I need to know immediately. Make sure every one of the intel guys knows this and tell Colonel Stroud to come see me as soon as he arrives this morning."

"Yes, sir. I will remind all the guys of our responsibilities. White Wolf."

Flannery winks at me. "Right, babes, White Wolf. Today and tomorrow are probably the most dangerous days of this entire deal. Things can spin out of control, and we have to stay a step ahead."

White Wolf is the name for a set of procedures and protocols to warn unarmed military aircraft of impending threats. Large reconnaissance aircraft have few defenses. Their best defensive tactic is to drop like a rock from their operating altitude (typically between 20,000 and 30,000 feet). The pilot puts the aircraft into a severe dive toward the earth's surface—terrestrial or maritime.

The pilots know that their best chance of survival is to dive for the wave tops and get down to the water as fast as possible. Then the pilot must pull up the nose just before hitting the water. This maneuver requires daring, skill, and physical strength. Airplanes like the US Navy's P-3 have mechanical flight controls and the act of pulling the big aircraft out of a dive requires the pilot to pull so hard on the yoke that he risks dislocating his shoulders.

Once the plane reaches the sea, the pilot will level off and fly for home as fast and as low as possible. This maneuver makes an escaping plane very tough for Soviet fighters to track and follow. Most Soviet fighters don't have very sophisticated radars, and they have a very difficult time differentiating a low-flying plane's radar signature from the multitude of radar returns received from the signals bouncing off the wave tops.

The reports we receive from our rescue aircraft are consistent—lots of Soviet interference and very little or no debris visible on the surface. Soviet fighters do their best to make it difficult for our aircraft to operate near the crash area, harassing them at every turn. Toward midafternoon, a kind of exhausted calm descends on the CAF.

I'm sitting a couple of rows below General Flannery, reading a press report about Secretary of State Shultz's press conference in Washington earlier in the day. Shultz revealed to the worldwide media that the critical intelligence on the shootdown came from a Japanese SIGINT site and that the Japanese have detailed recordings of Soviet communications, including transmissions from the Su-15 pilot who fired the fatal missiles. The secretary's statement causes a frenzy in the United States and amongst our Japanese allies. The Japanese government is concerned over Shultz's revelations of its intelligence collection capabilities and its close intelligence collaboration with the United States.

The press also is reporting widespread revulsion around the globe over what appears to be an intentional act of murder by the Soviet Union. The administration, and especially Secretary Shultz, fosters the notion that the Soviets acted with premeditated malice. I don't agree they acted with malice of forethought, but they are responsible for 267 deaths.

Our assessment is that the shootdown is the result of a series of Soviet mistakes. But our view is ignored by the most senior leaders in the Administration and Congress. Unfortunately, neither the CIA nor the NSA initially supports the Air Force intelligence assessment. Our notion that the Soviets' actions resulted from confusion is lost in the stampede to assign blame. The global media laps up the anti-Soviet rhetoric, and its reporting echoes the narrative coming out of official Washington. The incessant White House drumbeat assigning criminal intent to the Soviets is raising tensions with the Kremlin to ever more dangerous levels.

In Japan, we continue preparations to deter a potential fight with the Soviets. The Navy deploys more F-4s to Misawa Air Base and more F-15s from Okinawa join them. AWACS command and control aircraft and RC-135 and Navy EP-3 intelligence collectors also land at Misawa. The 7th Fleet steams ships northward, through the La Perouse Strait, toward the crash site in the Tatar Strait.

The US SAR effort is concentrated around a small island off the southwest coast of Sakhalin called Moneron because that's where the Soviets are concentrating their own search. The Russians know better than we do just where the Korean airliner crashed into the sea.

The narrow Tatar Strait is becoming more and more crowded with ships and aircraft as the day goes on. When great numbers of large, complex machines are in such close quarters, collisions and accidents become almost inevitable. The crash of the Soviet Tu-16 that I witnessed a couple of years ago during the naval exercise in the Sea of Japan is a case in point.

Late in the day, there are reports on Japanese television that Japanese fishermen, who were fishing illegally in Soviet waters on the night of the shootdown, acknowledged that they saw a large flash and heard an explosion near Moneron Island around the time the crippled airliner smashed into the waters of the Tatar Strait. If those reports are accurate, then Moneron Island must be the right place to look for wreckage.

At this point, of course, no one expects to find survivors. What is puzzling, however, is the relative lack of human remains. Oddly, large numbers of shoes are showing up on beaches on Hokkaido Island. A human limb and one torso also have washed ashore. But there are no other signs of the victims of this tragedy.

Saturday, 3 September 1983—Afternoon

I sleep in for a few hours the next morning. When I get to the watch center it is nearly noon. We are falling into a tense routine. I go down to the CAF and check on my team.

As I ruminate over the situation depicted on the CAF's big situation board, Master Sergeant "Pops" Parent bursts onto the operations floor and announces, "We have detected a credible threat to an active EP-3 mission! White Wolf alert!!!"

General Flannery looks up from a book he is reading and asks for the CAF staff to show him where the US Navy plane is flying. The senior air controller in the CAF immediately gets on the radio to call the Navy pilot. I see the controller's lips move rapidly above his clenched jaw, but I can't hear the warnings he is passing to the EP-3 flight crew.

I wave at Pops to come up to the top row of the dais where General Flannery and the other senior officers are gathered. A one-star general, vice commander of 5AF, is standing next to Flannery.

I ask Pops to brief General Flannery and the other senior officers crowding around the top level of the dais about the threat. "General, we are tracking a flight of two MiG-23s. They intercepted the EP-3 a few minutes ago. The Soviet ground controller told the MiG pilots that the EP-3 is a border violator and ordered them to destroy the target. We know, sir, that the EP is NOT in Soviet airspace. The Soviet pilots almost certainly know it, too. However . . ."

"However, they will follow their orders." General Flannery finishes Pops's thought for him.

Pops nods.

Flannery tells the CAF commander. "Tell our F-15s to go to their forward CAP orbit immediately. Apprise them of the MiG threat. Make sure AWACS is aware of everything we know."

There is a flight of four F-15s providing fighter cover for the reconnaissance aircraft. Their standard orbit is over the northern coast of the island of Hokkaido. Flannery's order moves the F-15s to the forward CAP orbit, putting them in position to attack the MiG-23s that are threatening the EP-3. This means we could be moments away from aerial combat between US Air Force F-15s and Soviet MiG-23s.

Another CAF controller calls the F-15 flight leader and passes along General Flannery's order. The flight leader acknowledges the order, and all four F-15s light their afterburners and race forward toward the MiGs. While we can't hear the two-way communications between the CAF and the EP-3 pilot, strangely, we *can* hear the F-15 flight leader's voice transmission through the ceiling speakers in the CAF.

The lead controller, who is talking to the EP-3 pilot, turns around in his seat and yells at General Flannery that the big plane is in a dive, heading for the wave tops. Now the survival of the two dozen Navy crewmembers depends on the skill and nerve and strength of the two pilots.

The F-15 flight lead reports that they've reached the forward CAP position. Meanwhile, the MiG-23s are diving toward the sea, attempting to maintain visual or radar contact with the big EP-3. The weather isn't great, it is getting late in the afternoon, and seeing a plane against a seascape of rising and falling waves is a tough challenge for the Soviet fighters' radars.

The Air Force major leading the flight of F-15s reports that he has acquired the MiG-23s on his search radar.

General Flannery yells at the controller, "Tell the major to stand by for my order." He barks at the CAF commander, "Colonel, where is the Navy plane?"

"Sir, we are checking the EP-3's status now."

The 5AF vice commander stands beside the seated General Flannery. "General, we must splash those MiGs whether they shoot down the EP-3 or not. This is clearly hostile intent. It's an act of war."

Flannery responds without looking at the brigadier, "Let's get that EP-3 home safely. That's the priority right now."

The lead controller turns around to face the top of the dais and yells, "General, AWACS reports that the EP-3 is on the deck, and the MiGs followed him down there. The MiGs don't seem to be closing on him. The Soviets may have lost lock on our guy."

I turn to my team a few steps away from me. I noiselessly mouth, *"What are you seeing from the Soviets?"*

Sergeant Weatherby mouths the words, *"Nothing new."*

Everyone is on edge, waiting to see if the Navy plane escapes the MiGs.

A few seconds pass, and the F-15 flight lead's disembodied voice can be heard through the ceiling speakers. "Tally ho on the MiGs. No joy on EP-3. In position to engage."

Flannery yells, "Tell the major to stand by and keep his powder dry. Make sure he knows that the orders are coming directly from me. He is to stand by until I direct otherwise."

"Yes, sir." The controller talking to the F-15s keys his mike and conveys General Flannery's instructions.

The other controller, who is working with the EP-3 says, "Sir, the

EP commander thinks he is clear of the MiGs. General, he thinks he can make it."

"Okay, let's make sure. Keep the F-15s ready to go."

I hear the vice commander say to General Flannery, "Boss, those MiGs are aggressors. We have every right to splash them. The F-15s have them dead to rights."

This time Flannery turns his chair to face the one-star. I cannot make out exactly what he says to his "vice," but I can see the younger general's face turn beet red and twist into a sickeningly sour expression. Flannery clearly doesn't agree with him. A small gaggle of senior colonels standing alongside the vice commander fidget uncomfortably.

The lead controller yells over the noise in the CAF, "The EP-3 is 'feet dry'! He is heading to Misawa. They made it! They made it!"

Hearing this welcome news, Flannery immediately orders the F-15s to return to their CAP position over Hokkaido.

Everyone in the big room breathes easier. Maybe we've dodged a direct confrontation and there won't be any shots fired.

A few seconds pass, and we hear the major in command of the F-15s say, "General Flannery, I understand you can hear me. We have the MiGs. I can splash them right now. We have them. They tried to take down our Navy plane. I have them."

Flannery immediately responds, "Advise the major that my specific orders are, 'Stand down. Re-establish your former CAP position ASAP. We aren't starting World War III today.' Tell him to repeat those orders back to me over the radio."

The tension in the room is almost unbearable. For his part, Flannery seems completely unruffled. The vice commander and the colonels surrounding him are practically standing on tiptoe, awaiting the major's response.

We hear the major's voice again over the speakers. Oddly, the transmission is crystal clear. The major's voice breaks slightly, caustic and brittle with frustration. "Sir, flight is to stand down and re-establish standard orbit ASAP. We don't need to start World War III today."

Flannery replies, "Tell him I am proud of him. I know he was ready to do his job if we needed him. Tell him to come see me when he flies through Yokota before he goes back to Okinawa."

Wow, how can Flannery know exactly what to say and how to say it under such pressure?

Then we hear the major's voice again—the transmission is still clear and strong. "General, appreciate your words. You know I had those bastards. I really had them, General." Now, he sounds chastened, like an Air Force Academy cadet quietly receiving demerits for an acknowledged infraction.

"I know you had them, babes. You did your job. I am proud of you. Stay sharp. This isn't over. We may need you again."

The controller relays the general's message to the F-15 flight lead.

The flight commander responds, "Thank you, sir. We'll be ready."

And just that quickly, the world returns to spinning on its axis in the correct direction.

I see the vice commander shake Flannery's hand and I hear him say. "General, you were right. You made the right call." His face turns red once again.

Flannery smiles. "I just didn't think we needed to start World War III this afternoon." Now I see the relief on Flannery's face. He stands and addresses everyone in the CAF. "Guys, I need you to stay sharp. You see how fast this situation can get out of control. We dodged a bullet. You all did a great job. You gotta stay ready. This is probably not the last incident."

I look down from the dais and see that there are about thirty people in the CAF. Each one of them is looking at Flannery and listening to him intently. I know what everyone is thinking—they're relieved and happy as hell that Flannery is in command.

The gravity of the incident hits me about twenty minutes later when I'm back in the watch. Flannery's cool head and sober thinking just prevented a shooting war with the Soviets.

What happened to the EP-3? It returned safely to Misawa Air

Base, but not without cost. Later, we learn that all the intelligence operators in the back end of the plane received numerous injuries as a result of their roller coaster ride to the wave tops. Several have concussions, and some have broken arms, wrists, or legs.

We also hear that the EP-3 pilot dislocated both of his shoulders as he pulled the big plane out of its emergency dive. It took tremendous strength to pull on the yoke and prevent the aircraft from crashing into the sea. It turns out that the pilot is a huge guy, a former lineman on the Naval Academy football team. Go Navy!

Everyone is thrilled that the Navy plane escaped. Flannery's recall of the F-15s is even more important because he prevented aerial combat between the two superpowers. I have no doubt the outcome of that fight would have been two "splashed" MiG-23s. We just dodged a bullet that could have led to a war—possibly a nuclear war—between the United States and the Soviet Union.

Later, as dusk falls on the Tatar Strait, the Soviets send fighters to intercept a small NHK-TV plane that is overflying the crash area. NHK is the Japanese equivalent of the United Kingdom's BBC. The Soviets believe erroneously that the TV plane is a border violator. My team reports the threat to the CAF. Of course, unlike the Navy EP-3, the CAF has no means of communicating a warning to an NHK aircraft.

Flannery sends a new flight of four F-15s to the forward CAP point—just in case. We wait tensely to see if the Soviet fighters shoot down the TV reporters. We're helpless to do anything to prevent an attack. The CAF alerts the Japanese Air Force to call NHK headquarters in Tokyo, but there is no way for NHK to communicate with their plane that far from home and, even if they could, any warning would come too late.

Miraculously and suddenly, the attack on the NHK place is aborted by the MiGs, and the oblivious TV reporters never skip a beat in filming KAL 007's debris field. General Flannery recalls the

F-15s, once again avoiding aerial combat between our fighters and Soviet aircraft.

Much later, we learn more from the Japanese SIGINT team at Wakkanai about the aborted engagement. It seems the lead Soviet fighter pilot refused to shoot down the civilian Japanese plane. He asked repeatedly for the ground controller to repeat his orders and each time he responded to the controller that he could see that the small plane had "NHK" written prominently on the fuselage and tail. The exasperated fighter pilot finally asserted that he was low on fuel and must return to base. The lead pilot's actions prevented what would have been a tragic and inflammatory incident. Fighter pilots, including Soviet pilots, are trained in their responsibilities to protect civilian aircraft under international law.

The NHK aircraft incident is the last serious scare in the immediate aftermath of the shootdown of KAL 007. The Soviet Pacific Fleet continues to harass our 7th Fleet ships and some close calls almost result in collisions at sea. Gradually, however, the risk of war with the Soviets in northeast Asia begins to recede.

In Washington, however, the political and nearly theological rhetoric continues to escalate. President Reagan gives a nationally televised speech in which he calls the KAL 007 shootdown the "Korean Air Lines massacre" and a "crime against humanity."

We're told that the overall commander in the Pacific, Admiral Crowe, will visit US Forces, Japan, and that he wants a full briefing on the events surrounding the KAL 007 tragedy. I get word from Colonel Stroud that General Flannery wants me to be the principal briefer.

We put together a few charts summarizing the events of the night of the shootdown and its aftermath, including how General Flannery avoided a shooting war despite Soviet provocations.

I stand at the podium at the front of our secure briefing theater, waiting to brief Admiral Crowe and his entourage. Crowe folds his large frame into a seat in the front row. General Flannery introduces me as the primary briefer and sits down next to the admiral.

Crowe studies me for a minute and starts to laugh. "Nice to see you again, Captain. Have you heard recently from your good friend, the commanding admiral at CINCPACFLT?" This would be the four-star commander of the Pacific Fleet with whom I crossed swords in July.

I smile and reply, "No, sir, but I expect to get a Christmas card from him this year."

Crowe roars with laughter and twists around in his seat to address his large entourage of admirals and general officers. "This young captain briefed me this past summer, right after I arrived at PACOM. He told me that the Russians would shoot down any airplane that they believed was flying in their airspace—even a civilian airplane—no questions asked. He had tracked their increased alert status out here for months and its impact on our intel flights. He used his head and got it right."

Crowe turns back to me and exclaims loudly. "I call him 'the man who could see the future.' So what prognostications do you have for me today, Captain Nostradamus?"

PART TWO

THE MAN WHO SAVED THE WORLD

"We have to learn to live as brothers,
or we will perish as dinosaurs,"

Lt. Col. Stanislav Petrov, Soviet Air Defense Forces

CHAPTER EIGHT

OPERATION RYaN

Colonel Ivan Levchenko, GRU,
Air Defense Forces of the Soviet Union
Moscow, Russia, USSR and Khabarovsk, Russia, USSR

Wednesday, 31 August 1983—Morning

I climb out of my staff car into a cool and grey August morning in Moscow. I sigh and rub my sore right knee. I'm exhausted. The last few days—the last few weeks, in fact—have been a whirlwind of hard work, numbing travel, and shattering stress. My life has been consumed by the USSR's most important intelligence program—Operation RYaN. This morning will be devoted to yet another high-level meeting on this topic.

Regrettably, my wife has gone to her parents' home near Kiev for several weeks. She hates Moscow and is unhappy that I'm stationed here. She loved our last assignment, which was truly a once-in-a-lifetime experience, unimaginable to most Soviet citizens. We lived for three years in West Germany, where I was assigned to the Military Liaison Mission (MLM). Our rented home was in a suburb of Frankfurt, and I worked in the section of the Soviet MLM focused on the Americans. My job there was to observe

American and NATO military exercises and develop intelligence on our adversaries' warfighting capacity throughout the NATO region. For a military intelligence officer—a GRU officer like me—there is no more prestigious or desirable assignment. I interacted weekly with American officers, coordinating, learning about the operational tempo of the US Air Force and its allies. During that time in Germany, my English language skills improved dramatically.

For her part, my wife Boyka thrilled to the freedom she enjoyed in West Germany, shopping at the American military exchange stores, and driving to Paris on the odd weekend. It was the happiest time of our married life and the best job I have had thus far in my career.

The MLM was established in the late 1940s after World War II as one means of preventing the outbreak of World War III. The Soviet Union posts officers like myself adjacent to the NATO forces, mainly in West Germany. Our presence on the enemy's territory enables us to monitor for signs of preparation for actual combat. The MLM was established as a "confidence-building measure." We are a tripwire that will provide warning of war or, ideally, prevent one.

The other three postwar powers—the United States, the United Kingdom, and France—have their own MLM operations, based in and around Berlin. Their mission is the same as ours. All the officers assigned to the MLM on both sides are multilingual intelligence professionals, who collect information on the other side both overtly and covertly.

I was reassigned from Germany to Moscow in late June of this year, and Boyka immediately declared herself miserable in the capital city. Blonde, beautiful, and sophisticated, she is enamored of Western culture, clothing, and food. My wife is a professional-caliber violinist and could have performed as a soloist with orchestras or as first violin in string quartets had she not chosen to follow me from place to place in my career.

Most importantly, Boyka is a Ukrainian—through and through. Her first name literally means "inhabitant of Western Ukraine," if you can believe it. Her sister, Oxana, is also a great beauty and is a fervent Ukrainian nationalist, to boot. They grew up just outside of Kiev in a small village.

Boyka's father served as a tank commander in the Great Patriotic War. He's a proud Ukrainian, and he is equally proud to have served in the victorious Soviet Red Army in the greatest war in history.

So, you see, Boyka's city is Kiev, not Moscow. Her family's religion is Roman Catholicism, not Russian Orthodoxy. And since we have no children, she has remained especially close to her parents and only sister. We met more than twenty years ago when I was a cadet at the air force academy in Kiev and while Boyka was studying violin at the Tchaikovsky Music Academy of Ukraine. Her musical talent is beyond my comprehension and Boyka continues to practice daily. I fear her unrealized musical career must be a disappointment to her. She has the talent to be at the top of her profession.

One should understand that she is far more beautiful than I am handsome. Boyka is blessed with the type of beauty that stops men dead in their tracks on the street. How did I manage to marry her? Well, as a student in Kiev, I was very popular at parties, and I had a great sense of humor, an uncanny ability to spin an amusing tale. She was intrigued. The final thing in my favor is that, in my final year at the academy, I was recruited by Soviet Military Intelligence—the GRU. Joining the GRU meant additional schooling, of course, and it also offered the opportunity for assignments abroad. The prospect of being one of the very few Soviet citizens who might be able to live abroad excited Boyka, and I think it was instrumental in her agreeing to marry me.

That said, we love each other deeply. She has always supported my career and has been a wonderful wife to me, which makes our current separation acutely painful. I wish I could have given her children, but our attempts to create a family came to nothing. Believe me, it was not for lack of trying on my part.

Much of my military career has been spent outside of Russia—in Poland, East Germany, and West Germany. Living abroad makes

Boyka happy. Moscow makes her profoundly irritable. So, she is away, and I am working day and night on RYaN.

Unknown to the public—of course—Operation RYaN is the largest intelligence program underway in the USSR. It was born out of a growing sense amongst the Kremlin leadership (especially that of the KGB) in early 1981 that the USSR was falling behind the West by virtually every measure—militarily, economically, and technologically—and that the Western powers' increasing boldness and belligerence toward the Soviet Union might be a precursor to war. Ominously, RYaN is an acronym that translates into English as "nuclear rocket attack." It implies a surprise attack, and we Russians are wary of surprises. After all, we remember when Hitler surprised us in 1941 with his Operation Barbarossa.

The RYaN operation itself is a combined KGB/GRU collection effort that I was first briefed on when I was with the MLM in West Germany. At the beginning of 1982, I was ordered to make RYaN my top priority in my annual work plan. The emphasis on RYaN intensified in February 1983 under orders from the Kremlin. The RYaN project directs intelligence officers around the world to discern preparations by America's Reagan Administration for a surprise nuclear attack on the USSR—a first-strike offensive, if you will. The operation has intensified as the time nears for the Americans' deployment of Pershing II nuclear ballistic missiles and ground-launched cruise missiles (GLCMs) to West Germany and England, respectively. Those missiles will afford the Western alliance the capacity to fight a "limited" nuclear war—a war that could decapitate the Soviet leadership and its ability to retaliate against the West.

Operation RYaN was launched jointly by General Secretary Leonid Brezhnev and Yuri Andropov, then head of the KGB. Andropov succeeded Brezhnev, upon the latter's death in November 1982, and is now himself the General Secretary of the Communist Party of the

Soviet Union—the most important and powerful position in the country.

In the summer of 1982, I attended a meeting on Project RYaN at the Soviet Embassy in London. There were a handful of senior KGB and GRU officers in attendance, all stationed at various locales in Europe. Amongst those who presented briefings was a KGB officer assigned to London—Oleg Gordievsky. His briefing summarized the RYaN-related findings the KGB had compiled over the last eighteen months. The presentation was well-crafted, but it seemed to me that there wasn't a great deal of substance to back up any assertions that the West might be planning a war. During my time in West Germany, I had never observed the Americans or other NATO forces do anything that would lead one to believe war was imminent. Gordievsky himself seemed to have limited confidence in his own briefing. It appeared to me that he was going through the motions to satisfy his bosses.

After Gordievsky briefed, the meeting broke for lunch and I happened to sit next to him during the meal. I found Gordievsky extremely astute and knowledgeable about the West. As if to reinforce his knowledge, he spoke to me exclusively in English.

The most important result of the London meeting for me was my newfound friendship with this KGB man—Oleg Gordievsky. We agreed to stay in touch. He visited me in West Germany several times over the next year. My wife and I visited with Oleg and his wife Leila in London at Christmastime in 1982—one of the more romantic and memorable experiences of our time in the West. My wife still talks about hearing the choir sing beautiful English Christmas carols at St. Martin-in-the-Fields church, just off Trafalgar Square—it was a magical time.

The last time I saw Gordievsky in person was when he attended my MLM farewell dinner in Frankfurt, just as I was about to depart for my current assignment in Moscow. We have kept up a regular letter-writing correspondence, although I must admit that he is a more faithful letter writer than yours truly.

Wednesday, 31 August 1983—Afternoon

My current position is deputy intelligence chief for the air defense district that protects Moscow from air and missile attacks. My driver collects me at my office, in the headquarters of the Order of Lenin Moscow Air Defense District, promptly at 1:00 PM to take me to today's RYaN meeting at the headquarters of the GRU. As you may know, the actual name for the GRU is the Main Intelligence Directorate of the General Staff.

Today's meeting on RYaN is relatively uneventful. I provide a brief update from the perspective of the Air Defense Force. Officers from our sister services give their updates. It seems to me that everyone is growing exhausted and bored by the effort of providing RYaN reports to our respective headquarters. Privately, many of my GRU colleagues are acknowledging the futility of RYaN. Officers in the field are filing reports filled with nonsense—feeling the pressure of the Kremlin's insatiable appetite for "news." They know it's become a reporting game, and we at headquarters know it, too. But the Politburo, especially General Secretary Andropov, demand that we feed the machine that RYaN has become.

Back in my office by mid-afternoon, I am tackling a pile of reports when a junior officer from the air defense watch center appears at my office door in an excited state.

Anxiously, he reports, "Comrade Colonel Levchenko, Petropavlovsk is reporting a border violation. They are attempting to contact the intruder. Your presence is requested by the officer of the watch immediately, sir."

"A border violator? An American plane? Are you certain this isn't just an exercise? It's the middle of the night there. What time is it in Petropavlovsk, Captain?"

"Comrade Colonel, it's about 1:30 AM local time at Petropavlovsk. On the first of September, of course, sir. Tomorrow."

We proceed to the bunker which houses the Moscow Air Defense District's watch center. I do quick calculations as we walk. Petropavlovsk is about 7,000 kilometers from Moscow, and there is a nine-hour difference in time zones, with the Kamchatka Peninsula being nine hours *ahead* of Moscow.

The chief of the watch briefs me on the situation. In his excitement, the young major gesticulates wildly at the map board and stumbles over his words.

"Sir, there was an American RC-135 just here, flying east of Kamchatka during the night, probably—we think—awaiting our ICBM test launch from Central Asia. The launch didn't occur, and the Americans apparently broke off their orbit—about here, sir—and began to fly directly towards Kamchatka. It took some time for the air defense units out there to react. Once they finally did, they launched several fighters to intercept the American, but—well, sir—they failed. Petropavlovsk is now reporting that they have lost radar coverage and that the American plane is flying west over the Sea of Okhotsk. We have no way of tracking it at this point, sir."

Stunned by this report, I respond, "Good God. Who's been informed in our chain of command? Does the Ministry of Defense know of this?"

"Sir, I believe that the Far Eastern Air Defense District headquarters at Khabarovsk has informed both the General Staff and the Ministry of Defense."

This news is astounding and could lead to a war with the Americans. "Major, get on the secure phone and make sure that the appropriate people are aware. How about Marshal Konstantinov? Does he know?"

"I have not informed the marshal, sir. I wanted to apprise you first."

I rush out of the bunker and race to the office of Marshal Anatoly Konstantinov, commander of the Moscow Air Defense District.

When I reach the marshal's outer office, I find that his aide is focused on reading computer printouts—probably detailing obscure logistical or operational readiness details. He isn't pleased to be interrupted by a GRU colonel.

The aide looks up, "Comrade Colonel, what do you require?"

"I have urgent news from the watch center that I must convey to Marshal Konstantinov."

He sighs heavily. "Sir, the comrade marshal is about to depart for the day. He's attending an event tonight at the Kremlin and must hurry along home to prepare." He returns to reading his printouts. I've been dismissed as far as he's concerned.

What an arrogant asshole. "Yes, yes, I understand. Nonetheless, I must see him immediately to inform him of important developments."

Reluctantly, the aide gets up from his desk and escorts me into the marshal's office. The marshal is reading reports and doesn't acknowledge us.

The aide clears his throat ostentatiously. "Comrade Marshal, this GRU officer claims to have news of 'important developments' that must be presented to you immediately."

Konstantinov has a hard, lined face with extraordinarily narrow eyes like a snake's. I find those eyes extremely unsettling.

"Colonel, what is it? I have only a few moments before I must depart."

"Sir, there is an incident—still ongoing—in the Far East. I respectfully request your presence in the bunker so that you may be fully briefed."

The marshal sighs and pays me full attention. "The bunker? Why? Have you started World War III?"

The aide stifles a laugh.

"It involves the Americans. It already has been reported to the Ministry of Defense and the General Staff. It's imperative, in my view, that you are briefed fully."

Upon hearing the full story in the watch Center, Marshal Konstantinov recognizes the importance of the news from the Far East. He sends his apologies to the Kremlin concerning tonight's event, and he and other senior officers remain in the bunker with me through the evening.

As time passes, we get reports that the intruder has reappeared on our radar systems and that the plane is now just east of Sakhalin Island. We closely follow reports of the furious action that ensues in the airspace around Sakhalin. I don't quite know how to react when we get word that a Sukhoi fighter from Sokol Airbase on Sakhalin has shot down the intruding plane. It's just after 7:45 PM Moscow time when word arrives that "the 'target is destroyed." The words give me an eerie foreboding. I'm gratified that our air defense troops were able to knock down the border violator; however, I'm concerned about the lack of definitive identification of the intruding plane. What did we just shoot down? Everyone assumes it is an American Air Force RC-135. But why would the Americans conduct such a provocative mission? If it is an American Air Force plane, the ramifications will be enormous. How will Reagan react to the USSR killing an entire aircrew? Those American intelligence planes carry about two dozen crewmembers. This single, momentous act could make RYaN a reality.

Once the shootdown is confirmed, Konstantinov orders the Moscow center to place our district's units on alert. Shortly thereafter, he tells me to leave the bunker and return with him to his office. My immediate boss, a one-star general, is on leave and is not in Moscow. As a result, I'm the marshal's senior intelligence officer.

Once we arrive back at Konstantinov's office, the marshal has orders for me. "Levchenko, you will go tonight to Khabarovsk. This has been directed from the highest levels of the Air Defense Force. You will lead a team—you pick the men—that will assess why the Americans conducted this mission and what they achieved. Colonel, you will have the authority to interview the regional air defense commander at Khabarovsk. Then you'll fly to Sakhalin and interview the senior air defense commander there and the pilot who shot down the American plane. You'll do your assessment and report back here directly to me. I want an unambiguous report, a thorough review—understood?"

"Yes, Comrade Marshal Konstantinov. Sir, as you know, I am the lead officer of the command for Operation RYaN. Will those duties be assumed by someone else—by another officer that I should ensure is prepared—to serve in my absence?"

Konstantinov looks blankly at me. "Colonel, I believed you to be one of our best and most intelligent officers. Was I wrong? Is it not self-evident that this American operation, which resulted in the destruction of one of their most expensive spy planes and an entire aircrew, is of great importance to Operation RYaN? It must be linked directly to RYaN. If this malevolent American action is not part of their preparation to launch a nuclear war, then what is it?"

I turn a bit pale and nod.

"Dismissed."

"Yes, Comrade Marshal."

Before I can make my exit, Konstantinov calls in his aide. Then the marshal orders me to stay and sit down.

Bizarrely, he begins to commiserate out loud with his aide, who is now standing beside me. "I hope Levchenko is up to taking on this task. He comes highly recommended, but he has only been with the command a couple of months. I want to know more about him."

The marshal tells his aide to retrieve my personnel file.

I remain seated in front of the marshal's desk. There's an extremely awkward silence.

My file is found quickly, and the aide lays it on the center of the marshal's desk. He turns to leave the office, but Konstantinov waves him back in and gestures for him to take a chair next to the one in which I'm now sitting.

The marshal opens the personnel file that he had perused only briefly this summer during my interview with him when I was first assigned to his staff. He studies it closely and reads *aloud* to his aide, even though I am sitting right there. This is truly bizarre. "Let's see what we have here. All right, Levchenko is forty-four years old and was born in Crimea, near Sevastopol. He's Russian, not Ukrainian. Well, that is good, at least. His official photograph . . . my God, it is awful. Remind me to tell him to have it retaken."

At this point, the aide glances at me nervously and uncomfortably.

The marshal continues his narrative. "God, that red mustache—I know the style is popular, but Christ. All right, I see that he has a talent for foreign languages. He reads, writes, and speaks German, Polish, and English. As a child, he spent twelve years at one of those special English language schools—the one in Sevastopol. That means that he was taken from his parents when he was about six years old to attend an English-language boarding school. He must have been frightened and sad to be taken at such a young age from the warm bosom of his family."

As he makes the last statement, the marshal glares right at me.

He continues. "All right, so he must be well-versed in American history and literature if he spent twelve years at that special school. He then graduated with honors from the Kiev Higher Engineering Radio-Technical College of the Soviet Air Force. I know this school well. I gave the commencement address there last year. It is one of the USSR's best military academies. Ugh, he's married to a Ukrainian woman that he met while at the academy. Well, like I said, at least *he* isn't Ukrainian."

The marshal pauses to ask his aide, "What do you know about this colonel? Does he go drinking with the other guys after hours? What's his story?"

The aide smiles awkwardly, looks over at me. "I don't really know him, sir. He doesn't seem to socialize. I've heard that he is a very hard worker—much more so than his boss, if you'll permit me to say so, sir."

This comment elicits a knowing laugh from Konstantinov, who

continues to read from my file. "All right, so he received his commission as an Air Defense officer, but he is now in the GRU. It says here that he attended the MDA—the Military-Diplomatic Academy—a three-year post-graduate school in intelligence—do you know it?"

The aide is in nearly as untenable a position as I am during this absurd scene. "Ah, yes, Comrade Marshal, I have heard of the school, yes, sir. It's just outside of Moscow, I believe—right?"

"Indeed, and it's highly selective and rigorous. The academy trains career GRU officers. Let's see here . . . Levchenko's career includes assignments in Poland, East Germany, and West Germany, and rapid promotion to full colonel. His most recent post was the West German assignment with the Military Liaison Mission in Frankfurt. Clearly, the GRU thinks highly of him."

Konstantinov finds the section covering my time in West Germany to be of particular interest, and he continues reading to his aide, "Levchenko was with the Military Liaison Mission attached to the Americans in Frankfurt. You know, this is an important posting and goes only to the best and most trustworthy GRU officers. This colonel will have had exposure to Americans like no one else on my staff. Very interesting. If anyone can sort out what the Americans were up to in the Far East tonight, then it ought to be him."

The aide nods vigorously in agreement.

Konstantinov closes my file, ignores me, and inquires of his beleaguered aide, "So you know little of Levchenko?"

"Comrade Marshal, I only know him as a newly assigned GRU officer. He seems polite and reserved. As I said, he has a reputation for hard work. And sir, I didn't know that we have officers assigned with the Americans at Frankfurt. That is very interesting."

The marshal looks up at his aide. "Yes, the famous Military Liaison Mission—one of the few ways a Soviet officer can live in the West. I hope he used his time there to do more than shop and that he developed a real understanding of how the Americans think. Dismissed. *Both* of you."

Thursday/Friday, 1-2 September 1983

After the bizarre episode with the marshal, I walk back to my office and make phone calls to the three officers I want for my team—two majors and a rather dour but capable lieutenant colonel. It takes some time to track them down and for my staff to make last-minute travel arrangements. By midnight, we're assembled and waiting to board a Soviet Air Force Il-76 that will fly us across eight time zones (one less than to Kamchatka) to Khabarovsk, the headquarters of the Far Eastern Military District.

The Il-76 Air Force transport that carries the team also is transporting equipment to a Soviet Strategic Rocket Forces base in Siberia. Our plane stops at Belaya Air Base, near Irkutsk, to offload the equipment and refuel. This makes a long trip even more painfully long, and the big plane doesn't land at the airfield near Khabarovsk until nearly 9:00 PM local time on 2 September.

A car is waiting to take my team immediately to the headquarters of the Far Eastern Air Defense District headquarters.

The commanding general's aide ushers me into an outer office. I stifle a yawn and stare at the peeling wallpaper curling toward the ceiling. I'm desperate for a cup of hot tea. None is offered.

At last, General Colonel Valeri Kamensky calls out of his office in a deep voice to his aide to bring the colonel from Moscow in to see him. The general's enormous office has such harsh overhead lights that I squint and blink my eyes involuntarily.

General Kamensky, a dark-haired, anxious Ukrainian, asks in a harsh voice, "Colonel, are you unwell? Do you suffer from an eye condition?"

"No, Comrade General. I'm fit. It's been a long day." I add with a slight chuckle to lighten the mood. I immediately realize that this is a mistake.

"Colonel, do you find this situation comical?"

"Not at all."

Kamensky squeezes an elegant writing pen in his left hand, points it menacingly at me, and scowls, "Very well. State your business."

"Comrade General, I am ordered here to investigate the malicious American intelligence mission that led to the current situation."

Kamensky storms, "The current situation! Do you believe that you, or anyone in Moscow, understands the current situation, Colonel? None of them comprehend what I have been dealing with out here since April. The American provocations never cease. We are on alert . . . constantly. My troops are exhausted, my equipment is wearing out, and the enemy is relentless."

I have not been invited to sit down. I shuffle my feet and shift my weight to relieve the pain in my lower back.

Kamensky's tirade continues. "Colonel, you say your task is to investigate a mission—that mission the other night, specifically—that the enemy conducted in my district? Do you know *anything* about the American intelligence operations in this region? You are not even a pilot. You have been stationed in Europe—never in the Far East. Why would Moscow send you to investigate such a matter? I don't know who you are. I do not know you, and you don't know this region." He waves his hand, dismissively.

"General, I was ordered here by Marshal Konstantinov to look into this matter. My orders are to determine the American intentions, especially in light of the heightened tensions with our main enemy."

That elegant pen is about to burst in Kamensky's hand, "Yes, this is well known. Tell me, Colonel, what type of aircraft did my troops destroy? What type of American intelligence airplane?"

"Comrade General, I understand that the target was a US Air Force RC-135."

Kamensky's neck veins bulge, "Wrong, wrong, wrong. That is not the type! My men shot down a Boeing airliner with two rows of portholes. What type would that be?"

"Two rows? I believe that only could be a Boeing 747. But I don't know of any American Air Force intelligence missions that use that model aircraft."

"Ah, not until this time! Moscow doesn't know this?"

A 747! Can this be true? The Americans don't use this type for reconnaissance. Could it have been a civilian airliner? How is this possible? What are the Americans playing at? How can this be explained?

Kamensky is finished with me. "Colonel, it seems you have quite a mystery to solve. You will fly tonight from here to Sakhalin. That is where you will begin your investigation."

This is not what I expected. I want my team to interview Kamensky's staff. This episode may have ended in the sea off Sakhalin Island, but it all started over the Kamchatka peninsula. Both regions are under Kamensky's command, and I need to investigate the entire story, not only the endgame over Sakhalin.

I pause for a moment. "Yes. Nevertheless, there are important facts I would like to ascertain here at your headquarters. Surely, your staff will have the best overall understanding of the events of that night, since they played out across your command area from Kamchatka to Sakhalin."

"Colonel, you must go to Sakhalin. Talk to General Kornukov. He knows the entire story. I authorize you to talk to Major Osipovich— yes, he is the pilot who destroyed the intruder. Talk to him."

Clearly, I have no choice in the matter and must fly this very night to Sakhalin Island.

"I will gather my team and fly to Sakhalin tonight."

His tone softens a bit. "I'll have my personal plane prepared and waiting for you. Dismissed."

"Yes, sir."

I reunite with my team at the airfield.

They're agitated about news they have heard while I was having my interview with the general. The Western press is claiming that the downed aircraft is a Korean Air Lines passenger jet—a Boeing 747, and not an American Air Force RC-135.

One of the young majors asks, "Sir, didn't General Kamensky inform you of this development?"

"Yes, although General Kamensky was more interested in being obstinate than informative. He told me the plane was a Boeing 747; however, he neglected to mention that it was a civilian Korean airliner. Anyway, we are ordered to fly immediately to Sakhalin. The general also doesn't want us to interview his staff here in Khabarovsk."

The guys look at me like I must be kidding them.

I exhale a sigh from deep in my chest. "All right, comrades, we will do our duty and go interview the guys at Sakhalin. We have a mystery to solve, I'd say. Why would the Americans use a civilian airliner?"

As I settle into my seat for the flight across the Tatar Strait to Sakhalin, I consider this news. A civilian airliner. Why? If this was an intelligence mission, then it was incredibly—outrageously—provocative. Is this flight connected to Operation RYaN? Are they provoking us with a civilian airliner to provide them an excuse to launch a surprise attack? Is this further evidence that the Americans are attempting to provoke us into a world war?

CHAPTER NINE

MISSILES AWAY

Col Ivan Levchenko, GRU, Soviet Air Defense Forces
Sakhalin Island, Russia, USSR

Saturday, 3 September 1983—Morning

M y team and I arrive at Sokol Air Base on Sakhalin Island at
about 2:00 AM on Saturday. We touch down in a war zone. The
airfield is a turned-over beehive of activity with men running around
to prepare fighters for combat operations—fueling them, arming them
with cannon shells and missiles, and inspecting engines and avionics.

Peering through the aircraft's porthole, one of my majors, who
was stationed at Bagram Air Base in Afghanistan until six months
ago, exclaims, "My God, it looks like we're going to war. This looks
like a base in Afghanistan."

The tumult on the airfield would be entirely appropriate for the
war zone in Afghanistan, but it seems bizarre in the middle of the
night in peacetime—and we are on Soviet soil, not in Afghanistan.

The main fighter unit at Sokol is a fighter-interceptor regiment
outfitted with Su-15s, and it's a Sokol-based Su-15 that shot down the
Korean airliner. Early this year, one of the fighter units subordinate
to Sokol began to transition from its Vietnam War-era MiG-21s to

modern MiG-23s. Those MiG-23s routinely deploy for rotational duty to the austere, remote Burevestnik Air Base in the Kurile Islands. That was the base that failed to respond to the overflight by US Navy aircraft on 4 April 1983, thus playing a humiliating role in the drama that has unfolded in the Far Eastern Air Defense District over the last five months.

All the fighter regiments and air defense units in this area are subordinate to the overall commander on Sakhalin, General Major Anatoly Kornukov, whose headquarters is at Sokol. I have never met General Kornukov, but I'm aware of his reputation as a consummate survivor. Not only did he weather the storm over the fallout from the failure of the MiG-23s to launch and intercept the US Navy fighters last April, but he had also previously survived the defection of one of his pilots in 1976. That pilot, Captain Viktor Belenko, flew his state-of-the-art MiG-25 fighter to a Japanese airfield and into the waiting arms of the Americans. US Air Force intelligence and the CIA gained a wealth of information about the latest Soviet technology by dissecting the MiG-25. Somehow Kornukov survived both failures, and he is one of General Kamensky's principal subordinates. General Kornukov is center stage in the current craziness, and now he is preparing his units for war with the Americans.

My team is exhausted and famished when we finally sit down in the small café in the Sokol's operations building. Quickly swallowing tepid tea and mushy sandwiches, the team chats nervously about the preparations for war they have just seen and the task ahead. I leave my tired officers to finish their meal, and I walk across a darkened street to Kornukov's headquarters building.

Once again, I wait impatiently outside the office of a general officer. It is now 3:00 AM on the 3rd of September. The general's aide finally tells me that Kornukov won't see me now. He is too busy preparing his units for combat. I am told to get some sleep and he'll see me sometime later in the day. At this point, I'm too exhausted to argue. I stand up and leave the office.

I walk down a long hallway to a conference room that my team has been provided to use as a base of operations. My guys have found their way here after departing the café.

I tell them, "The general is too busy to see me right now. Let's review the key questions we need to answer. Firstly, why did Kamchatka get confused about what was happening? We know there was an American RC-135 in the area and the Korean plane apparently flew near the American plane. Did our radar operators think that the two different airplanes—the Korean airliner and the American air force mission—were the same plane? Secondly, did the Americans intentionally use a civilian airliner for a brazen intelligence collection mission? Thirdly, did the Americans intend this to be a war-inducing provocation, an escalation beyond their overflight of the Kurile Islands last April? Lastly, what does this mean for the future? Will the Americans attempt more provocations, and is there a pattern of behavior that demonstrates that Washington has a plan to incite a confrontation they can use as a pretext for a nuclear strike on the USSR? Any questions? Am I missing anything? I need you guys to really think. If you come up with ideas or theories, I want to hear them. Right?"

I look at the men and realize that they're too worn out to think. A few hours of rest will refresh them. "Guys, let's get a few hours of sleep and reconvene at 0800."

I make sure that the men are housed properly before I go to my own room to rest. I set the bedside clock alarm for 7:30 AM.

I awake from a deep sleep abruptly. Freezing, I pull the heavy cover tight to my chest. I collect myself. What did I dream? Why do I feel so cold?

In my dream, it was just before daybreak, and I was walking from my home village in Crimea toward a town perched proudly on a rock outcropping on the far side of a deep valley. The town's four towers gleamed like alabaster as the sun rose behind them. The strange town beckoned me to cross the chasm, but I can see no way to get across it. Suddenly, a bridge appeared before me as if made from sunshine itself. Tentatively, I crossed slowly over this sun bridge. Dropping my eyes, I peered down into the deep cavern below. As soon as I reached the distant end of the miraculous bridge, the shimmering white town faded until it finally disappeared. I found myself on a high cliff overlooking the sea. I stood and stared down, down, down to the sea, to the roiling waves. The sea was dark green and grey, spinning with whirlpools. There was a square hole in the water, into which the sea poured with tremendous ferocity. It was a doorway leading into the abyss. Suddenly, I felt very cold. The cold became so intense, so vivid, that I awakened.

This strange dream disturbs me, but I don't have time to dwell on it. What does it mean, if anything, about the shootdown and the task ahead?

My men are waiting for me at a dirty table in the café adjacent to the flight line. They still look dead tired when I sit down with them at 8:00 A.M.

"Guys, we're going to have a tough time today. Firstly, they won't want to talk to us about the shootdown because they're suspicious of our motives. They'll try to keep us at bay like General Kornukov did with me last night. Secondly, they all believe that war with the Americans is imminent. We're nothing but a nuisance keeping them from important combat preparations. Lastly, be prepared to be treated like a bunch of idiots from Moscow who know nothing about the Far East."

My most senior man, a highly experienced, taciturn lieutenant colonel named Kirilenko, asks, "And what do you think? Is war with the Americans a real possibility? As you say, the officers out here certainly think so."

I consider my answer carefully. "I believe the situation is dangerous. One error, one intemperate decision, could lead to unintended consequences. I'm worried—I won't bullshit you. The troops out here are under extreme stress, and they're exhausted from nearly half a year of nonstop alerts. We don't want to be seen as interfering with their operations. If we do that, then you know they'll close their mouths to us about everything. All of us need to be sensitive to what we hear and what we observe. This is a time for all of you to be diplomatic. We need them to be comfortable enough to talk to us. Questions?"

Kirilenko asks, "Sir, where do we start?"

"Go to that conference room they gave us last night and start compiling a list of the people we need to talk to, by position, since we don't know most of their names yet. Compile that list and then brainstorm on a set of questions. Focus on what our guys think the Americans were doing that night. Focus on the Americans' actions, not on those of our people. Once you get them to give their opinions about the Americans, they naturally will open up about other things. Understand? Don't think like a cross-examining lawyer; think like a colleague who just wants to learn what the hell the Americans were doing. Show them that you care about them and have empathy for the situation they dealt with the other night. Understand?"

One of my majors asks, "Sir what will you do? And when should we plan to meet with you again?"

"I am going to the regimental headquarters to talk to the commander. I need to arrange to talk to the Su-15 pilot who shot down the border violator and I need to have the commander's permission. I'll plan to meet you in the conference room at noon. All right?"

Upon leaving my team, I immediately regret not retaining at least one of the men with me. An unaccustomed feeling of loneliness and vulnerability comes over me as I open the door to the regimental headquarters of the Su-15 fighter unit.

I walk down a dingy hallway to the regimental commander's office suite, where I find a tired-looking aide and announce my intention to see his boss as soon as possible.

His sleepy eyes go wide with hostility, and he says icily, "Comrade Colonel, it is doubtful that the commander will have time for you.

As you may know, we are on a war footing here."

I don't have time for this crap, and two can play this game. "Captain, I appreciate that your regiment is seeing to its readiness for a possible confrontation with the Americans. Please understand, however, I'm not requesting to see your commander. I am demanding it. If you do not comply immediately, then I will contact the regimental political officer, and I will have you placed in his custody pending further punitive action. I carry the authority of the chief marshal of aviation of the Soviet Air Defense Forces. Any officer who thwarts my mission will receive the harshest treatment. Given the events of last April in these parts and the severe punishments doled out to officers far senior to you, I believe you understand what I mean. Am I making myself clear, Captain?"

"Yes, Comrade Colonel, you make your position crystal clear. Please follow me to the commander's office."

Now I really wish I had brought one of my men with me.

The colonel commanding the regiment at Sokol has been in his position since late April. The man he replaced was relieved of his command and demoted. Reportedly, he received additional harsh treatment, although I am not privy to the details. In any event, the new commander's predecessor was one of the officers held responsible for the failure of the fighters at Burevestnik Air Base to get off the ground during the airspace violation by US Navy fighters.

Colonel Yevgeny Gritchko, the regimental commander, has the look of a man fighting his way through a continuously regenerating jungle. And by the look of the ashtray on his desk, he has smoked a prodigious number of cigarettes over the last few hours. He must be the most beleaguered man in the Soviet Union.

I try a nonconfrontational approach. "Comrade Colonel, I am Colonel Levchenko. I trust you have been informed by Khabarovsk of my mission here."

Lighting another cigarette, he responds with venom in his voice, "Yes, I know your mission—it is to spy on my units. Believe me, the men out here had their fill of 'inspectors' from Moscow last April. I have no time for you. We are preparing for war with the Americans. You are free to go."

Wow, he has balls. Okay, we will play it his way. "Well, Colonel, unfortunately for you, I am not free to go. I am under orders from the chief marshal of aviation. I will interview the pilot who shot down the Korean airliner and anyone else I deem necessary, including you. If you refuse me, then I will have no option but to report you to the chief marshal, after I have you arrested. Don't test me on this, comrade."

He glares at me and lights another cigarette. "It is not possible for you to interview Major Osipovich. He is far too busy in his duties. You don't seem to understand that the Americans are flying their aircraft around the crash site. They are provoking us and threatening to violate our borders again. I cannot permit any further border violations. That is my responsibility and that is *my* charge from the chief marshal of aviation. World War III may well start today, and I must have my units ready."

Good God, it is shit-for-brains like this guy who will *start* World War III. "Yes, I fully appreciate your heavy responsibilities. You have my word that I will do my best to interview your men without undue interference. Surely, Major Osipovich will have a few moments for me today."

The regimental commander's exasperation is building, and he lights another cigarette from the stub of the one he is finishing. He yells, "Captain, get Major Osipovich up here immediately. Have him meet this GRU colonel in my conference room. Colonel, this is your one shot with the major, so don't fuck it up."

An exhausted rage is welling up in my throat, but I control it. "Colonel, you will not dictate to me how I conduct my interviews, nor how many I hold. But I assure you I will be efficient and respectful of all of your officers and their time."

I leave his office and stride down the hall to his conference room. Although I desperately want my team present for the crucial interview with Osipovich, I can't risk missing the now-famous man who shot down the Korean airliner. I ask the aide to make a phone call to summon my team. He refuses, claiming that he is far too busy to "herd my cattle." This is fucking unbelievable. I decide not to press the matter and I sit down in the conference room and await the arrival of Osipovich. He surprises me by appearing promptly.

Thick fingers and even thicker hair and a heavy, sullen face—that is my first impression of Osipovich. Everything about him seems to be thick—thick voice, thick neck, and thick veneer over his psyche. A veteran fighter pilot, his attitude is one of nonchalant aggression. What is the source of such an attitude? Where did he learn aggression and learn how to kill? He hasn't been fighting in Afghanistan. He is too young to have flown against the American air force in Vietnam. No, this killing instinct is deeply sown in his genes. I have seen this attitude before in special forces—Spetsnaz—guys. You can readily identify the killers—their quiet seething and preternatural detachment. I see the killer in his eyes. This Osipovich didn't need to be taught.

Well, here we go. I begin, "Major Osipovich, it is an honor to meet you."

He coughs a cigarette cough. I am always amazed by these pilots. They train their bodies hard. Lots of work in the gym to build resistance and strong muscles against the G-forces, but they also drink and smoke like gigolos. They pride themselves on their physical condition and flout it. They drink copious amounts of vodka and smoke cigarettes. They flaunt their superiority to mere mortals. They can remain superior to us even while they inflict harm on themselves, which is why they do it.

Major Osipovich addresses me with an air of superior detachment. "Yes, Colonel, I understand you wish to ask me questions and that I am bound to talk to you."

"Well Major, I am here to *learn* from you. I want to understand what the Americans were up to a few nights ago. Why did they penetrate our airspace? What do you think their action means?"

Osipovich shrugs his shoulders. "How would I know, sir? The Americans are always provoking us. That's what they do. We live it every day out here."

"Yes, but surely the events of the other night were unusual—unique, even, wouldn't you say?"

The major squints his eyes. "The Americans sent their air force spy plane into our airspace. Do you know that they also violated our airspace with navy fighters in the spring? You say it is unusual or unique. I don't know. It doesn't seem that unusual to me."

Jesus Christ, why don't I have one of my guys with me? I'd like some moral support. "Why didn't our fighters intercept the plane over Kamchatka? Why did they fail?"

He shrugs. "Colonel, I cannot speak for the Kamchatka guys. I have heard that several of their radar sites were not operational, or at least not fully operational. It's fucking hard to find a plane in the middle of the night if you don't have radar vectoring you from the ground. It's fucking hard to find a plane at night even *if* you do have good radar support. Have you ever flown an intercept mission? At night? It isn't easy."

"Major, I am not a pilot, so I cannot even imagine the difficulty of flying such a mission, especially at night. I am curious, however, why the units on Sakhalin succeeded while the Kamchatka guys let the Americans get away. Why is that?"

"Well, Colonel, we had the advantage of going second. We had far more warning of the intruder than Kamchatka did. We had time to prepare. And our radars here on Sakhalin actually work, unlike theirs. Even for us, it was difficult. We sent many fighters from our two Sakhalin bases, and *we* almost didn't find the airplane. Like I said, it isn't easy."

"All right, what did you see? Was the plane you intercepted an American Air Force plane? Did you think it was a commercial airliner? What did you think?"

"Colonel, I could see that the plane had two rows of portholes. I saw that. It looked like a Boeing 747. Okay? It didn't matter to me. The

Americans take lots of civilian planes and make them intelligence planes. Why should a 747 be any different?"

"Major, with respect, have you ever been briefed by your intelligence unit that the United States has a military intelligence aircraft based on the Boeing 747 airplane? I mean, let's get realistic here. Did you ever see an intelligence briefing that said the Americans use 747s for missions like this one?"

He grimaces. I've ruffled his feathers. "Look, what I know is that the Americans always pull a rabbit out of their hat. No one can ever know their tricks. I'm a fighter pilot, not a professor of American studies or an intelligence officer."

This guy is smart—he isn't going to be drawn into a discussion about American intent, or comment on the quality of the intelligence he gets. "All right, all right, Major. I know you've been debriefed several times already, but I need to hear your words—your recollections—directly from you, please."

He sighs deeply and coughs. "Like I said, we had several fighters in the air. I was directed by the controller to go forward and intercept the intruder, which was classified officially as a military target. I had no reason to doubt it. The intercept took a long time. When I finally got to within visual range—remember, it was the middle of the night, and visual range was limited. I reported back to the ground controller that I had acquired the target. I saw the blinking lights. I flew around the target, and I saw it had two rows of portholes—some of the windows had lights glowing. I knew this airplane was a Boeing 747, but that meant nothing to me. I mean, as I said before, it is easy to turn a civilian plane into a military one, and the American air force does it all the time."

"All right, Major, what did you report to the ground control officer? Did you tell him it was a civilian plane?"

"No, Colonel, I didn't give the ground a detailed description. You must understand—the ground did not *ask* me for a description. Remember, this plane was already classified as a border violator. You understand? It was a military target!" He's quite exercised now.

I speak in a calming voice. "Yes, I understand, Major. What happened next?"

"The controller told me to try to contact the intruder. I pulsed him with my radio but there was no response. Then the ground told me to fire warning shots across the front of the cockpit. I fired about 200 rounds, for all the good it did."

"What do you mean, Major?"

"Well, my cannon was loaded with armor-piercing rounds, not incendiaries. I fired the rounds, but they don't light up at night. So I may as well have been pissing at the plane. No one in the cockpit was going to see anything."

"I see. And you rocked your wings to get their attention?"

"Of course. I followed all the procedures, but it was no use. It was a very black night, and my speed was much greater than the intruder's. It's doubtful that they saw me. However, at a crucial point, the target slowed further and gained altitude. So I thought that maybe he knew he had been intercepted and was trying to get away. Perhaps this was an evasive maneuver. I told ground control that the target was taking evasive action. We were running out of time, you know. The target was about to leave our airspace. Like I told you, my airspeed was much greater than his, and it was impossible to stay abeam. And when he took this evasive maneuver, well, I risked losing him entirely, or stalling my own jet. It was precarious and everything was happening in seconds. There was no time to lose."

The pilot glares at me. Is Osipovich being evasive? It doesn't seem likely. His story rings true to me. I'm beginning to appreciate just how desperately challenging and precarious his mission was that night. He almost let the target get away, and if he had, it would have been his ass. I encourage him to continue with a friendly wave of my hand.

"Well, Colonel, I really risked losing him. I knew the ground controller was getting terribly nervous and he thought that we might let the intruder get away—you know, like they did over Kamchatka.

Anyway, we had already flown over Sakhalin—the island is very narrow at that point. There was a clear risk he would get away. There was a MiG-23 nearby and I feared that the controller would take the mission away from me and give it to him. I couldn't allow that to happen. Suddenly, I heard the controller say, 'destroy the target!' Well, that was easy for him to say. I had already expended 243 rounds from my cannon. How should I attack him?"

Major Osipovich pauses again.

"So, Major, you thought you were running out of options, as well as time?"

"Yes, I only had seconds to react. I thought to myself—ram him. You can ram him before he leaves state airspace."

"Wait, wait, you are saying that you considered ramming the intruder? Ramming him with your fighter? You would have been killed yourself!"

"I was desperate. I couldn't let this bastard go. I decided to take a different action. I flew around, turned, and I was on top of him again. I had to calculate immediately the physics of the intercept. It was a dilemma."

He pauses again. I had no idea. He considered ramming the target! Unbelievable. Then he had to calculate the mathematics of the intercept in his head—at the same time that he was considering committing suicide by ramming the intruder.

"What did you do, Major?"

"I decided I must get behind him to execute the attack. Time was passing—we were nearly in international airspace. I dropped down a couple of thousand meters below and behind him. Then I hit my afterburners, armed my missiles, and pulled up my nose sharply. Suddenly, I got the lock-on signal. I had him! I fired one missile, then another. I told the controller, 'Missiles away.' I saw the first one hit the rear of the target—around the tail. It looked like the other missile struck the left wing and tore it in half. I told the controller, 'The target is destroyed.'"

I can see that he is reliving those adrenaline-fueled moments. His eyes are red and filling up. His mind is replaying the awful event. He pauses again and goes quiet.

I break the silence. "It clearly was a difficult task. Did you follow the airplane as it fell?"

He collects himself. "Not really, Colonel. I was too low on fuel. There was a MiG-23 from Smirnykh with me. He had more fuel, and he followed the target down to the sea. I don't really know what he saw—not much, I'd guess. Anyway, I had to return to base immediately due to my low fuel levels."

"Major, do you believe this was a legitimate target?'

A wave of panic briefly passes over his face, but it's ephemeral. "Yes. We acted legally. Even if this turns out to be a Korean airliner, it is obvious that it was on a military mission. They flew right over Petropavlovsk, for fuck's sake! We did nothing wrong. We defended our borders. I executed the mission I was given."

He composes himself and looks at me with stony eyes. His impenetrable nonchalance has returned. "Colonel, I need a cigarette. Am I free to go?"

"Yes, Major. Thank you for your assistance. I may need to talk to you again if I have any follow-up questions. I will let your regimental commander know. Thank you again."

In reality, I doubt that I'll need to talk to him again. I want to debrief my team and I head to the other building where they are holed up in the conference room. Is the major credible? He seems sincere and without artifice—I don't think he is bullshitting me.

My team has been busy. They have collected a large list of questions on long pieces of paper and organized them on the conference room table. They look up when I walk in the door.

"I can see you all have been working hard, guys. I just talked to Major Osipovich. I would've preferred to have you all there with me, but it was not possible for me to leave the regimental conference room, and the regimental colonel's aide refused to call you on my behalf."

They all smile knowingly.

"The most interesting thing that I got from talking to Osipovich is how close we came that night to losing the Korean airliner. He actually considered *ramming* the 747 to prevent it from getting away. Ramming it! Can you imagine? He was playing three-dimensional chess in the dark with the Korean airliner that night."

Lieutenant Colonel Kirilenko is the first to speak. "Maybe he should have let it get away. He gave the Americans a major propaganda coup and an opportunity to create mischief. Reagan may launch World War III now. Do you believe the major's story, Colonel?"

"Yeah, I do. I think the essence of his story is true. I imagine that others may disagree with some of the details, but he seems credible to me, and he didn't hesitate to share details. What is clear is that the mission that night was complex and challenging, and success was not guaranteed. I think that he's representative of the general view out here, which is that they did their duty and stopped a border violator from escaping. Full stop."

Everybody looks at me and then at Kirilenko to gauge his reaction. He nods in agreement—at least that's how I read him.

Kirilenko proceeds to brief me on the list of officers—by position—that the men want to interview. Then he has each of the men take turns going through the list of questions they have compiled. Their work is impressive. It is clear to me that they are working well together and challenging each other's assumptions and lines of inquiry. I smile to myself as they wrap up the impromptu presentation. I have chosen well and wisely—this is a great group of officers.

"Well done, comrades. I am impressed with your thoroughness. I leave it to you to decide how to divide up the work and the interviews, while I attempt to see General Kornukov again. Let's reconvene here in the conference room at 1800 today—okay?"

They look eager to get on with their work as they respond affirmatively.

Saturday, 3 September 1983—Midday

I don't relish approaching General Kornukov's lion's den again, but here we go. When I arrive at the general's office, his aide offers me a cup of tepid, weak tea. At least it is a peace offering of sorts.

As soon as I enter his office and see Kornukov, I know I am in trouble. He is a stocky, ruddy-faced ball of aggression. No seat is offered.

He bleats, "Well, Colonel, what do you want?"

I pause to swallow the tea that has erupted from my stomach back up to my mouth. "Ah, good day, Comrade General Kornukov. My team is tasked with assessing the reasons for the provocative American action of two nights ago. I respectfully request the cooperation of your staff in completing our mission."

Kornukov stares through me with angry eyes. He is silent.

I break the silence. "General, may I ask your indulgence? May I sit down, please?"

The general waves his red hand toward a chair.

Seated, I start again. "General, in your long experience in the Far East, have you ever seen an American provocation anything like this one?"

Kornukov's eyes turn even more venomous. He must think to himself, *why has Moscow sent me this idiotic goat?* "Colonel, of course the Americans haven't done anything like this before. Why do you ask such a stupid question? Is the GRU this bereft of knowledge and common sense?"

"My apologies. Shall we start with what you think transpired two nights ago?"

Kornukov looks indignantly at me but begins to speak. "The Americans had an RC-135 mission flying off the east coast of Kamchatka, awaiting our ICBM test, which didn't occur. We believe that the intruder airplane is an American mission that flew right through the RC-135 orbit in a clever ploy designed to confuse our radar operators on Kamchatka. Then the intruder continued its mission to spy on our naval base—our nuclear submarine base—at Petropavlovsk. The fighters from Kamchatka launched but failed to find and intercept the intruder. The radars on the west coast of Kamchatka lost track of the border violator as it began its journey over the Sea of Okhotsk."

He takes a deep breath and continues. "By contrast, *my* radar troops on Sakhalin acquired the target and tracked it with high competence as it approached the east coast of our island. I launched fighters from Sokol and Smirnykh. Major Osipovich, one of our regimental deputy commanders here at Sokol, intercepted the intruder over Sakhalin. He endeavored to contact the Boeing plane, per international regulations. The intruder ignored his attempts. I was ordered by General Colonel Kamensky to get the airplane to land before it left Soviet sovereign airspace. This was not possible because the violator ignored Osipovich and took evasive action in a clear attempt to flee into international airspace. I was told that if the border violator refused to cooperate with our pilot that we were to shoot it down before it departed sovereign territory. Thus, I ordered our man into firing position, and he was given target destruct orders. He carried out his orders before the border violator departed Soviet airspace. That, Colonel, is what 'transpired' two nights ago. Kamchatka failed. My troops succeeded."

I'm impressed by his extemporaneous speech. "Did Major Osipovich know that the plane was a civilian airliner? Did he identify it as a Boeing 747? After all, the American air force doesn't use 747s as intelligence collectors."

"Colonel, I don't know. Ask him yourself. He carried out his orders, as I did. I expect the GRU to tell *me* why the Americans used a 747—a civilian airliner, if that is what it was—for this mission. My mission is to defend the sovereign airspace of the USSR. My job is not to determine what mischief is in the devious minds that run the CIA and the American Air Force. I thought that was the job of the GRU!"

No one out here seems to care for the GRU. "Sir, did General Kamensky order you to shoot down the intruder, even if it was identified as a civilian airliner? It seems to me that this is a crucial point."

Kornukov's neck turns an odd shade of crimson as he responds. "Colonel, General Kamensky was in constant communication with me. He also was in communication with the highest authorities in Moscow during this event. Are you implying that he and the senior leadership of the Ministry of Defense ordered the shootdown of a civilian airliner with no cause? I don't care for this line of inquiry, Colonel."

Nor do I care for you, General. "I would like to interview key officers who were on duty that night, in addition to Major Osipovich. With your permission, of course. The most important thing is to try to determine the intentions of the Americans. What is it they were playing at that night? This is not an investigation of the performance of your troops, Comrade General."

The general isn't buying it and replies sarcastically, "Yes, fine, Colonel. Of course, this isn't an investigation of my troops by a cadre of Moscow errand boys. I understand completely."

More seriously, he continues. "And let me say this: I was not prepared that night to permit a border violator to get away under any circumstances. I made this point clear to General Kamensky at the time—during the intercept itself. As far as I am concerned, the fact that this plane had overflown Kamchatka proved it was a military target. There was no need for an absolute identification. It was self-evident on the night of the events that this plane was on a military intelligence mission. If you talk to my officers, they will tell you the same thing I did. We did our duty that night to protect the motherland. I offer no apologies for securing our borders—not to you and not to any other asshole from Moscow."

Well, that's clear. "Sir, did you know that Major Osipovich considered ramming the 747 to prevent it from escaping?"

This point is news to the general, and his eyes go wide. He recovers his composure and says, "Well, in wartime, one sometimes must take desperate measures. I imagine that Osipovich knew the stakes that night. I nearly took him off the intercept because he was taking too long to accomplish the task. Now I am busy. You are dismissed, Colonel."

Jesus fucking Christ, what an obstinate, arrogant ass he is. Guys like him will get us in a nuclear war with the Americans.

Saturday, 3 September 1983—Early Afternoon

I have one last interview to conduct here at Sokol, with the lieutenant colonel who was in charge of the Sakhalin air defense sector's response to the border violator on the night of the shootdown. In the meantime, my men have been busy interviewing other officers who were involved in that night's events. My team also will conduct telephone interviews with key officers at Petropavlovsk later this afternoon.

I stop by the flight line café for a quick bite of lunch before heading to the air defense operations center and my final interview. I am anxious to get the interview over with, compare notes with my team, and wrap up this investigation.

I doubt we'll learn much that is new, or that anything of much importance will happen here on Sakhalin now.

CHAPTER TEN

BIG WARS START IN SMALL PLACES

Colonel Ivan Levchenko, GRU,
Air Defense Forces of the Soviet Union
Sakhalin Island, and Moscow, Russia, USSR

Saturday, 3 September 1983—Afternoon

U nsurprisingly, the food at the airfield's café has not improved since this morning, but at least the tea is hot. I sit and allow myself the luxury of my own thoughts for a few minutes.

I wonder how Boyka is doing. I cannot bear to have her decamp to Kiev indefinitely. If that were to happen, I will become a staggering drunkard or God knows what. Anyway, we must find a way to live together in Moscow.

When I was a student at the advanced college in Moscow—the Military-Diplomatic Academy—I thought that Boyka would enjoy the capital city and its social scene, and especially the great art it has to offer. That didn't work out. In those early days, Boyka felt like an unwanted foreigner—a Ukrainian beauty in a city of smug Russians who looked down their noses at anyone from the "provinces." Her withering opinion of the city and its inhabitants was formed then and has never changed.

Oh well, I must carry on with my mission. I gulp down the last of my tea and head over to the air defense operations center building. Interviewing men who question my motives is becoming extremely tiresome.

Anxious to complete my last interview of the day, I arrive shortly after 2:00 PM at the security desk outside Sokol's air defense operations center. The junior lieutenant in charge of security scrutinizes my identification card and asks me to wait. There is one dilapidated chair in the waiting area and shortly after I sit down in it, I fall into a deep sleep. I'm still jetlagged.

A metal drawer closing loudly awakens me. I look at my watch and it is nearly 3:00 PM. Christ! I shift in the chair, and the lieutenant looks at me with undisguised amusement.

He clears his throat. "Comrade Colonel, it took time to verify your clearance credentials; however, everything is in order. You may go into the operations center when you are ready."

Falling asleep in front of a kid like this lieutenant is embarrassing. "Yes, Lieutenant, I'm ready. I'm to see Lieutenant Colonel Burakovsky. Can you confirm that he's on duty this afternoon?"

"Yes, Colonel, he is commanding the day shift today. I must warn you, sir, that he is extremely busy. The situation with the Americans is very complicated today—treacherous."

The lieutenant enters a code into the security pad on the door to the operations center and he escorts me inside.

Pandemonium. The scene in the air defense operations center is one of frantic activity. My focus immediately goes to the situation map that dominates the front of the room. Junior personnel are busy updating the locations of ships and aircraft that are seemingly fighting for position like hockey players around the net. They've converged around a small island called Moneron in the Tatar Strait. That's the crash site, where the Korean airliner smashed into the sea.

Our Pacific Fleet has numerous ships in the area, searching for wreckage and the all-important black boxes from the plane's cockpit. We have several search planes and intelligence aircraft orbiting the site. Lastly, the Air Defense Force has pairs of fighters flying combat air patrol over the scene.

As if the Soviet assets were not sufficient to clog up the narrow Tatar Strait, the American Navy has a flotilla of ships flooding into the area, along with several search-and-intelligence aircraft orbiting in the limited airspace over the Strait. To make matters worse, the Japanese Coast Guard has ships in the area and the Japanese news media are flying small aircraft taking photographs around the site. What an unholy mess!

The technicians working on the situation board are doing their best to keep track of all the ships and planes converging around Moneron Island. If the big board is an accurate representation of what is happening in the Tatar Strait, then the conditions are ripe for confusion and accidental conflict with the Americans. An incident in the air or unintentional collision between our ships could spark a conflagration.

As I take stock of all this chaos, an unexpected wave of hot shame washes over me. I suddenly see myself the way the Sakhalin-based officers do—a pinhead colonel from Moscow, conducting an inquisition of loyal officers while they are on the front lines battling with the Americans. As I contemplate these feelings, I feel someone tap on my shoulder to get my attention. My reverie broken; I turn to face Burakovsky—the very officer I've come here to see. He's a man of medium height and build, with a face that is a blend of European and Tatar features. His eyes bore into mine with a healthy self-assurance.

He introduces himself and says, "Comrade Colonel Levchenko, I understand you wish to talk to me about the Korean airliner. As you can see, we're very busy here, but I can spare a few minutes for you right now."

I smile to show my appreciation and say, "Lieutenant Colonel Burakovsky, it is a pleasure to meet you. Yes, I want to talk to you about the night of the shootdown and what you think the Americans were up to. Is there an office or quiet place where we can talk?"

Burakovsky gestures toward an alcove with chairs and a small table, "Colonel, we can chat over there. All right?"

We sit down in what is a relatively quiet spot amidst the manic activity of the operations floor.

Burakovsky keeps one eye on the floor and wastes no time in getting to the point. "Colonel, there are only two possibilities regarding the Korean plane's intentions. One, it was an American-directed intelligence collection flight. Or two, the Korean aircrew made a grave navigational error that took them off their normal track. If the second scenario is true, then the Korean crew was oblivious to their mistake and the fate that awaited them."

Holy shit! No one else has suggested a navigational error as the possible cause of the mysterious flight. This lieutenant colonel now has my full attention.

I am intrigued. "Tell me, if the intrusion wasn't intentional, then do you think that the Americans' outrage about the shootdown is justified? We, in the GRU, are seeing reports that the Western press is braying about the nefarious Soviet actions that led to the shootdown of an unarmed civilian airliner. What do you make of that, Burakovsky?"

"Colonel, I cannot comment on the Western press. I don't know if the flight wasn't intentional. I am merely stating that there are only two logical scenarios—the flight was either an intelligence collection mission or a tragic mistake. There are no other scenarios. I've been an operational air defense officer for more than twenty years. I have never seen the Americans risk the lives of civilians to conduct an intelligence collection mission. It seems unlikely to me, even given the fraught relations between our two countries." This Burakovsky is a savvy customer and brutally honest.

"Tell me, how could an experienced Korean Air Lines crew make such a catastrophic navigational error? I mean, these crews fly the trans-Pacific route routinely. How could they make such a fundamental mistake, and wouldn't they, or air traffic control, have realized the error?"

Burakovsky considers his response for a moment. "I don't know *how* they may have made the initial mistake. As for air traffic control, the Western countries don't have positive air traffic control over the Pacific. Their ATC relies on the airliners to report on their own positions and there is no way for ATC to independently verify that those positions are accurate. All I'm saying is that there are only two possible scenarios, and a navigational error is one of them."

As I let Burakovsky's comments sink in, my thoughts are interrupted by a commotion that has erupted on the operations floor. A young officer is calling for Burakovsky.

"Colonel Burakovksy, come here quickly, sir! We have confirmed radar signals that an American aircraft is violating our border!"

Burakovsky jumps up from his chair like he has been launched from a cannon and shouts, "Captain, what is the aircraft type, and where precisely is it located?"

"Sir, it is a US Navy P-3, probably the intelligence version and not the anti-submarine version, based on its flight route. According to our radar reports, the P-3 is in our airspace."

I follow Burakovsky onto the ops floor and my eyes focus on the board, which shows the American flight as a border violator.

Burakovsky swings into action. "Where is our closest combat air patrol—the closest one to this reported location?"

A different captain appears. "We have a flight of two MiG-23s from Smirnykh that can effect an intercept rapidly. The fighters are right over Moneron Island."

I stare at Burakovsky. He is facing a momentous decision. If he orders the MiG-23s to attack the American plane, he risks an escalation to a shooting war. If the P-3 really is a border violator and if he were to permit it to escape, he risks his own neck, especially in the current highly charged climate.

Burakovsky picks up the red phone that connects him directly with General Kornukov. He's asking for guidance from his commanding general. From what I can determine, the flight of two MiG-23s is easily in range of the P-3, which is a slow-moving turbo-prop airplane. The weather over the strait isn't great and it is just before 3:30 in the afternoon, so dusk at this high latitude is not far off. It seems to me that a successful intercept will be tricky but feasible. The question is, should we try?

General Kornukov answers that question with a direct order to shoot down the border violator. Doesn't the general understand the consequences of shooting down an unarmed American reconnaissance plane—especially one with a crew of two dozen US Navy personnel? What will Reagan do? Let the goddamn airplane go, for God's sake! Our radars are notoriously imprecise. It's probably not even in our airspace.

The pandemonium on the operations center floor ratchets up another gear and orders are passed to the MiG-23s to intercept and engage the US Navy P-3. I cannot believe this is happening. I'm a powerless observer of this madness. I move to a position where I can overhear the orders that Burakovsky is issuing. He tells the pilots to arm their missiles and engage once they are in a firing position. All of this is happening so fast, no one has time to consider the consequences. The only objective of Burakovsky's team now is to shoot down the border violator before it leaves our airspace. I cannot imagine that the Americans would be so careless as to cross into our airspace under any circumstances and especially not now. I know their navigation systems are quite precise and their flight crews are highly trained. An intentional intrusion or a navigational error—both seem very unlikely scenarios to me.

Suddenly, one of the young officers is shouting. "Colonel Burakovsky, we have radar tracking four fast movers—American fighters. They appear to be on course to intercept our MiGs. They are supersonic."

I hear Burakovsky mutter, "Holy Jesus fucking Christ . . ."

Then he turns to the chief controller who is vectoring the MiG-23s. "Alert the pilots that the Americans are coming after them. They are probably F-4s or F-15s. Whatever they are, they are closing fast. Tell them they need to execute the attack on the P-3 now!!!"

For the first time, Burakovsky notices me standing nearby. He grimaces at me, shrugging his shoulders. Holy shit. Am I about to witness the first shots of World War III? I'm praying for the P-3 to escape. I am confident that if he gets away safely, then the Americans will call off their attack on the MiG-23s. Well, let's say I am *pretty* confident they won't attack, but in the heat of the moment, who knows?

Moments creep by. It is clear from Burakovsky's demeanor that the MiGs must be about to engage.

Suddenly he shouts. "What the hell? What do you mean the P-3 is escaping? Are the MiGs following him down to the sea? They need to follow him down to the water, find him, and get him!"

Someone on the floor reports. "Colonel Burakovsky, it looks like the American is no longer in our airspace. He is on the wavetops. Our pilots have lost him, they followed him down to the sea, but they lost track of him. He is getting away."

Burakovsky shouts, "Where are the American fighters? Are they on top of our guys? Get our guys out of there, now!"

I am impressed with Burakovsky. He immediately pivoted from intercepting the P-3 to protecting our MiGs. Now the storyline has switched from whether we will start World War III by shooting down an American P-3 to whether World War III will begin when American fighters shoot down our MiG-23s. I am sure that the Americans won't lose sight of our MiGs like we lost the P-3. I'm feeling sick to my stomach, and by the expressions I see on the operations floor, I'm not the only one.

Seconds crawl by. Suddenly, there is a cry from the floor. "The Americans are in position. They probably have a firing solution." Oh, God. Here we go.

In a moment, the same voice shouts again. "It looks like the Americans are breaking off—turning away."

Burakovsky stands up straighter. "Confirm that the American fighters are returning to their previous orbit. Are they returning to that orbit?"

"Yes, Colonel, it appears that they are turning back—they are breaking off their attack."

Burakovsky's chest puffs out. "Have the MiG-23s return to base at once. I want them back on the ground, and I want those pilots debriefed as soon as possible."

It feels like the entire room exhales. It's almost like one can see the pressure in the room evaporate like a mist. I begin to breathe normally again. The war won't start here today. Everyone can sense the universe rebalance.

I lean into Burakovsky and whisper. "Thank God, sanity has prevailed."

He manages a weak grin. His face is a sickly pale, and his eyes are red. His blood pressure must have been skyrocketing just a few moments ago.

I shake his hand and depart the operations center. There will be no more interviews today. Or tomorrow for that matter. Walking unsteadily, I make my way out of the operations building. I feel empty. World War III nearly began a few minutes ago, and I could do nothing but stand there and watch helplessly. I feel like the ground is heaving beneath me, like in an earthquake. When have I felt this way before? Oh yes, I remember feeling similar sensations the day my father died. My world was crashing around me. The horizon tilted. The difference, of course, is that this time the world nearly did crash all around me.

Perhaps the worst has passed, and we will get through this crisis without blowing up the planet. Silently, I give thanks to the American officer who called off his fighters and stopped the attack on our MiG-23s. If big wars start in small places, then we managed through luck and an anonymous officer's good judgment to avoid starting a very big war in a very small place today.

I walk across the street toward the main headquarters building. It's dusk and getting cold. What a climate this is to live in. I do sympathize with the poor guys who are stationed on this godawful island for years on end. As I open the door to the headquarters building, I'm accosted from behind by a young officer.

"Comrade Colonel Levchenko, with respect, Lieutenant Colonel Burakovsky sends his compliments and begs you to return immediately to the operations center."

Christ! What's happened now? "Captain, why does he want me to come back?"

"Sir, I am not at liberty to say, but please, come with me."

The captain and I head back to the operations building at a trot. Immediately upon entering, I see that Burakovsky is dealing with a new crisis. He sees me and motions me to stand next to him. Good Lord, what now?

A Japanese NHK television aircraft has been identified as a border violator. Two MiG-23s have been sent to intercept it. Burakovsky himself is on the radio, talking to the MiG-23 flight lead. He grimaces at me and speaks into the microphone. "Comrade Captain, have you identified the border violator?"

Burakovsky points to a headset on the table and indicates that I should put it on. I comply and affix it to my right ear. I can hear the crackly transmission from the lead MiG pilot, who says, "I have intercepted a slow-moving prop plane. It has the letters 'NHK' written on the side. It's too slow for me. I have deployed my speed brake, but I can't slow down enough to stay with it."

Burakovsky responds, "Our radar reflects that this plane is a border violator. Can you confirm this?"

There is a pause, and the pilot keys in to say, "I can't confirm. I think I am over international waters, but it's hard to say."

Burakovsky takes in this information. "If this aircraft is violating the border, then I must give you orders to contact it and attempt to get it to land."

The fighter pilot responds, "This is impossible. Like I said, I'm too fast for him. There's no way for me to contact this plane. It *is* a civilian aircraft. It has NHK on the fuselage—that's a Japanese television station. It's also getting dark out here. I'm not sure that the civilian pilot can even see me."

"Captain, if you cannot contact this intruder, then your orders are to shoot it down. Our radar reflects that he is a border violator."

"Colonel, with respect, I can't verify that this plane is a border violator, but I can confirm that it is an NHK civilian plane. Colonel, my wingman and I are low on fuel. We're returning to base. I repeat, I am low on fuel and returning to base."

Burakovsky's face is white again. He takes a long pause and keys his microphone. "Understood, Captain, you must return to base as a result of low fuel levels, which will be reflected in my official log."

A junior officer on the ops floor shouts, "American fighters are approaching the area at supersonic speed."

Christ. The Americans must have intercepted Burakovsky's target destruct order on the NHK plane. Now they are hunting our MiG-23s.

Burakovsky shouts into his mouthpiece. "Captain, American fighters are flying to your position. Return to base! RTB now!"

Here we go again. The MiGs light their afterburners and race for the Soviet coastline. If they weren't truly low on fuel before, they will be now that they've lit the afterburners. There are tense moments until our MiGs reenter Soviet airspace. Surely American fighters won't follow them there.

There's another cry from the operations floor. "The American fighters are turning away from our coastline. It appears they are breaking off the attack."

Burakovsky throws his headphones onto the desk in front of him. He stands back, puts his hands on his hips, then on his temples.

He closes his eyes. Leaning forward, he puts his hands on the desk and sits down. He's shattered by this latest episode. What would the Japanese and Americans have done if our MiGs had shot down an NHK television plane?

For my part, I can't believe this moment. We've just avoided another calamity. Thank God for that young pilot. 'I am low on fuel and returning to base.' Those words ought to be inscribed on a monument somewhere. Unfucking-believable. Here we are on the brink of Armageddon again, and a young pilot is the one to pull us back!

My team reconvenes as planned in "our" conference room. The men report on their interviews, most of which provide information generally consistent with what we already know. The most interesting was by telephone with a pair of colonels from Petropavlovsk. The colonels confirmed several of their large, search radars were inoperable on the night of the shootdown. The big arrays had been damaged weeks earlier by a late summer Arctic gale that nearly blew the radars completely over. The unsavory truth is that the commander of the Kamchatka air defense zone lied to his boss, General Kamensky, about the radars' condition after the storm. He reported they had been repaired and were operational when that was not at all true. He'll find himself on Kamensky's chopping block for certain. I can only hope that Kamensky doesn't shoot the messenger—me.

I arrange for my team and I to fly back to Khabarovsk in the morning so that I can brief General Kamensky before we begin the long trek home to Moscow. We have dinner together that night at the officers' mess, where one of my majors produces a bottle of very good vodka for us to share. I am so proud of these guys. They did a really good job in tough circumstances.

Sunday, 4 September 1983

We are scheduled to depart Sokol Air Base for Khabarovsk at 0800 on Sunday morning and I stop by the operations center around 0600. Burakovsky is back on duty. He tells me there has been no significant air activity since the near-shootdown of the NHK television plane. However, there have been several incidents at sea, where our Pacific Fleet ships have blocked US Navy ships from getting close to the Korean airliner crash site. The US Navy has filed official complaints claiming infringement of freedom of navigation. No matter how much the Americans complain, our Pacific Fleet will not permit the Americans to dive on the crash site. We must get the aircraft's black boxes before the Americans do. Our navy divers have been busy locating the wreckage on the sea floor and they are prepared to dive on the wreckage field. Maybe they will find the black boxes today.

I also stop by General Kornukov's office before our flight to Khabarovsk. He deigns to see me for a few minutes, and I provide him with the highlights of the report that I will present to his boss, General Colonel Kamensky.

Kornukov tells me my report seems fair and reasonable. He is especially pleased that the commander on Kamchatka is chastised for lying about the state of his search radars. He wishes me a safe return to Moscow, and I depart for the flight line.

The flight to Khabarovsk is uneventful, and I muse aloud to my men that the acute military crisis appears to be passing. There's still some danger, given that forces on both sides are on high alert, and there remains a risk of confrontation in the close confines of the Tatar Strait.

The political crisis, however, is building in intensity. The United States's anti-Soviet rhetoric concerning the Korean airliner shootdown seems designed to provoke the Kremlin. Even if the Americans didn't use the Korean airliner for an intelligence collection mission, and even if Burakovsky is correct that the Koreans made a fatal navigational error, Reagan is using the incident to escalate tensions. Could the crisis prompt a nuclear war? I don't know, but this could be the accidental trigger that makes pieces of the RYaN puzzle fall into place.

As I try to put the Korean airliner tragedy in perspective, it seems to me that it's a flashing red warning light of sorts. The Americans will see the event as further evidence of nefarious Soviet intentions and justification for their deployment of Pershing II missiles to Germany and new ground-launched cruise missiles (GLCMs) to Great Britain.

Of course, I don't buy the Kremlin's paranoid worldview; however, I agree with Andropov that the new missile deployments to NATO threaten Moscow with a decapitation strike—a first strike designed to destroy the leadership of the Soviet state. To the extent that the Korean incident stokes the flame of Reagan's already inflammatory rhetoric, it also will feed the fire of paranoia in the Kremlin.

To my great surprise, General Colonel Kamensky hosts me for lunch in his office in Khabarovsk. I share my findings with him over an excellent assortment of seafood. He listens silently and is attuned to each point I make. The state of the radars on Kamchatka alarms him. He asks me to pause my briefing while he tells his aide to schedule a call with the Kamchatka sector air defense commander after lunch.

As I conclude, Kamensky sighs like he's dead tired of the entire business. "Well, Colonel, you have done a thorough job in a short amount of time. I want to learn more about this possible Korean navigational error. If this wasn't an intelligence collection flight—and, I remain convinced that it was—then we will need to understand how such an error could have occurred."

At least he isn't rejecting the navigational theory out of hand. "Sir, if our divers recover the airplane's black boxes, then we may find clues to unlock the more mysterious aspects of this episode. Then we will see whether the navigational error theory holds up. In the meantime, I think the prudent approach is to assume that the flight was an intelligence collection mission until we have solid evidence to the contrary. That is what I shall report to Moscow."

General Kamensky ponders my statement for a moment. "Well, Colonel, I think shooting down the Korean plane was a national security imperative. I know we acted legally and properly. I am proud of the actions of the troops on Sakhalin. On the other hand, I'm deeply distressed over what happened, or rather didn't happen, at Kamchatka."

Kamensky rises and shakes my hand. He wishes me and my team a safe journey back to Moscow. And with that, the Far Eastern chapter of my mission is over.

Monday, 5 September 1983

We all are exhausted when we finally land in Moscow. The flight is long and made more tedious by the need for a refueling stop in Siberia. I thank each of my team members as we deplane and ask them to keep my executive officer apprised of their whereabouts over the next week or so, as I may need to reach them on short notice.

I have my driver take me directly to my office from the airfield. I want some time to catch up on work there and collect my thoughts. My main task is to compose a formal briefing summarizing the results of our mission to the Far East for my boss, Marshal Konstantinov, and our big boss, the chief marshal of aviation, Alexander Koldunov, the commanding officer of the entire Soviet Air Defense Force.

Tuesday, 6 September 1983

After a couple of days of silence on the matter, the Kremlin's news agency, TASS, reports that the Korean airliner flew into Soviet airspace without clearance and that its navigation lights were not illuminated. The television news reporters read the TASS statements verbatim, of course, with no editorial commentary. TASS also asserts that the civilian plane was warned but failed to respond and that the flight was a planned provocation. *Pravda,* our official state newspaper, states,

"The crude violation of the Soviet state border by the South Korean plane and its deep penetration into the Soviet Union's airspace was a deliberate, pre-planned action pursuing far-reaching political and military aims." All of this is madness and a public relations fiasco, to boot. The Kremlin offers no apology for the loss of life. As the Americans would say, the Kremlin is circling the wagons.

President Reagan has a television address in which he calls the shootdown the "Korean Airline Massacre." Reagan calls it a "monstrous wrong" and a "crime against humanity." It seems that Reagan knows exactly how to twist the knife and attack the Kremlin's brittle psyche.

The Russian soul is an old soul—much older than the Bolsheviks. It is highly sensitive to slights and charges of barbarism and inhumanity. We are products of the Tatar conquest, our mixed Asian-European racial makeup, and our orthodox religion. We are not children of the Enlightenment. We are children of autocracy, orthodoxy, and serfdom. Our tsarist rulers fashioned themselves after the French court to demonstrate their refinement and sophistication. None of it worked. The West, especially the Europeans, still consider us barbarians.

I must be circumspect in how I craft my briefing—careful in tone and in how I state my conclusions. Careers are at stake, including my own. My assessment also will influence how resources are allocated in the future. Will the Far Eastern Military District get newer radars? Fighter aircraft? Communications gear? Intelligence systems? Much is on the line, and everyone is aware of it. Meticulous preparation and objectivity are necessary.

Wednesday, 7 September 1983

I finish preparing my briefing early in the morning. I take a break to call my wife's childhood home outside Kiev. Boyka's mother answers the phone with her soft voice. I can barely hear her say "Hello."

"Hello, mama, how are you, my dear?"

"Ivanko, is that you?" She's surprised to hear from me. God, I hate the Ukrainian diminutive *Ivanko,* but I love my mother-in-law. I just wish she'd call me *Vanya* if she is going to use a diminutive.

I bite my tongue and reply, "Yes, Mama, it is Ivanko. How are you and your beautiful daughter?"

"I am old, Ivanko, and I feel especially old today because of the heavy rain. It makes my joints sore. Your Boyka is fine. She is staying at her sister's house for a few days."

Staying with her sister? "I see. Well, can you give me Oxana's phone number? I don't have it with me here at the office. You see, I want to come to Kiev to visit."

"I'll get you Oxana's number—I have it written down just here. Somewhere. I simply can't recall phone numbers anymore." I can hear her shuffling around the kitchen looking for her younger daughter's phone number.

"Thank you, Mama."

After a few minutes, I get Oxana's number and make the call. Oxana's husband Oleksander answers the phone.

"Hello."

"Yes, hello Oleksander Petrovich, this is Ivan Ivanovich calling from Moscow. I hope you are well. I understand that Boyka is staying with you and Oxana for a few days. Is she there now?"

"Ah, it's Ivanko. Don't be so formal! Why are you being so formal? Just call me Sasha. Hey, are you keeping tabs on those fatheads in the Kremlin? Have they shot down any civilian airliners lately?"

I can't help but smile. "Oh, well, my dear brother, these are difficult times. Is Boyka there?"

"I bet you are a busy bee with this Korean airline thing. No, Boyka isn't here. She and Oxana are in downtown Kiev shopping today. I told them not to go out in this heavy rain. But you know those sisters are stubborn. They've been inseparable recently."

"Can I ask you for a favor? Please tell Boyka I called and that I want to talk to her today. I'm planning to take leave later this month so that I can visit her. All right? Have her call me back. I'm anxious to talk to her."

"All right, Ivanko. I will tell her when she gets back. Where should she call you—at the office or at home?"

"I will be at the office today until about 7:00 PM. After that, I will be at home. Oh, and remember that Moscow time is one hour ahead of Kiev. Thank you."

"I know. Goodbye, Ivanko."

The sisters are inseparable? That isn't a good sign. Perhaps Boyka won't want to leave her sister and come back to Moscow. I can't face that.

I catch up on work and answer questions posed by the guys finalizing my briefing. I get home much later than I'd hoped. I'm disappointed when Boyka doesn't call me. I tell myself that she probably called earlier when I was still at the office. Maybe Oleksander didn't give her the message? Or is there another reason? I'll call her again tomorrow—early in the morning.

Thursday, 8 September 1983

I'm awakened by the bedside phone ringing at 4:00 AM. Who's calling me so early? For a second, I think that it must be Boyka, but it's far too early for her to call.

I answer the phone, and it's my office calling to tell me that my briefing has been moved up to 0700 today. I'm told that Marshal of the Soviet Union Ogarkov will hold a televised press conference tomorrow about the Korean airliner shootdown, and my briefing is needed as soon as possible.

Ogarkov is going on television? He's chief of the General Staff and one of the three or four most powerful men in the entire Soviet Union. Boy, the old men in the Kremlin must be very worried to take this step. They know that Reagan is winning the global public relations war. It's one week to the day since the Korean airliner shootdown.

Shit, now I won't be able to call Boyka this morning like I planned.

Marshal Konstantinov greets me outside of the secure conference room where I'm to present my briefing. It's just before 7:00 AM.

He gives me a stern look. "This is an important day for you. It's vital that you give Chief Marshal of Aviation Koldunov your best assessment of the events. He and I will meet with Marshal Ogarkov later this morning. My staff will prepare maps and charts for his big press conference tomorrow, based on the information in your briefing."

I come to attention. "Yes, I understand."

We enter the conference room and I take a seat next to Konstantinov. I'm the junior officer in the room. Chief Marshal of Aviation Koldunov appears exactly as the clock strikes 7:00 AM.

He sits down and declares, "Good morning, comrades. Colonel, I'm told you have done good work out in the Far East. Now, before you begin, I want to set the table for Marshal Ogarkov's press conference tomorrow. All right?"

Everyone nods in assent. This should prove interesting.

"The main message that Marshal Ogarkov will convey to the world is that Reagan and his henchmen are dead wrong about the events of the first of September. We've determined irrefutably that the intrusion of the South Korean plane into our sovereign airspace was a deliberate and thoroughly planned intelligence operation. It was directed by the main centers of the United States and Japan. We have tapes of the Su-15 pilot, Major Osipovich, from that night. He fired his cannon across the bow of the airliner and provided them other warnings. The Americans have denied this happened. Reagan is accusing the USSR of intentional, cold-blooded murder. This will be refuted with vigor. We also have a new recording of Osipovich from that night in which he says the intruder was flying without navigation lights flashing."

Jesus Christ. I am fucked. My briefing highlights the theory that the Korean airliner may have been off course due to a navigational error. Moreover, Osipovich told me that the plane he shot down definitely had its navigation lights on! This "new recording" that the chief marshal references must be a fabrication. I still think we were within our rights as a sovereign country to shoot down the KAL plane, but we have no evidence that definitively proves it was on an intelligence collection mission. Unfortunately, that's the story that Ogarkov plans to tell the world tomorrow.

It's time to present my briefing. As I begin, I acknowledge that the presence of the US Air Force RC-135 near Kamchatka created confusion. I convey the facts about the inoperable radar systems that handicapped our ability to track the Korean plane. The faulty radars added to our troops' confusion about the whereabouts of the American RC-135 and the identity of the intruder.

Koldunov stops me at that point. "Yes, there was confusion because the Americans intentionally masked their flight routes. I can assure you that Marshal Ogarkov is aware of the shortcomings of the radars on Kamchatka. He knows that the condition of the radar systems unintentionally aided and abetted the nefarious American plan. Of course, he won't report any radar problems to our enemies tomorrow."

After the interruption, I continue. "There also is a theory that the Korean aircrew made a catastrophic navigational error that caused them to deviate from their intended course. If true, that would mean that the Koreans penetrated our airspace unintentionally."

Koldunov scoffs. "Yes, and I believe in flying giraffes, too. No, Colonel, there was no navigational error. I've heard this theory, and it's nonsense. This was an intentional overflight of the most sensitive nuclear facilities in the Far East by our main adversary and their Japanese and Korean lackeys."

This briefing is a total waste of time. Nonetheless, I must continue, and I do my best to be even-handed about the events of that night and the actions of our men on the scene in the Far East.

Before I can conclude the presentation, Koldunov stops me to make his own closing comments. "Levchenko, you've done a fine job.

This is very thorough work. You and your team are to be commended. I know you've done your best to present an objective assessment in the finest tradition of the GRU. I must disagree with you on some areas of speculation in the briefing—like the navigational error theory—but I appreciate the fact that you had the professional integrity to present your findings in their entirety. It seems to me that your presentation largely supports the conclusions that Marshal Ogarkov will present to the world tomorrow."

Well, he's not entirely wrong about that—not entirely wrong.

Koldunov turns to the other officers at the conference table and says, "Comrades, we know what happened on that fateful night. We must always remain vigilant in our duty to protect the homeland. Our troops, particularly our forces on Sakhalin Island, did their utmost when duty demanded it. I am proud of them. Marshal Ogarkov is proud of them and he has made this known to Comrade General Secretary Andropov. Oh, I almost forgot something quite interesting. I understand that the new American 24-hour news channel will cover Ogarkov's press conference tomorrow. I think they call it the Cable News Network, or CNN! Can you imagine that?"

With that, the chief marshal of aviation stands up and nods to the officers around the table, thanks me for the briefing again, and departs.

Marhsal Konstantinov stands up. "Levchenko, you did well. The chief marshal and I appreciate your thoroughness. Make sure you are in the office and can be reached to answer questions my staff may have for you until we get through Ogarkov's press conference tomorrow. Understood?"

I nod in assent.

What an anticlimax the meeting with the big guys has proven to be. At least it's over, and I can still try to reach Boyka in Kiev this morning.

I call my sister-in-law's phone number as soon as I get back to my office. This time Oxana answers.

"Hello, Oxana, it's Ivan Ivanovich calling. How are you, sister?"

"Oh, hello, Ivanko. Yes, Sasha told me you called yesterday. How are things in the big city? Are you keeping us out of World War III? Those fatheads in the Kremlin seem bent on starting a war. We are counting on you to stop them, brother!"

"Yes, well, you know things are not as bad as all that, Oxana."

"Really? We listen to Radio Free Europe here and it sounds like Ronald Reagan is blaming you Russians for murdering innocent civilians on that Korean plane. Everyone in Kiev thinks a war is just around the corner. And I hear that Ogarkov is going to hold a press conference tomorrow. Is that true? Dear God, the idiots in the Kremlin must be very worried if they plan to trot that fool Ogarkov out in front of the cameras!"

Jesus, why do I have to listen to this crap from her? I hope my phone isn't tapped. "All right, Oxana, all right. Is Boyka there? I want to speak to her."

"Yes, she is here, but she's still sleeping. You know it is only 7:00 AM here now, and we aren't in the military. We don't rise before dawn like you and the rest of the glorious defenders of the homeland! Or did you forget Kiev is in a different time zone from Moscow? Why don't you call back at a more civilized hour? Goodbye, Ivanko."

Jesus! She hung up on me! Unbelievable.

I'm busy the rest of the day and well into the night reviewing briefing material for Ogarkov's presentation. I do my best to ensure his charts are accurate and that the maps he will use are illuminating and not misleading. By the end of the evening, I decide the presentation is as good as it's going to get, and I head for home. Unfortunately, I'll have to wait until tomorrow to call Kiev again.

Friday, 9 September 1983

The office this morning is abuzz with anticipation. I've had a television set moved into my conference room to allow a gaggle of my officers to watch Marshal Ogarkov's unprecedented press conference. I sit at the head of the table and watch intently as Ogarkov begins.

The chief of the General Staff holds a microphone in one hand and a briefer's pointing stick in the other. He has maps and charts showing the path of the Korean airliner and the reactions of our Air Defense Forces. Early in the presentation, Ogarkov plays an audiotape of Major Osipovich's interaction with the ground control officer. The tape demonstrates that the pilot fired cannon bursts in a futile attempt to raise the attention of the Korean aircrew. This is a legitimate tape and matches my interview with Osipovich. The Americans have been alleging to the world that no warnings were issued. This tape refutes that contention and will prove embarrassing to the Americans. Unfortunately, Ogarkov also plays the bogus tape in which Osipovich claims the Korean airliner's navigation lights were not illuminated. Perhaps it's a small point, but why lie about the navigation lights when we have a valid tape of Osipovich firing warning shots?

Reporters are permitted to ask questions. Marshal Ogarkov handles them well, if somewhat dismissively. Our top officer prepared well for this press conference. It concludes without any gaffes.

Through the TASS news service, the Kremlin announces that Ogarkov's press conference is a great success. TASS emphasizes that America's narrative about the shootdown is inaccurate. This has a positive, albeit limited, effect around the world. Most observers around the world begin to see that *both* the USA and USSR are using the tragic incident for political grandstanding. Meanwhile, both sides maintain dangerously high levels of military alert. This may yet end badly.

I will admit that my attention wandered a bit during Ogarkov's television appearance. After all, I knew what he was going to say, and my mind is focused on what I will find in Kiev when I finally see my Boyka.

CHAPTER ELEVEN

HOMECOMING

Colonel Ivan Levchenko,
GRU, Soviet Air Defense Forces
Kiev, Ukraine, USSR

Sunday, 11 September 1983

Finally, I'm on an Aeroflot flight to Kiev. I settle into my seat and contemplate the state of my marriage during the ninety-minute flight. After days of trying, I reached Boyka on the phone last night. It was a short conversation. She was in no mood to talk. I'm trying to keep a positive state of mind about Boyka and our relationship.

My brother-in-law, Oleksander, collects me at the airport outside of Kiev. He's a trim guy with an angular face—not handsome but interesting-looking. He's a born politician who never shuts up and has an opinion on every topic under the sun. Lack of knowledge is no impediment to his pontifications. He serves on the city council of Kiev, and he believes in Ukrainian autonomy, if not outright independence. He's strongly anti-Soviet, but the foundation of his political outlook is a hatred of all things Russian. Moscow is the enemy, whether the rulers are tsars or Bolsheviks.

Did I mention that he never shuts up?

"So, Ivanko, did you watch your General Staff chief's press conference on Friday? What an idiot Ogarkov is! Is he the best the Kremlin has to offer? Ogarkov? The Americans must be quaking in their cowboy boots!"

"Well, I think the press conference went as well as could be expected. Ogarkov has a tough job."

Oleksander smirks. "Really, Ivanko, how tough can it be to shoot down an unarmed passenger plane? I guess the USSR is safe if the Americans invade us using United Airlines or Pan Am! God forbid they should send their bombers to attack us!"

Even I have to laugh a bit at this comment.

"Ah, see, Ivanko, you still have some sense of humor. The barbaric Muscovites haven't ridden you of all your humanity!"

"Tell me, brother, how is Boyka? I've barely spoken to her since she left this past summer."

He sighs. "God, Ivanko, I don't know. I'll tell you something. You and I made a big mistake in marrying these sisters. Men are cursed when they marry truly beautiful women, don't you think? You always are worried about other men. You always are worried you aren't good enough, no?"

I consider the implications of that statement. I admire his candor and his willingness to share what most men would hide. However, I fear where this conversation may be headed, so I shut it down.

When we arrive at Oleksandr's house, I see Boyka's face in silhouette at the front window as we park in front on the street. Is she waiting for me?

My brother-in-law and I enter the front door. Boyka walks toward me and kisses me on both cheeks. It's a formal and polite greeting. What does it mean? It's easy to forget how beautiful Boyka is when one doesn't see her in the flesh for a few months. She can be rather intimidating.

Oxana has tea and snacks waiting on a table in the small parlor. I'm touched by her solicitude. Oxana says, "Welcome the conquering hero, home from the wars. Of course, it's not precisely home and maybe not precisely wars, but what the hell. And where is home when you are a military man—when you live like a nomad?"

Oleksander hangs up his jacket in the front hall closet. "Leave the poor boy alone, Oxana. He wants to see his wife and make love to her—not hear your philosophizing!"

Boyka looks at me and smiles. That smile looks promising.

Oxana pours me a cup of tea. She ignores her husband and says, "Well, everyone thinks we're going to war with the Americans. Reagan is going to bomb us into the stone age. Those antediluvian morons in the Kremlin are too senile to do anything halfway intelligent. All my friends want to know what my esteemed GRU colonel brother-in-law thinks. Well, brother, what do you think?"

Oleksander scowls. "Oxana, I told you to leave him be. First you call him a nomad and next you want him to solve world peace. Give *him* some peace, for God's sake."

Oxana is relentless. "My dear husband, I don't expect him to solve the world's problems, I merely want to hear what he *thinks* about them. Who else do we know who sits at the right hand of God the Father in the Kremlin? And goddamn it, people are genuinely scared."

I think my sister-in-law deserves a frank response. "Oxana, things are tense with the Americans; however, I am confident that we will weather the current storm. I know you don't think much of Marshal Ogarkov, but he did a good job at his press conference. He deflated some of the American claims and I think it will have a calming effect on passions in the West."

Oxana and Oleksandr exchange a glance. She says, "If *you* believe that is true, Ivanko, then I am somewhat reassured."

Finally, my wife speaks. "You must be tired, Vanya. We're going to stay at my parents' house. They have room for us—more room than here. Oxana, I'd like to leave now."

Oxana objects. "What? He just arrived, and my own sister is taking him away already? Who will I spar with? I have more questions for our esteemed colonel."

Boyka laughs. "There will be time for you to fight with Vanya. I promise."

Oxana is undeterred. "You know I prefer Ivanko to Vanya. He was born in Crimea, he went to school in Sevastopol, and he graduated from the Kiev Air Force Academy—he is more Ukrainian than most Ukrainians, even if he is a Russian. He should be called by a Ukrainian name!"

"Sister, I think you actually are proud of my husband! You know his history so well. You prefer Ivanko, but he prefers Vanya and so do I."

"Boyka, I have never said I'm not proud of him. He's a full colonel now. We're all proud of him and we're lucky to have someone of his intelligence advising those cretins in Moscow!"

I'm thankful when Oleksander intervenes. "All right, you two, that's enough. Ivanko, grab your wife's bag and let's get in the car."

I'm more than happy to obey him.

My wife's parents greet us at the door of their trim, little house. They live in a quiet village that has retained its quaint character even though it is now a suburb of sprawling Kiev. I haven't seen my in-laws in close to five years. My mother-in-law hugs me and kisses me with real emotion. She's crying so hard that she trembles in my arms. My own mother died when I was at the Air Force Academy and Boyka's mother has mothered me since. I'm moved by her emotion and tear up myself. I can feel that she doesn't want to let go of me.

My wife's father has shrunk. He was a tank commander in the Great Patriotic War. He's always been short in stature but thickly muscled. Now he's shriveled and old. Nevertheless, he takes the luggage firmly from my hands and carries the bags upstairs to our room—the room my wife and her sister shared growing up.

The old man says, "Full colonels don't carry their own bags, my son."

Oleksander says goodbye.

Upon my father-in-law's return from upstairs, the four of us assemble in the modest parlor. Boyka's father produces a bottle of chilled sparkling wine, while his wife lays out an assortment of local chocolates. He pops the cork and pours generous portions.

The old man rises from his chair and raises his glass. "I want to propose a toast to my son-in-law, Colonel Ivan Levchenko, of the Soviet Air Defense Forces and GRU! It's an honor to have a full colonel in the family. Welcome back to our home, Ivanko."

I feel myself tearing up again. My parents have both been dead for more than two decades now. Much like his wife, Boyka's father has filled a crucial parental role for me.

I compose myself and say, "Thank you, sir. This is a warm welcome, indeed. And I want to propose a toast to your wife, my mama, who has always welcomed me as her own son."

We all drink deeply and have a taste of chocolate and sit in silence for a few moments. I sense we're all a bit overwhelmed by the emotions we're feeling.

Boyka stands up. I assume she is about to propose another toast. Instead, she has an announcement. "Vanya and I have been separated for some months now. I want to see him in private, Mama."

My father-in-law raises an eyebrow and reaches into the cabinet next to his chair. He pulls out a bottle of excellent vodka. Smiling, he hands it over to me and says, "Take this, son, and we will see you both in the morning."

I blush a little as Boyka takes my hand and leads me upstairs. Her childhood room is quite small, with a single window and a low ceiling. Boyka leads me to the center of the room and kisses me. I'm not sure what she wants me to do, so I simply stand there with my hands at my sides. She steps away from me and takes off her clothes, staring into my eyes. Soon she is naked. Looking at beauty like hers is like staring into the sun on a summer day. The sight of her is almost too powerful to take in for long, but I can't look away.

Later that night, after vodka and lovemaking, Boyka is ready to talk. "Vanya, it wasn't until I saw you walk through Oxana's door this evening that it all fell into place. I love you but I feel lost. I don't fit in Kiev any longer and I don't want to live in Moscow. But I must be with you. I know that much." She takes a couple of deep breaths. "I want to be with you. How long did we live abroad?"

I do a quick calculation, although the number is already well-known to me. "It would be a total of eleven years given our time in Poland, East Germany, and West Germany, yes."

I feel her nod agreement in the darkened room. "We've been married for twenty-one years, and the best years were the ones abroad. I want to be with you, just not in Moscow."

"I'll do anything to make life in Moscow more bearable for you."

She doesn't respond, so I add, "Look, I have to go back in a few days, and then I have a trip planned to several of our air defense centers. I may even get to see our old friend Petrov and his little wife—you remember her?"

Boyka smiles at the memory. "Yes, she is so tiny—like a doll. She's a lovely woman—so warm and friendly."

"I will be back in Moscow by the first of October. Can you join me then? We can work on things—on how to make it better for you."

She kisses my cheek, and says, "All right. I will join you in October. Let's see how we can make it better. I don't want us to be apart any longer." She rolls over and lies on top of me. "Now, show me again how much you love me, Vanya."

CHAPTER TWELVE

THE MAN WHO SAVED
THE WORLD

Colonel Ivan Levchenko, GRU, Soviet Air Defense Forces
Serpukhov-15, Russia, USSR

Monday, 26 September 1983

It's more than three weeks since the Korean shootdown, and the world is still going crazy. Accusations continue to fly between Moscow and Washington. I've never seen relations between the superpowers this strained. One wrong move and all hell could break loose. One wrong decision by someone in high authority and everything could turn to dust.

I've been on the road for over a week, visiting installations all over the Moscow Air Defense District. My meetings have been sobering. Our forces have been on alert since the Korean airliner incident. Everyone is tired and tense. I've developed greater empathy for the commanders in the Far East who told me that their men and machines were at the breaking point at the time of the shootdown.

This morning I arrived at Serpukhov-15, a closed, military city and home to the National Missile Defense Center, some 120 kilometers south of Moscow. This city is by far the most important stop on my journey, and it's the last before I return to Moscow. The Missile Defense Center fuses information from multiple sensors: satellites, Arctic Circle radars, regional radars, SIGINT sites, and even human intelligence reports from our agents based in the United States. If any center should have a finger on the pulse of Western preparations for a missile strike on the USSR, it is this one. I hope that the officers stationed here have insights about the Americans that will inform my own thinking as well as Operation RYaN.

As busy as I am, Boyka is never far from my mind. I'm thirsting for her and our reunion in Moscow on the first of October.

Despite how much I miss my wife, my spirits are high this morning. My best friend and classmate from the Kiev Air Force Academy, Lieutenant Colonel Stanislav Petrov, is based at Serpukhov-15. He and his family have been here for several years, and Stas' is a key player in the new OKO missile defense satellite program. *Oko* means *eye* in Russian.

Stas' is a brilliant engineer. He was an outstanding student at the Kiev academy, excelling at mathematics and physics. Taciturn, he was never the life of the party, as I tried to be while we were in school. But he is as solid as an oak tree and the most reliable friend I have ever known.

Stas' job title at Serpukhov-15 is a real mouthful—he's the deputy chief of the Department of Military Algorithms. He's responsible for ensuring the accuracy and validity of the computer programs that process and fuse the raw data pouring into the Missile Center from the OKO satellite constellation, the Arctic Circle radars, and regional radar systems spread throughout the USSR. This is extremely challenging work and requires a disciplined yet creative intellect like Stas'. We'll have lunch together later today and I look forward to catching up.

My first meeting at Serpukhov-15 is with the one-star general who is the center commander. He's not "read into" the RYaN program, but he is smart and guesses that my visit is not routine, given the strained relations with the United States. He confirms his troops are acutely attuned to any possible indication of American hostile intent. One step he's taken is to request the GRU increase the number of intelligence personnel in the United States that monitor the American ICBM, bomber, and nuclear submarine bases. I'm impressed with this officer and his careful preparations. As we conclude our meeting, he suggests that the best way for me to understand the center's mission is to observe the overnight watch in the missile defense operations center tonight. This appeals to me, and I immediately agree. I excuse myself to be on time for my luncheon appointment with Stas.'

I drive across the base to the officers' housing area, where the officers' club is located. When I walk into the club's dining room, Stas' is already waiting for me at a table. He stands as I approach. I haven't seen him in over five years. He looks fit and younger than I expected.

I smile broadly and say, "Stas', how are you, my brother? You look wonderful. This job must agree with you!" We embrace and kiss three times.

"It does! I like this job. But, Vanya, *you* look tired! Your colonel's shoulder boards must be very heavy. I'm content to be a lieutenant colonel, at least for a couple more years!" He sits down and looks at me with a big grin on his face.

"Well, Stas', you always were the smarter one."

I inquire after his wife, who I first met more than twenty years ago, "How is Raisa—your lovely little Raya?"

My friend's handsome face goes grey, and he says morosely, "She's unwell. She is sick, very sick. She wanted to see you. She desperately wanted to see you, but she cannot bear for you to see her like this— like she is now."

This news hits me like a hammer to the head, "My God, Stas'. I'm devastated to hear this. Little Raya. Is it that serious?"

Stas' grimaces. "Deadly."

We both go silent, and I ask, "How are your children doing?"

"They are confused. They don't really understand what's happening to Raya—you know. They're sweet kids—like their mother, not like me."

We eat in silence for a while. The silence is not uncomfortable. It's soothing. It occurs to me that I don't think Stas' ever had another girlfriend—only pixie-like Raya.

At the end of lunch, Stas' announces that he must go home to check on his wife and get a few hours of rest. Late this morning he was informed that he will command the overnight shift in the Missile Defense Center tonight. The officer who was scheduled to work the night shift is sick, and Stas' has been ordered to substitute for him.

I'm delighted to hear this. "Stas', that is good news for me. Your commanding general told me this morning that I should observe the overnight watch. Is that okay with you? I don't want to get in the way of your work."

Stas' entire face brightens. "Vanya, that's terrific. It'll give us more time together, and you can see the operation in action. I look forward to seeing you at shift change. We can have a late dinner in the watch—okay?"

I hug him as we part. "See you tonight, my brother."

I return to my visiting officers' quarters, go for a run, and then get a few hours of sleep before arriving at the Missile Defense Center at 1900. After I am checked into the secure facility's operations floor, I see that Stas' already is reviewing the status of the sensor systems with the outgoing watch commander. I give them space to do their work. I probably wouldn't understand much, if any, of their technical talk anyway.

Stas' assumes official command of the facility at 2000 hours—8:00 PM. I observe the respect the officers and enlisted guys have for Stas'—their substitute commander.

My friend motions for me to sit next to him at his command position, which overlooks the operations floor, with a clear view of the huge situation map that dominates the room.

As Stas' settles into his seat, he says, "You know, Vanya, I don't mind watch duty, except that it keeps me away from Raya. Anyway, it's a nice break from my normal routine, and it allows me to observe how our systems are operating and whether we need to adjust the processing algorithms. It's very important to get an operational 'feel' for a new system like the OKO satellites. The feedback I get from the watch analysts is invaluable to me and my algorithm team."

I nod knowingly, even though I don't have much experience with these high-technology sensor systems. "Stas, the OKO satellites were launched about a year ago—right? How are they working—are they reliable?"

Stas' crinkles up his nose. "Oh, God, they are *not* ready for operational use. The higher powers, you know, declared them fully operational prematurely. The OKO birds *will* be good systems, but they need a lot of refinement—software fixes to improve accuracy and reliability . . . lots of work."

I take in this startling information. As far as I know, no one at my headquarters in Moscow is aware of what Stas' has just told me. We have been told that OKO is fully operational.

He gestures toward the operations floor and smiles. "You see these guys on the floor? The permanent watch crew likes to poke fun at me. They call me the 'professor.' It is true that I look more and more like an academician as I get older. Anyway, I am one of the experts on the OKO satellites, and they respect that—I think—but you never know."

Stas' directs my attention to the large board that indicates the health of the OKO satellites. "As it happens, we are having trouble with one of the OKO birds tonight. It's wobbling in its orbit, but the other four birds check out just fine. I also have access to the big early warning radars that populate the northern zones along the Arctic Circle. Analysts in the center—in a separate area beyond those walls—work with their computers to analyze the signals arriving from the ground-based radars and the satellites' infrared and electro-optical sensors. We have limited access to agents living in the United States whose job is to observe the American Air Force's intercontinental ballistic missile (ICBM) fields with high-powered optical and infrared devices. Those agents can confirm if a launch has occurred from the

American ICBM silos. Thus, we have a multilayered approach to gain warning of American missile launches—satellites, ground radars, and in-place agents."

As usual, Stas' is right on top of things, no matter how complex. It's good to hear all this directly from him, and he points to the displays on the wall as he describes things to me, which improves my understanding.

Stas' then tells me that he must focus on fixing the one OKO satellite that is wobbling in its orbit. "Officially, the new system became operational last year, but I see the bugs and shortcomings. We get false alarms—erroneous signals that can lead to false conclusions. One must exercise caution when receiving any signals from OKO and gauge their reliability with care. We'll be wringing out the issues in this system for many years."

He smiles and jokes, "Job security is a good thing, and I have it!"

It's nearly midnight and Stas' and his team have fixed the wobbly satellite. Everything else is operating normally, and we have time to relax a bit. We've just finished our simple supper—sandwiches and tea.

Stas' stretches his arms and yawns. "Vanya, I think we've had our excitement for tonight's shift. Getting that satellite back online was pretty exciting—right? I bet your MLM days in West Germany were boring by comparison!"

I laugh. "I have no idea what you did to fix that satellite. These technologies are way beyond me. It's amazing you can do a software patch that quickly. I'm impressed!"

Monday, 27 September 1983

I look at the big digital clock on the wall and it reads five minutes after midnight. I can't help but close my eyes for a moment after our modest meal and I drift off to sleep, only to be shocked into alertness by a deafening noise. Loud horns blare and the huge map board lights up with red letters indicating a **Missile Launch Warning.**

The operations officer shouts excitedly. "Missile incoming from a base in the western United States. Time of detection at 00:15.03."

The entire room erupts. Men leave their consoles and yell excitedly at each other. It's a scene of anxiety and confusion.

Stas' immediately takes control of the room. He speaks loudly and clearly to the men on the floor. "Everyone back to your stations— back to work. Listen up and carry out my orders. Understand?"

He asks his operations officer, "Level of verification?"

The ops officer responds in a loud voice, "Level of verification— maximum, sir!"

Stas' gets on the radio to the chief analyst in the electro-optical analysis section. "This is the commander. Are you seeing indications of missile launches from anywhere in the western United States? Anywhere west of the Mississippi River?"

He awaits the answer and looks at me with controlled terror in his eyes. Stas' speaks into the radio phone. "I need an answer immediately; don't hedge."

The ops officer is back in front of us. "Comrade Colonel, the launches seem to be coming from Grand Forks Air Force Base in North Dakota, where it is late afternoon. The electro-optical sensors won't be able to see anything clearly due to the sun beginning to set. This base is right on the line between daylight and nighttime in that part of North America. It will create a very ambiguous situation for our analysts."

Stas' looks at me and mouths, *"Jesus Christ."*

He turns back to the ops officer. "Alert the early warning radars in the Arctic. They must report immediately if they see any American missiles breaking the horizon over the pole. Do we have agents observing Grand Forks? Can we get a message to them?"

The ops officer shrugs. "Comrade Colonel, we should have agents, or at least one guy, observing the American missile fields around Grand Forks. We can send him a coded message and pray that he receives it. But this, sir, will take time."

"Do it, Major. Now!"

Stas' is perspiring heavily, and the room is steeped in a desperate apprehension one can feel. Or, at least, I can feel it. Everyone is working with a frantic resolve.

Stas' looks me in the eye and says, "We have to wait for confirmation. There are indications of one or two American ICBM launches. They aren't going to begin World War III with just one or two missiles. They would launch hundreds at one time. This must be a false alarm."

This makes sense to me, and I try to reassure him. "I am glad you're in command tonight. You're the right man in the right place at the right time. What's the next step?"

"I have to call my immediate superior and inform him."

While Stas' prepares to call his boss, the deputy watch commander—a major—sidles up to me. "Comrade Colonel, you must talk to Petrov. Moscow needs time to stage a retaliatory response to the Americans' attack. Every moment we delay brings us closer to catastrophe. You need to get him to act now, sir!"

"Comrade Major, are you suggesting that we launch our ICBMs based on a single missile launch warning? Are you serious?"

"Colonel, it is our duty to respond."

"Major, I think Colonel Petrov is taking appropriate action. Let him work through this. He needs your support."

The major turns away sullenly. Clearly, he disagrees with me.

Stas' calls his superior, a full colonel. He explains the situation and that he must issue a report to Moscow, but that his professional judgment is that the launch indications are false alarms from the OKO satellites.

Stas' hangs up the phone. "The colonel was at a birthday party tonight and I woke him up. He isn't happy that I awakened him from his drunken stupor. He told me to handle it and not to bother him again. Goddamn drunk."

"Stas', you shouldn't be on your own. I think you should call the commanding general and have him come in immediately."

He grins. "I am not on my own—you're here, aren't you? But you're right, I'll call the general right now. It'll take him just a few minutes to get here. His quarters are in the next building and he's probably awake. He hasn't been sleeping well since the Korean shootdown."

Seconds after Stas' hangs up the phone with the general, the horns blast again and the big board lights up again with a new message— **Missile Launch Warning.**

The ops officer intones in a nervous voice. "New missile-launch indications from the western USA. Time is 00:21.05. Level of confirmation—maximum—one-to-three missile launches."

The entire staff on the operations floor repeat the same actions taken just minutes ago. They attempt to confirm the launches through every sensor system available to them, but everything the analysts see is inconclusive. They can neither prove nor disprove that the Americans are launching ICBMs at us.

Stas's face is red. He is perspiring profusely and breathing hard. Yet, he issues orders calmly and professionally. His deputy has returned with several other officers. They are demanding loudly that he inform Moscow of this latest launch and confirm its legitimacy.

The recalcitrant deputy watch commander screams, "Colonel, there will be no time to retaliate if the American missiles begin striking their targets. A confirmed American ICBM launch means nuclear war! We have no option but to respond. We are sworn to defend the motherland!"

Stas' stares at his deputy, calmly. "Major, are you finished? I am not about to start World War III based on reports from a satellite system I know to be flawed."

His deputy begins to respond angrily.

Before he can speak Stas' tells him in a steely voice, "Major, you are relieved!"

The unbowed officer looks at me, the senior officer present, for support. I give him none. "Major, you heard the commander. You're relieved. The rest of you—return to your stations."

The disgruntled officers disperse.

Coolly, Stas' types a message to the Ministry of Defense in Moscow. It reads, 'Indications of multiple American ICBM launches received. The only indicators we have are from OKO. There is no corroboration from other sources. I believe the OKO indicators are false alarms.'

Stas' completes his message, looks at me, and whispers, "I'd better be right."

The commanding general joins us minutes later, out of breath and perspiring. He sits down next to me with a loud plop and asks Stas', "Petrov, what is the great crisis?"

Stas' summarizes the situation for the general, who looks in horror at the alerts on the status board.

The general leans over to me. "Well, Colonel, what do you think of this? Is Petrov right that these indicators are false alarms?"

Normally, it isn't my place to weigh in on such operations; however, nothing about tonight is normal. "There is no one better qualified than Petrov. He's the best man you have to make decisions about OKO and these indicators. I pray he's right."

Just as Stas' and his crew are collecting their wits, there is another blast of horns and a huge message across the big board—**Missile Launch Warning**. More reported American ICBM launches. This time the OKO satellites report there are between six and ten launches! This is beginning to look like a real attack from the United States.

The local time now is 00:35:15. Again, the ops officer confirms that the confidence level on the missile launches is *maximum.*

Stas' informs the general, "Sir, despite these latest alerts, we have no other corroboration of American ICBM launches. There are no positive reports from our agents in America. I believe OKO is transmitting false alarms. The absolute proof will come in a few minutes. If our Arctic Circle radars pick up ICBMs on the horizon, then we will know we have a real launch. We will know in minutes."

The general blinks his eyes rapidly. "Petrov, if the Arctic radars detect launches, then Moscow and the Kremlin—not to mention all of us in this room—will be dust in seconds. You *must* be right about all this. I understand your logic about the OKO satellites and false alarms. I am inclined to believe you are right. However, *you* must send the next message to the Kremlin. It will not have my signature on it."

My God, the general has placed the burden on Stas' to determine the content of his next report and send it on to Moscow. The pressure on everyone in the watch center is enormous, but Stas' must feel like Christ in the Garden of Gethsemane. My blood pressure surges in my neck and temples. Of course, if the Arctic radars confirm the missile launches, high blood pressure will be the least of my worries since we all will be dead in a matter of minutes.

Time passes slowly and Stas' turns to me and whispers so that the general can't hear him. "I think I'm right. But what if I'm wrong? I have massive doubts, Vanya. We now have just three minutes to wait until the Arctic radars report on the first missile salvo. Then we'll know if we will have a nuclear catastrophe."

The next three minutes crawl by. Agonizing is too small a word. I feel death on my shoulder and focus my mind on memories of happy times with Boyka. I will myself to make her face the final image in my brain.

Finally, the Arctic sites call in—they see no missiles passing over the North Pole! At least the first ICBM launch warning from OKO is a false alarm. The atmosphere in the watch center lifts like a hot-air balloon. A few more minutes pass, and the Arctic stations report on the second salvo—there are no missiles over the North Pole! Now, officers run up to the dais and hustle to Stas's side to shake his hand. Even the commanding general has a smile on his face. A few minutes later when the final salvo is reported as a false alarm by the Arctic sites, the room erupts in cheers praising Stas'.

One officer loudly condemns the Americans for playing an ugly trick on us tonight. He screams, "The Americans tried to fuck us tonight, and we fucked them right back!"

The crisis passes. Everyone in the joyous room knows that this small spark could have caused the end of our own lives and of all civilization. The ancient Hindu words that Robert Oppenheimer echoed decades ago at the first atomic bomb test in New Mexico come to mind, "Now I am become death, destroyer of worlds."

I thank God that Stas' was on duty tonight. Fate intervened to save us from a nuclear catastrophe. Stas' was here only because another officer got sick! Imagine! Our fates—and the fate of mankind—hinged on the mere chance that Stas' was called to be on duty tonight.

My old friend is truly the right man in the right place at the right time.

Stas' is a hero. A genuine hero. Officers around the room are hugging each other and shouting, "Bravo, comrade Petrov! Petrov for the Order of Lenin! Petrov, the man who saved the world!"

PART THREE

ABLE ARCHER 83

"I am become death, destroyer of worlds."

Bhagavad-Gita

CHAPTER THIRTEEN

DON'T GET COCKY

Captain Kevin Cattani, United States Air Force
Yokota Air Base, Japan and Ramstein Air Base,
Federal Republic of Germany (West Germany)

Wednesday, 28 September 1983

It's late morning when Lieutenant Colonel Stroud comes into the analysis cell and stops in front of my desk. He bends down and whispers. "Kevin, General Flannery's office just called, and they want you in his office in five minutes."

"Really? Any idea what he wants?"

"Nope."

"Okay, on my way."

I run up the two flights of stairs to the command section and walk down the long hallway to the commander's office. General Flannery's secretary tells me to wait a second, and she calls him on the intercom. I'm to go right in.

I walk into the general's office and stand off to the side of his desk. He's reading papers in a thick binder and doesn't notice me at first.

"Good morning, General Flannery."

He looks up from his work and smiles. "Morning, babes. How are you doing? Take a seat."

I sit down in front of his desk. "I'm fine, sir. How are you and Mrs. Flannery?"

He beams. "We are aces. Just aces. She's looking forward to going to Germany. I guess you heard about my new job?"

"Yes, sir. Congratulations on your promotion. That's really cool."

His eyes light up and he shakes his head gently. "Yeah, you know, I never thought I'd make four stars. Hell, I was surprised when I got my third one."

I'm not sure how to respond to that admission, so I don't. Flannery is being typically modest, but I also think that his surprise at being promoted is genuine. As a four-star general, he will be commander-in-chief of all US Air Forces in Europe (USAFE) and all NATO Air Forces—another "dual-hatted" position, somewhat like the one he has had in Japan, but on a much larger stage.

"Kevin, when do you PCS?" This is a common Air Force abbreviation for 'permanent change of station'—meaning a move to a new location and job.

"Sir, I'm leaving here on 7 November and I report into my new assignment in Washington on 15 November. I will take a short leave on the way to see my family in Virginia."

He ponders this for a moment. "Right. Do you have your heart set on this new assignment in D.C.?"

"Well, sir, it's a good job with a 'special' intelligence unit. I've been looking forward to being closer to home. I've been in Japan four years now."

He stares directly at me. "Got it, but you didn't answer my question."

I thought I had, but, of course, I really hadn't. I wonder where this is leading. "Sir, I guess you are catching me a bit off-guard. Is there another option for me? You know, another assignment?"

Flannery leans forward onto his elbows, "Look, Kevin, I want you to come to Germany with me. I know this is unusual, but these are unusual times. I need people around me I can rely on. You are one of the few intelligence officers I've known in my career who really gets it."

I'm flustered and manage to stammer, "Sir, I'm flattered and honored. I'm just a captain. What would my job be? Would it be at your headquarters at Ramstein?"

Flannery's face brightens as he warms to his proposal. "Yes, I want you to do current intelligence like you do here. I want you as my briefer. It won't be forever. There'll be other job opportunities. I have discussed all this with General Palumbo. He's the head of intelligence at USAFE—do you know him?"

"Only by reputation, sir. I've never met him."

He picks up the pace of the conversation. "The other thing is that I need you in Germany by 7 October. Could you handle that quick a move?"

Wow. This is a complete shock. I was looking forward to being back in the States after living overseas for so long. On the other hand, what will I miss if I don't go with General Flannery to Germany? The only thing I have to do before I depart Japan is sell my car, which will be pretty easy.

I also know I really don't have a choice in the matter. "General, if you need me, then I can handle it. Thank you, sir."

General Flannery beams again. "There's one more thing, babes. This next thing is a big deal, and it is secret info, too. Okay?"

I nod and wait for the other shoe to drop.

"This coming Saturday, the Secretary of Defense, Caspar Weinberger, will be visiting Tokyo. We need to brief him on the entire Korean airliner situation, which means I want you to brief him. It'll be early Saturday afternoon at the embassy downtown—at the CIA station. You and I will fly down together, Okay?"

The Secretary of Defense? Me? "Yes, sir, of course."

I go back downstairs to my office in a bit of a fog. What just happened? I sit down at my desk.

Once again, my boss, Colonel Stroud, looms over me. "What did the general want?"

"He wants to change my PCS orders and have me go to USAFE with him. I have to report to Germany on 7 October. That's only about ten days from now. My replacement won't be here until 1 November."

Stroud chuckles. "No shit. Wow. Well, you can't say no. As for your replacement, we'll muddle through."

"So, I need to do it? Go to Germany?"

My boss nods, slowly.

I stand up and whisper in Stroud's ear. "General Flannery wants me to brief Secretary Weinberger on Saturday—at the embassy. That is close hold, sir."

"No shit? Well, the general has a lot of faith in you. I won't tell anyone about the briefing on Saturday. I'll help you prepare.

Saturday, 1 October 1983

I meet General Flannery at Yokota flight operations at 1100 on Saturday morning for the helicopter flight to the US embassy. I've made this flight a couple of times since my hard landing on a high school baseball field back in April, but I remain leery of the reliability of Huey helicopters.

During the flight, I have time to think about how the main conclusions of my briefing don't agree with the public story being promulgated by the Reagan Administration. From the outset of the KAL crisis, my office and Air Force intelligence in the Pentagon concluded the shootdown was not a premeditated act of barbarism and that the Soviets were terribly confused on the night in question. Unfortunately, both CIA and NSA initially disagreed with our assessment, and our analysis became lost in the noise in the days immediately following the shootdown. Over the following days and weeks, both CIA and NSA came to agree with our initial conclusions, but by then, most of official Washington was convinced otherwise. Positions formed early and then hardened.

When the leadership in the White House, State, and Defense seizes upon a narrative, it is almost impossible for them to walk it back—especially when they themselves are leading the global outcry against the Soviets. I find myself getting more and more nervous as I think about the yawning gap between the intelligence community's view of the Korean shootdown and the Administration's harsh, anti-Soviet rhetoric.

At the Tokyo Embassy, we check in at the CIA station. General Flannery and I are met at the vault door by the CIA station chief himself, Mr. John "M." I haven't seen him since I left my old job with the red-haired major, and he gives me a warm welcome.

One of the CIA information technology guys helps me get set up in the secure room where I will present the briefing to Secretary Weinberger. Then General Flannery and I wait for the arrival of the secretary and his party.

The secure room is the size and shape of a plastic Airstream trailer. There's a large noise machine in a corner to defeat listening devices, which also makes it hard to hear and hard to be heard. As the time draws near, I'm feeling even more nervous about this briefing. General Flannery notices my tension and asks if he can do anything for me. I can't think of anything that'd help, except a stiff Scotch, but that won't do.

John M pokes his head into the room to tell us that the ambassador and the secretary have arrived. Mr. M escorts the small group into the room and the door is sealed shut with a vacuum-lid thud. The ambassador introduces me and General Flannery to Mr. Weinberger and his party. There are only two men with the secretary. One is Richard Armitage, the deputy assistant secretary of defense for East Asia and Pacific affairs. Mr. Armitage is built like a bowling ball—short and stocky and extremely muscular. His bald head heightens the effect. The other man is a tall, distinguished-looking Black officer. He's a one-star US Army general named Colin Powell, Secretary Weinberger's senior military assistant.

Everyone sits down, and General Flannery and Mr. M. give me the high sign to begin briefing. I get off to a rocky start. I am so nervous that I cannot find my voice. General Flannery looks at me with concern. I take a deep breath and calm down. I find my voice and hit my stride, but I'm horrified to see that Secretary Weinberger has fallen asleep. In my panic, I look at General Flannery for guidance and he motions for me to keep going.

The jet-lagged secretary sleeps through almost the entire briefing, including the controversial US Navy actions during FLEETEX 83. General Powell and Secretary Armitage, however, pay close attention and are visibly surprised by the Navy overflights. Still, they don't say anything, and I feel like I am briefing inside a sealed plastic bubble (which, in fact, I am) and all I hear is my somewhat brittle voice straining over the incessant hum of the noise machine.

As I'm concluding, General Powell asks me a couple of pointed questions concerning the Soviet response to the Korean airliner— essentially, *what did they know and when did they know it?* Mr. Armitage joins in.

The sound of their familiar voices serves to awaken the dozing secretary of defense, who opens his eyes abruptly. "Captain, why did the Soviets intentionally shoot down a civilian airliner? What possibly could have motivated them to conduct such a monstrous, criminal act?" Weinberger speaks with the precise elegance of a high-priced Manhattan lawyer.

This is the line of inquiry I've been expecting and that has made me so uncharacteristically nervous. By this time, the entire intelligence community agrees that Air Force intelligence had it right from the outset—that the tragic shootdown was due to a deadly combination of Soviet errors. I look nervously at General Flannery, and he gives me a sign to take it easy with my answer. Here we go . . .

"Mr. Secretary, there was confusion—even disagreement—in the intelligence community concerning Soviet intentions, especially during the first few days after the shootdown."

I now have the secretary's full attention and it feels like his eyes are boring a hole in my forehead.

I continue. "I believe it is safe to say, sir, that now the entire intelligence community views the shootdown as the result of a number of faulty assumptions and hasty decisions that the Soviets made that night. Coupled with the hair-trigger alert posture throughout the Soviet Far East, their erroneous assumptions about the identity of the plane led to the tragic event. I realize that the common wisdom in Washington is that the shootdown was an intentional, criminal act."

The secretary makes a chapel with his two hands and puts his fingertips to his nose. "Captain, the Soviets knew exactly what they were doing that night. There is no excusing what they did with commentary about 'hasty decisions and faulty assumptions' or a 'hair-trigger' posture that contributed to their criminal actions. The USSR's leadership is responsible for the conduct of its military, just as I am responsible for the actions of the United States Department of Defense. We must hold them to account. Any other approach with Moscow is hopelessly naïve."

Mr. M., the CIA chief, turns his large frame toward the secretary. "Sir, no one is excusing what the Soviets did that night, and they are responsible. I have to stress that the captain is accurately reporting the intelligence community's conclusion that the Soviets acted out of fear and confusion, rather than from a premeditation toward mass murder."

Weinberger turns to face the senior CIA man. "Well, it is immaterial at the end of the day. The act is what they must be judged on. The *act* resulted in the deaths of hundreds of civilians, including 62 Americans and a sitting US congressman. We all know the perfidy of Moscow. Look, I appreciate the work you all are doing out here. But US policy is based on a hard-nosed, realistic appraisal of Soviet actions. That will not change."

With that, the secretary stands up and thanks all of us. He and his team head for the airport, where they are to fly immediately to Seoul to meet with the South Korean president and other senior officials to discuss matters pertaining to the shootdown.

I feel like I let everybody down. I feel that was the worst briefing of my life. Quietly, I gather my materials and lock them in my secure pouch. Then I leave the CIA station and take the elevator downstairs.

I meet General Flannery and Mr. M. at the embassy entrance. "Gentlemen, I apologize for briefing so poorly. I wasn't on my game."

Mr. M. shakes my hand. "You did fine. You got the message across. And you handled the secretary's question appropriately. This is a lesson for you, and I don't mean about briefing, per se. I mean that what you just witnessed is the difference between being an intelligence officer and a senior policymaker. We support them as best we can, and then we have to get out of their way. Understand?"

I nod. "Yes, sir. I think I do."

What I can't get my head around, however, is that the most senior officials in our government are promoting an explosive narrative of Soviet intentions. Their rhetoric is increasing already sky-high tensions and making a war, or at least an armed confrontation, more likely.

Friday, 7 October 1983

As ordered, I arrive in Germany on 7 October and report to Ramstein Air Base, in the western part of West Germany. This is my first time in the country. Germany is lovely at this time of year, and I am looking forward to exploring the countryside, if I ever get any free time. I am scheduled to report to General Palumbo on Monday. I have the weekend to get settled in my new quarters and find a car to buy.

Monday, 10 October 1983

My appointment to meet Brigadier General Leonard "Lenny" Palumbo is scheduled for 1000. I arrive five minutes early to General Palumbo's suite and check in with the executive officer, a full colonel, who immediately starts in on me.

"Captain, why are you late for your meeting with the general?"

Taken aback, I look at my watch. "Sir, I have the time as just before ten. Was I supposed to be meeting with the general earlier?" I feel a hot surge of panic.

The colonel sits back in his chair and glares at me. "You should always arrive fifteen minutes early to a meeting with a general officer. That makes you late. I don't know how you did things in Japan, but that's how we roll in Germany."

I mumble, "Yes, sir." What an asshole. I'll have to watch out for this guy.

Just as I am about to sit down, the general's secretary tells me to go into his office.

General Palumbo is "heads down," with his reading glasses on, studying a document with great intensity. Rubbing his forehead with his palm, he doesn't acknowledge my presence. I stand at attention in front of his desk.

He looks up and seems startled to see me. "Okay, Captain, what's up?"

I salute. "Captain Cattani reporting for duty, sir."

Palumbo still seems surprised to see me. He looks at the daily planner on his desk, takes off his glasses, and barks at me. "Oh, you're the kid from Japan that General Flannery wanted."

It is as much a question as a statement, and I nod. "Yes, sir, I am Captain Kevin Cattani."

He stares at my forehead. "How long were you in Japan? I have your file here somewhere. Let me see where it is." General Palumbo rummages around his desk and discovers my personnel file and holds it up like it's a rare treasure map.

"Got it. Okay, well, sit down, Captain. You know I didn't ask for you to be assigned here. I rarely make 'by-name' requests for people, and I know I didn't ask for you because I don't know you. I understand General Flannery wants you, but I don't like anyone going over my head to get assigned to my staff—understand?"

His rapid-fire delivery speeds up as he gets more excited. He pauses for air and looks down at my file. I remain silent.

"Why is the first half of your tour in Tokyo classified? I need to know what the hell you did over there." He continues reading. "How the hell did you get a meritorious service medal *and* a commendation medal as a lieutenant? Nobody does that." The general pauses and looks hard into my eyes. "Do you know a red-haired major at the Tokyo Embassy?"

I nod and start to respond, but quickly ascertain that his questions—at least at this point of the interview—are purely rhetorical.

"So you worked for that red-headed son-of-a-bitch! It also says here that you were the guy that reported the KAL 007 shootdown? What a frickin' mess that is. It's got things in Europe all stirred up. By the way, how good is your Russian?"

"Sir, my Russian is a little rusty, but I hope to get a refresher at the NATO School while I'm stationed here."

General Palumbo sits back in his chair. "Why does Flannery think so highly of you? It's weird for a four-star to request a captain—really unusual. Do you know that he wants you to be his primary morning briefer?" He slams his left hand down on the top of his desk. "I make those assignments, not the four-star! Did I already tell you that I didn't ask for you to be assigned here?"

I'm feeling deflated. "Yes, sir, you did say that already."

He stares at me again. "Did you know that General Flannery put you in for another meritorious service medal?"

"No sir, I did not."

He goes silent for a few seconds. "You know that I have a reputation as a briefer? Do you know that? Being one of my briefers is a tough business. I already have a couple of majors who are very good briefers. Why do I need you?"

I fail to respond because I have no clue how to answer him.

He sighs and concludes the interview. "All right. Since you worked for the red-haired major over there, you must have something on the ball. If you survived working for him, then . . . well. How well do you know the Soviets in this part of the world? You are going to have to get smart real fast. I want you to spend this week with my Soviet desk analysts and learn all you can about their order of battle, current exercises, the whole nine yards, okay? You are briefing the four-star at his first staff meeting after change of command next Monday, so you need to be ready. Dismissed!"

Monday, 17 October 1983

I work diligently over the next week to learn about Soviet operations in Europe. Of course, in the time allotted, I just scratch the surface.

The following Monday, I'm at work by 0200 to begin preparing for the morning briefing to General Flannery scheduled for 0800. In the commander's conference room, General Flannery greets me warmly and asks me how I'm settling in. He takes his seat at the head of the table. I sit against the wall and scan the faces of the senior officers gathered around the conference table. Unsurprisingly, I'm the most junior officer in the room, but I'm used to that. When it's my time to brief, I walk to the podium and wait for General Palumbo to give me the sign to begin. Palumbo nods. Then I look at General Flannery and he gives me a thumbs-up, which is my cue that he's ready.

I go through my normal briefing ritual. I look at the big screen behind me to make sure that the audiovisual tech has the correct slide displayed, adjust my reading light, open my briefing book, and remove my glasses and place them on top of the podium next to the microphone. Only then do I begin to present the morning briefing, which focuses on increased Soviet air and missile activity at nuclear-weapons-equipped bases in Poland and East Germany. The Soviets look to be gearing up for a big exercise; however, they have not notified NATO through the MLM of any exercise plans. This is highly unusual and may be a breach of the post-World War II Potsdam Accord. I tell Flannery that this unusual development is probably part of the general ratcheting up of readiness we have seen from the Soviet side since the Korean airliner was shot down.

The briefing goes smoothly, and General Flannery asks a couple of questions that I handle adequately. After the four-star's staff meeting concludes, I go back to my cubicle in the current intelligence shop. As I sit down to record the questions I was asked during the briefing, my desk phone rings.

I answer it and I'm shocked to find General Palumbo on the other end of the line. He growls. "Captain, get down to my office right away!"

I immediately head toward his office, wondering what the hell this could be about. Did I do something wrong? As I approach Palumbo's outer office, I'm intercepted in the hallway by several full colonels who want to know what went wrong during the briefing. Somehow word has already spread that General Palumbo summoned me to his office. I get to the general's outer office and his deputy, a very senior colonel, tells me that he is disappointed in me and that he will go in to see the general with me. He wants to know what happened in the four-star's staff meeting so he can "fix it."

By this point, I'm exasperated. "Colonel, nothing happened. It was strictly 'no runs, no hits, no errors, no one left on base'—totally routine."

The colonel mutters. "Well, something sure happened."

I'm ushered into General Palumbo's office and the colonel follows me in. General Palumbo is in the same pose in which I found him one week ago, studiously reviewing a document with his reading glasses perched on his nose.

Finally, the general looks up at me and the colonel. He appears a bit confused and points at the colonel. "What the hell is he doing here?"

The colonel responds, "Sir, I thought it best that I accompany the captain so that we can address deficiencies in a timely manner."

Palumbo looks as if the colonel just landed from Mars. "Deficiencies? What the hell are you talking about? Look, I don't need you in this meeting. I just want to talk to the captain."

Flummoxed, the colonel retreats from the general's office and shuts the door.

General Palumbo glares at me. "How do you think things went today in the staff meeting?"

"Well, sir, I thought that the briefing went well, and I handled the questions adequately."

He contemplates my response and says, "Yeah, I agree. You were great. Don't change anything."

Confused, I stand at attention and wonder if I'm dismissed.

The general is finished with me. "You can go. And tell all those nervous Nelly colonels out there to calm the hell down."

I start to leave the office and as I'm turning the doorknob, the general pipes up.

"Oh, one more thing, Captain."

I turn back toward his voice. "Yes, sir?"

"Yeah, one more thing. Don't get cocky!"

CHAPTER FOURTEEN

GORDIEVSKY AND PALUMBO

Colonel Ivan Levchenko, GRU, Soviet Air Defense Forces
Moscow, Russia, USSR and Frankfurt,
Federal Republic of Germany

Monday, 17 October 1983

Today dawned cold and snowy in Moscow. This is the first real snow of the season. If this storm is any indication, it promises to be a long, dreary winter.

After that terrifying night with Petrov, I returned to Moscow on the first of October, eagerly awaiting Boyka's return to the capital. Sadly, due to a sudden illness that overtook her father, Boyka could not join me until yesterday. We had a sweet reunion, and I loved her with an intensity that surprised both of us. The trauma of that awful night when I feared I would never see her again was the source of my passion.

Of course, I can't tell Boyka what happened at Serpukhov-15. No less than Minister of Defense Ustinov has ordered each of us who were present that night to sign documents swearing we will never share the story with anyone *as long as we live*. The embarrassment would be too great for the Kremlin leadership. It also would lead to global outrage. Can you imagine the consequences if the Western press were to learn that the Soviet Union erroneously detected an American ICBM strike and that only the cool thinking of a uniquely talented lieutenant colonel prevented planetwide Armageddon?

Despite Petrov's heroism during that crisis, my dear friend is the one who has been disciplined. His purported offense is that he failed to keep a detailed commander's log of the events of 27 September, and breached protocol in other petty ways. I fear Stas's military career is over. They need a scapegoat to divert attention from the flaws in our expensive OKO satellite constellation. Petrov is the designated goat. His real crime is that his competence uncovered that the OKO system never should have been awarded operational status. Powerful men's careers depend on OKO's deficiencies remaining secret. So, Petrov will pay.

Yes, the man who saved the world will pay. The man whose actions prevented the instant death of hundreds of millions of people will pay. It makes me want to scream or chain myself to Lenin's Tomb in protest. It's true what they say: no good deed goes unpunished.

Cruelly, my old friend is dealing with this massive injustice while caring for his dying wife. The enormity of the unfairness overwhelms me, and I can't talk to anyone about it. I can't commiserate with Boyka. Last night she sensed that something is bothering me terribly. But I can never tell her the source of my pain.

Friday, 21 October 1983

I'll attend another RYaN meeting at GRU headquarters this afternoon. NATO has announced its plans to conduct a nuclear weapons exercise called Able Archer. The Americans and NATO have conducted this exercise in past years to test and exercise their nuclear command and control systems. Given the fraught relations between the West and the USSR, the timing of this year's Able Archer exercise is imprudent at best. I've no doubt that the alert posture of our nuclear forces will increase accordingly.

I arrive at GRU headquarters for the RYaN meeting just after lunch. The conference room is packed with officers. The meeting is kicked off by the chief of the General Staff, Marshal of the Soviet Union Ogarkov. This is extraordinary, truly astonishing, Marshal Ogarkov himself being here. The Marshal tells us that this year's Able Archer exercise demands extra scrutiny by the GRU. His tone is somber. According to Ogarkov, highly sensitive sources have discerned that this year's Able Archer exercise will involve the participation of the most senior authorities of the United States and the United Kingdom. Their participation in a nuclear exercise like this one is unprecedented.

Ogarkov elaborates. "Both President Ronald Reagan and Prime Minister Margaret Thatcher are expected to participate in the final phase of this exercise. As you know, those officials are the 'national command authority' figures who authorize the release of nuclear weapons in their respective countries. Unlike any we have seen in the past, this exercise will take the NATO commanders through a full-scale simulated release of nuclear weapons. And at the climax—at the most crucial stage—they will have on hand the national command authorities—Reagan and Thatcher—to authorize the actual release of nuclear weapons.

"I do not have to tell you gentlemen what this means. NATO has never before included its top leaders in a major nuclear exercise. You must realize how serious this escalation by NATO is for the USSR. NATO can use this Able Archer exercise to mask their true intention, which may be to launch a preemptive nuclear strike. The Americans assert they need this exercise to prepare their command structure for the imminent deployment of their Pershing II and ground-launched cruise missiles to Germany and Britain, respectively. And that there is nothing alarming about it and Moscow ought not to be concerned. Well, I find it very alarming, and so should all of you. Here is what I want you to do. Pulse all your contacts in the West to determine their actual plans. Contact everyone in a position to know what's really going on. Follow every lead. I'm certain it surprises none of you that we are at the climax of the RYaN project."

As Ogarkov concludes, the conference room is as silent as a tomb. No one coughs, and no one shuffles their feet. Every officer in the room comprehends the gravity of the marshal's remarks.

As the meeting adjourns, I am surprised to see my acquaintance from the London KGB residence—Oleg Gordievsky. He has been seated unobtrusively in the back of the conference room. When Gordievsky sees me, he walks toward me with a purpose.

"Hello, Vanya, how are you and your beautiful wife? I was hoping that you would be at today's meeting."

"Hello, Gordievsky, it's a pleasure to see you again. Yes, RYaN has consumed my life since I arrived here this past summer. I appreciate your letters, and I miss seeing you in London and so does Boyka. I apologize for being a poor correspondent. I have spent more days on the road than in Moscow the last few months."

Gordievsky smiles. "I'm sure that RYaN and the Korean shootdown have kept you quite busy. I miss seeing you and Boyka. She lights up any room she enters, my friend."

His smile fades. He whispers. "Look, I want to talk to you while I am in Moscow. It's extremely important that we meet, especially after hearing Marshal Ogarkov's briefing."

So Gordievsky is not requesting a social visit. "Sure, we can go to my office now if you have the time."

He shakes his head vigorously. "No, no, thank you. First, I am tied up this afternoon at Dzerzhinsky Square. My KGB masters want me to check in with headquarters while I'm in Moscow. Second, our meeting must be unofficial. I am happy to invite you and Boyka to dinner. How about tomorrow night? She can't refuse a dinner out in Moscow on a Saturday night!"

I chuckle. "Yes, I'm sure she will be delighted to see you. Will your wife join us? Boyka enjoys her company so much."

Gordievsky's smile returns. "No, I'm afraid my wife is in London with the kids. I will make arrangements for the Hotel Metropol. I hope she likes the Boyarsky Restaurant."

With that, he turns and strides out of the room. This man is convivial, but he always has an aura of mystery about him. I feel I can never quite pin him down. I wonder what he's up to.

Saturday, 22 October 1983

We arrive early at the Metropol Hotel for dinner with Gordievsky so that Boyka and I can have a cocktail at the hotel's pleasingly decadent bar—the famous Shalyapin Bar with its 1920s-era American décor. As is customary, there is a jazz band making an earnest attempt to emulate the lively American music of the 1930s and 1940s. Boyka is wearing her finest gold dress and she has her blonde hair done up on top of her head. She looks like a countess from the court of Tsar Alexander I.

As we enter the bar, every man's eyes focus on the regal beauty walking beside me. This is a scenario I've become accustomed to over the years. I find it mildly amusing how blatantly men stare at her, ignoring me completely—erasing me from the scene like an unwanted and mistaken brushstroke. Candidly, I get a tingling of pride and sexual excitement from all this attention paid to my wife.

After a drink at the bar, we join Gordievsky in the sumptuous Boyarsky Restaurant. He's already seated at a reserved table, and the KGB man waves when he sees us enter. He rises and kisses Boyka's hand, bowing slightly.

"Good evening, Madame Levchenka. I'm so pleased you could join me. You look like a queen."

Boyka blushes and curtsies. She loves the attention.

Gordievsky pats my arm. "My God, Levchenko, your wife is even more ravishing than I recall. You are a very lucky man, indeed."

Boyka beams and replies charmingly, "Sir, your flattery is even more colorful than I recall."

She is as radiant as the surroundings of this old, elegant restaurant. We sit at one of the Boyarsky's famous banquettes with the KGB officer between us. Gordievsky orders the finest caviar on the menu for the table—a notable extravagance—and pairs it with a wonderful Blanc de Noir. Soon we're laughing and reminiscing about our time together in London. As the marvelous dinner unfolds, I feel myself relaxing for the first time in months.

Gordievsky orders brandy after we finish eating. He whispers that it's time for more serious discussion.

"Madame Levchenka, I must speak in confidence to your husband for a few moments. I beg your forgiveness."

Then he puts his lips nearly to my ear. "Vanya, you made important contacts with the Americans during your time with the Military Liaison Mission—no?"

"Of course."

He leans over and speaks directly into my right ear. "As we heard yesterday from the big man, it is time to reach out to the most trusted of those contacts. Since the Korean shootdown, relations are incredibly strained with the West. I see evidence of this every day in London. As you know, our top leaders are not talking to their Western counterparts. They only communicate by exchanging insults through the media. Therefore, it falls to us to open lines of communication with our Western contacts to prevent further escalation. Do you understand, my friend?"

I nod my head. "Yes, I understand. Things can spin out of control rapidly. That's what I've observed and what we were told yesterday."

Gordievsky nods several times and leans into me again. "The Americans and the British have no idea of the level of paranoia that exists in the Kremlin and within the KGB. This new exercise will present an opportunity for massive miscalculation on both sides. We must warn our contacts in the West that our leadership believes the West is fully capable of launching a nuclear first strike. It's madness, but there it is. You must go to West Germany and establish a channel with the Americans. Use the MLM. After all, the MLM was founded to prevent World War III and deescalate tensions—right?"

Of course, that's true and I add. "Yes, the MLM could be a useful tool. There are trusted relationships we can leverage—and facilities, as well."

"Yes, yes, and Colonel, we need to move quickly. With this NATO exercise on the horizon, we don't have much time to get in front of events." He leans in even closer. "Comrade . . . my friend, I'm convinced that the West is *not* planning a nuclear first strike. It's simply not part of their mindset. However, I also understand that circumstances and circumstantial evidence can cloud the perspective of our leadership. We who know better must help the Kremlin see the light, or the light may go out permanently. Those, my friend, are the stakes."

I can't disagree. My mind is swimming from the alcohol and Gordievsky's blunt remarks. I must decide how far I'm prepared to go—how far I'm prepared to go in contacting the Americans. Establishing a channel is dangerous. However, Marshal Ogarkov has given us permission—actually, an order—to do so.

Twenty minutes later, Boyka and I thank Gordievsky for a wonderful dinner. I shake Gordievsky's hand as we depart the Metropol. The night is very cold, and it's starting to snow again. The doorman secures us a cab for the short drive home.

As we prepare for bed, Boyka gives me a troubled look. "What did Gordievsky ask you to do tonight? I like him, but his mysterious manner worries me. He seems like a dangerous man." She is always looking out for my best interests.

"Yes, he may be a dangerous man. These are dangerous times. Basically, he wants my help to deescalate the tense relations with the West. I'm not sure what I can do. However, I do think that he's correct that something needs to be done, or we could find ourselves in a war that no one wants."

She looks frightened. "Are things that bad? I thought tensions were beginning to ease. After all, that Korean airliner was shot down nearly two months ago. You know I just don't want to see you hurt. I know how the powers-that-be behave. They delight in destroying careers. You must be careful."

I smile to reassure her. "Yes, I know. I know. No good deed goes unpunished, my love. I'll be careful."

Tuesday, 25 October 1983

Two important events occur today. One is expected and the other is not. The first event is that today is my boss's final day on the job—clearly expected. He'll retire at the end of 1983 and since he has a couple of months of unused leave, he's packing up his office today. His replacement has not been identified, and I'll be the acting chief of intelligence for the Moscow Air Defense District for the foreseeable future. The second event is somewhat more significant. The United States military invaded a tiny Caribbean Island called Grenada. Soviet intelligence was surprised. If the Americans can invade a small country without us knowing anything about it in advance, then what else might they be able to do without us knowing? It doesn't bode well for the looming Able Archer exercise.

Further inflaming the world situation, just two days ago terrorist explosions killed nearly 250 American Marines and almost 60 French paratroopers in Beirut, Lebanon. Now, American Marines and other US forces are in combat on the island of Grenada, battling both local troops loyal to the ruling Marxist regime and Cuban troops deployed there to rebuild the island's airfield. One would think that the tragedy in Beirut and the ongoing combat in Grenada would preoccupy the Pentagon. Nonetheless, plans for Able Archer 83 are proceeding apace.

In pondering my dinner conversation with Gordievsky, I have arrived at a plan of action. I will pay a visit to my old Military Liaison Mission colleagues in West Germany, under the auspices of my RYaN responsibilities. The MLM may have some useful details about Able Archer. My main task, however, will be to try to arrange a private meeting with General Leonard Palumbo, the head of US Air Force intelligence in Europe. I met him several times when I was with the MLM in Frankfurt and found him to be skillful and wise. He may be just the right man with whom to confer. I think highly of this American.

Friday, 28 October 1983

Walking into my old haunts at the MLM compound in Frankfurt feels surreal yet comforting after the events of the last two months. It also reminds me of how much Boyka and I enjoyed our years in West Germany. I know she'd be happy to return here at a moment's notice.

My first task is to interview my colleagues to get their assessment of what is really going on in NATO. As it happens, my meetings with the MLM officers reinforce my view that NATO is not planning to initiate hostilities. Certainly, the timing of Able Archer 83 is clumsy, in light of the extreme tensions between East and West. A less rigid NATO command structure might have recognized this and postponed the exercise. Nonetheless, I understand the inertia of military planning processes and with the imminent arrival of Pershing II and GLCM missiles, the nuclear force planners at NATO headquarters are probably insisting that Able Archer must go forward as planned.

My friends at the Soviet MLM office have arranged for me to meet General Palumbo for dinner tonight. General Palumbo has selected a quiet restaurant in a quaint old section of Frankfurt. I rely on him to ensure it is the best choice for a discreet meeting.

As I indicated, I met the American general a handful of times when I was stationed in West Germany. I know something of his background. He's the son of Italian immigrants and his father was a stonemason. He didn't attend the American Air Force Academy but graduated in 1955 from West Virginia University, which is in his hometown of Morgantown. He's a career intelligence officer—and I've found him to be a consummate professional. He's meticulous about his appearance, but not in a fussy way. A born storyteller, he sprinkles his conversation with genuinely funny anecdotes delivered with superb timing. At the very least, this dinner promises to be entertaining.

I have my driver take me to the center of the city, where we will dine at the Romer Pils Brunnen, known for its traditional Frankfurter cuisine. I'm looking forward to ordering the Kalbsschnitzel—veal fried in butter—and I skipped lunch today to ensure I have the fortitude to tackle this rich and hearty dish. Since it is November, they should be serving their delicious Carolus double bock beer, as well. One of the many things I miss about West Germany is the excellent beer, which comes in so many intriguing varieties.

The restaurant host tells me that I'm the first to arrive, and I decide to go back outside and wait on the street until I see the general's car drop him off at the front door. Then I allow him five minutes to secure our table and get settled. My intent is that General Palumbo be as comfortable as possible, given that a meeting such as this must strike him as profoundly unusual.

I reenter the restaurant and Palumbo stands up to greet me and shakes my hand with a wry smile on his face. "Welcome back to Frankfurt, Colonel Levchenko. I hope this restaurant is to your liking. The menu is very traditional."

I respond with a smile, "Sir, this is perfect. You chose well. I don't even have to look at the menu. As soon as I heard we were to meet here, my mind was fixed on the Kalbsschnitzel."

Palumbo's eyes sparkle. "Good choice. I hope you brought a good appetite! I know that your English is excellent, so I won't trouble you with attempting to use German or Russian. Okay?"

We each order a beer and make small talk about the German weather.

The waiter delivers our beers, and we order our meals. The seasonal bock is even better than I remember, and I savor its dark tones.

General Palumbo waits for me to initiate the conversation.

"General, thank you so much for agreeing to meet with me on short notice. I realize my request is unusual. But first, let me offer my condolences to you and your country on the tragedy that befell your Marines in Beirut."

Palumbo looks me in the eye. "Thank you, Colonel, I appreciate your comments. You must have something very important to tell me—to justify traveling here all the way from Moscow."

"Yes, sir, it is important."

The general taps his right index figure on the table and waits for me to continue.

"Sir, we both know that tensions between our two sides have reached a dangerous level and grown even more alarming since the Korean airliner shootdown."

The general continues to tap his finger.

I keep talking. "The political leadership on each side is ratcheting up the tension. They are not talking to each other. I am very concerned that we have no channels through which to communicate and help us deescalate tensions. During the Cuban Missile Crisis, your President Kennedy established a channel through his brother and our ambassador in Washington. No such conduit exists now. Based on what I have heard concerning talks between your Secretary of State Shultz and Foreign Minister Gromyko since the KAL 007 incident, their relationship is frayed to the breaking point."

General Palumbo nods and motions for me to continue.

I take a deep draught of beer and proceed. "Here is the crux of the matter. My leadership in the Kremlin believes that NATO is plotting a nuclear first strike."

I let that sink in. My dinner partner's eyes go wide, but he remains silent.

"Sir, with respect, they believe that Able Archer may be a cover for actual preparations for nuclear war. I don't believe that this is the case, personally; however, mine is not the view held in Moscow. This is why a channel for communication is so crucial."

General Palumbo stares intently at me—unblinking. He stops tapping his finger and takes a sip of beer. "Colonel, I am . . . astounded."

He pauses for a moment and says, "If your leadership has the degree of paranoia that you are claiming, then we are in deep kimchi. You are scaring the hell out of me. Is that your intent?"

"Sorry, sir, what is kimchi?"

Palumbo suppresses a laugh. "Kimchi is really smelly Korean food. Answer my question."

I decide to be bold. "General, my purpose is to get your attention, and if scaring the hell out of you helps me to do that, then so be it."

"All right, Colonel, you have my attention. For the life of me, I cannot believe your leadership actually believes that we are contemplating a nuclear first strike. Why the hell would they think that?"

I order another bock before responding. "General, think of it from our perspective. Your President has called us an evil empire, he has proposed a missile defense program to negate our nuclear capability, he is deploying a new generation of nuclear missiles to Europe, he has claimed we are the focus of evil in the world, and that we are guilty of premeditated mass murder by shooting down the Korean airliner. And just this week, your military invaded Grenada to overthrow a Marxist regime allied with our friend Cuba."

General Palumbo maintains a poker face during my testimony. I may have overdone it.

At last, he says, "Look, Colonel, I could give you a similar litany from our perspective, but what's the point?"

There is a lengthy pause in our conversation.

He continues. "All right, I agree that we need a line of communication. What do you propose?"

"Sir, I propose you identify someone for me to communicate with and that we schedule a meeting as soon as possible. Further, I believe he and I should meet at your MLM facility in East Germany—the Potsdam House. It will be far easier for me to get there than to travel to Frankfurt, much as I like it here."

That elicits a sly smile from the general. "Okay, Colonel. I'll identify a point of contact for you. I presume I should get word to you through the Soviet MLM office in Frankfurt?"

"Yes, sir, please utilize our MLM. Thank you for your frankness and this excellent dinner. I'll need to run ten kilometers tomorrow morning before my flight, but the Kalbsschnitzel was more than worth it!"

Palumbo smiles again. "I'm glad you enjoyed it. Thank you for your frankness, as well. I'm hopeful that this new channel will pay off. Colonel, I'm relying on you to make this work. I'll get you a good counterpart, but the depth of *your* knowledge of both sides is invaluable. I wish you success. Reach out to me through the American MLM if you need me. Good night, Colonel Levchenko."

"Good night, General. Thank you."

We part ways and I return to the Soviet MLM for the night.

At this late date, it's doubtful the Americans will change their plans for Able Archer 83. Still, while there is a chance of defusing the situation, I must take it.

My larger concern lies within the Kremlin. My leadership's paranoia is tuned to a fever pitch. The preparations that are no doubt underway for nuclear war will be very difficult to walk back. Just think of the momentum that built toward war across all of Europe in August of 1914. None of those leaders really wanted a major war—they didn't even think one was possible—but once the machinery of mobilization started, they were powerless to reverse the inertia.

CHAPTER FIFTEEN

POTSDAM HOUSE

Captain Kevin Cattani, United States Air Force
Potsdam, German Democratic Republic (East Germany)

Wednesday, 2 November 1983

My escort to the Potsdam House is Air Force Major Mark Stablinksi. He is a multilingual career intelligence officer who was captain of the gymnastics team at the Air Force Academy. He still looks fit enough to compete in that demanding sport. Stablinksi has a patrician air about him. I've learned that his family has a proud military history—both in the United States and its native Poland.

We are to drive to Potsdam via the Glienicke Bridge—the "bridge of spies," as it is known, for the numerous exchanges of Soviet and Western spies that have taken place on its rickety structure during the Cold War. The bridge used to be the highway link between Berlin and Potsdam; however, it has been closed to all public traffic since the erection of the Berlin Wall in 1962. It is used occasionally by diplomats and routinely by the Western Military Liaison Missions. It's the only crossing around Berlin the Soviets control. The other crossings between East and West Berlin, including the more famous "Checkpoint Charlie," are secured by the East Germans.

On this dreary, rainy November morning, our vehicle is stopped by the Russians for a thorough inspection. Major Stablinski is sitting in the front seat next to the driver, who is a US Army NCO—a Special Forces guy—a green beret. I'm in the back seat behind the major.

A very tall Soviet warrant officer steps up to the driver's window. The Army NCO rolls down his window and hands the Russian our identification credentials. The Soviet takes our papers back to his guard house where I can see him confer with an officer who must be checking our names against his roster of visitors to the East.

The warrant officer returns after a few minutes and leans his large frame over so he can look inside the car. He sees Stablinski and greets him like an old friend. The Soviet speaks a heavily accented Russian, which is tough for me to understand. "Ah, Major Stablinksi, are you off on a 'tour' today? Not such a nice day for a drive in the country, is it?"

Stablinski chuckles and responds, "No, my friend, no tour today. We're simply going to Potsdam House for a routine meeting. No excitement for me today."

The warrant officer walks around the front of the vehicle and approaches Stablinski's side window. Stablinski rolls down his window partway and I hear the Soviet say, "Well, Major, at least you will be inside and out of this chilly air. Who do we have in the back seat today?"

Stablinski rolls down his window all the way—and I feel a rush of cold air. Stablinski answers, "He's a captain who has a meeting at the house. Say, why did you stop us today?"

I can see now that the warrant officer has a huge mustache, like something from the Napoleonic era—it can't possibly be within Soviet Army regulations. "Major, you have three men in the car, which is unusual, no? I was curious why there are three and not two."

The Russian looks at me and pantomimes rolling down the window. I comply and feel another rush of cold air. The Russian warrant officer pokes his head inside and takes a good look at me. He turns his head toward Stablinski and says, "Jesus, Major, your captain looks like a teenager. You Americans must be desperate for officers. Hey, Captain, have you started shaving yet?"

I think for a second about how to respond and say, "Your wife told me that she likes a cleanshaven man to eat her pussy."

The warrant officer's eyes go wide and burn into me for a few seconds, and then he starts laughing. "Major, your captain has a sense of humor—a bad one, and his Russian is a bit hard to understand. Cleanshaven, my asshole—what shit. I suppose the young captain must be an American assassin, eh, Major? A baby-faced assassin? We should be very scared of what he might do. Okay, off you go."

He walks away, shaking his head.

Stablinksi turns around and snaps at me. "Christ, Cattani, are you fucking nuts? I hope you plan to be more diplomatic with our guest today."

"Major, I will mind my bearing with our guest. Don't worry. I'm just a little sensitive about shaving."

Stablinski turns and faces the front windshield again. "Evidently. Christ almighty. I hope your GRU contact doesn't have a mustache."

Our Army driver makes his way through the security gates on the bridge and we enter East Germany. Eventually, he guides the vehicle into the driveway of a white stucco villa—the home of the American MLM in Potsdam. The Potsdam House is an impressive building but not ostentatious. A few of the MLM guys spend their nights here, but most of the guys on tours (or missions) just pass through, using it, if at all, as a way station on their way into the countryside. I will meet the GRU officer on the second floor in a small conference room. I've been told that he is a colonel and probably will not give me his name. I'm in battle dress uniform like the MLM guys—and my last name is stitched on my chest above my right pocket. The GRU visitor will know who I am.

I go inside, get settled in the second-floor conference room, and wait for my contact to arrive.

About forty-five minutes later, I hear a car drive into the stone-surfaced driveway and park in front of the villa. I get up from the conference table and walk to a tall window that provides a full view of the circular driveway and small courtyard below. A man of medium build climbs out of the driver's seat. He is alone—he's driven himself to the meeting. I sense Stablinski standing beside me. With a smirk, he observes, "Well, Cattani, it looks like your GRU colonel has a mustache. Are you gonna freak out on me again?"

Stablinski leaves the room and goes downstairs to greet our guest and escort him to the conference room.

Major Stablinski and the GRU colonel enter the conference room. We shake hands and I offer the colonel a cup of tea. As I pour him a cup, I observe that our guest looks very fit—like a runner. He has reddish hair and a mustache—Stablinski was right about that. His features are even—nothing remarkable one way or the other except for his eyes, which seem to observe everything.

Stablinski leaves the room without closing the door. The GRU colonel notices this "oversight" (I'm sure Stablinski intended to leave the door open) and he closes the door himself. This simple gesture reveals a high degree of natural self-confidence, as if to say, *this may be your conference room, but I'm in charge.*

I can't quite believe that I'm alone with a GRU full colonel. He sits down and smiles at me in a very friendly way. The overall sense I get is of a highly intelligent, controlled professional. He smiles again and says in English, "Shall we get started?"

I answer in Russian. "Thank you, Colonel, for meeting with me today. It is an honor for me to meet you."

He looks at me with curiosity. "Where did you learn your Russian? Who was your teacher?"

Ah, this is a professional intelligence officer, indeed. He's asking me to reveal personal details. Or is he simply curious? "I learned at university. My first teacher was an elderly Russian woman, who grew up in Shanghai."

The colonel ponders my answer. "Shanghai—so her parents were Whites during the Civil War—they were monarchists, no?"

"Yes, sir, they were Whites. Her father was a general officer in the tsarist army."

"Yes, that explains your archaic Russian. Do you mind if we speak English?"

I think I should feel insulted, but I switch to English. "No, sir, I don't mind. English is fine."

He looks relieved. "Good. Okay. Where are you from, Captain? Where in the States?" I can already tell his English is superb.

Where is this going? "I'm from southern Virginia."

Levchenko looks pleased. "I thought I heard a Southern accent, but not a strong one. You have worked hard at losing it, I think. I hear a drawl, however, when you said, 'southern Virginia.'"

I suppose the polite thing to do is to reciprocate the inquiry. "And sir, where did you grow up?"

He looks surprised at my question. "Oh me? I'm from Crimea. But I am Russian—not Ukrainian. My wife is Ukrainian. Are you married? And how old are you?"

This is a lot of private information, but what the hell. "No, Colonel, I am not married. I am twenty-seven."

The colonel takes in that information. "You are very young to have been given such a heavy responsibility today, no? How long have you been in the Air Force? Forgive me, but I simply don't understand why your superiors have sent a young captain to parley with me. It doesn't make sense."

I was expecting this line of inquiry. "I was commissioned when I was twenty-one. Let me try to explain why I'm here—and not someone more senior. I know that you met with Brigadier General Leonard Palumbo, the head of Air Force intelligence in Europe."

He nods. "Yes, I know General Palumbo from my time with the MLM in Frankfurt. He's a good man. We met quite recently in Frankfurt. Do you work for him? I assume that you must."

I'm glad to hear that he likes Palumbo. "Yes, sir, well, not directly—I don't work for him directly, but I am assigned to his organization."

"Right, and who is this new general that commands the Air Forces in Europe—he has an Irish name—right?"

"Yes, Colonel, that would be General Flannery—he is the new commander."

Recognition flashes across his face. "Is this the same Flannery who commanded US Forces in Japan? He was in command during the Korean airliner incident just a couple of months ago, right?"

Where is he going with this? Is he just collecting or confirming senior officer intelligence? "Colonel, yes, it is the same man."

He seems excited—in a positive way. "He's the man who was in command when our MiGs almost shot down your P-3? And when your F-15s came after our MiGs—this is the same man?"

Jesus? How does a GRU colonel from Moscow know all these details? Almost no one in my own Air Force knows this stuff. How can he know about the EP-3 incident and the near-showdown between the MiG-23s and our F-15s?

"Yes, he is the same man. General Flannery was promoted to four-star general, and recently arrived in Europe as commander of all the NATO air forces."

He sighs—a sigh of visible relief. "Good. Good for him. So, Captain, what do you know about the KAL incident? You realize that incident is the trigger for much of the current tension—all the craziness we are seeing this autumn?"

Of course, I know all this. "Yes, sir, that event has led to a very dangerous situation."

The colonel is not satisfied with my answer. "Yes, yes, but what do *you* know about it? Is General Flannery responsible for the decision to call off your F-15s? Were you assigned to Japan? With General Flannery? Is that why you are here now?"

"The answer to all of your questions is 'yes'; however, with all due respect, I don't understand the relevancy."

He leans across the conference table. "My questions are relevant, Captain, because I need to know why a junior captain, who looks like a teenager, has been sent to talk to me about matters of enormous importance to the future of our two countries. That is why I need to know what you know, who you are, and why you are here!"

Taking a deep breath, I deliver my response. "Okay, Colonel, that is a fair point. I was on duty the night of the shootdown—I was the senior intelligence officer on duty. I served under General Flannery for two years in Tokyo, and I was there when General Flannery ordered our F-15s to stand down and not engage your MiGs. General Flannery could have started World War III that day. He pulled us all back from the brink. I know the details—at least the ones that our side knows."

He looks triumphant. "So the reason that I am meeting with a junior captain is that this *particular* captain is the personal envoy of the commander-in-chief of all NATO air forces—do I have that right? Why else would they send someone so junior? And Flannery had the good judgment not to shoot down our MiGs in the Tatar Strait—even though he was provoked and had ample justification. And if Flannery's judgment remains sound, then he has sound reasons for sending you here today. This is the explanation for why you are here." The GRU man beams a self-satisfied smile.

"Yes, Colonel. I can understand that you need a rationale for why I'm here for your superiors as much as for your own peace of mind. You are correct on all counts."

The colonel looks pleased. "Naturally. This is good. Maybe I am talking to the right man, after all. Why does General Flannery place trust in such a young man?"

"I suppose he thinks I got a lot of things right in the Far East. I think it is enough for our conversation for you to know that both General Flannery and General Palumbo trust me, and they've asked me to take this sensitive meeting with you. There is no disrespect intended, I can assure you. Since you know who I am, can you tell me your name?"

He looks surprised by my question. "Me? I'm Colonel Ivan Levchenko. I'm currently the acting chief of intelligence for the Moscow Air Defense district. Is that good enough for you?"

He looks amused—this GRU colonel. I respond, "Yes, sir. Where else have you served? You know all about me, after all."

The colonel smiles and says, "I served in the American section of our MLM in Frankfurt and I've had assignments in East Germany, Poland, and in the western USSR. I'm satisfied that I am talking to the right man. Let's get to the matter at hand, shall we?

"We're on the brink of disaster. Your President Reagan thinks we are an evil empire and that the shootdown of the Korean plane was a ruthless act of premeditated murder. On our side, Chief Marshal Ogarkov claims that the Korean flight was a pre-planned intelligence collection mission, meant to provoke the USSR and create a pretext for the USA to start a nuclear war. I suspect that both of us know that those perceptions are wrong and extremely dangerous. Can your General Flannery help us defuse this crisis before it is too late?"

"Colonel, I hope so."

He helps himself to another cup of tea. "Tell me, Captain, why is NATO conducting such a large nuclear war exercise now? It makes no sense, given how strained relations are between the Soviet bloc and the West, especially since the Korean shootdown. It makes no sense."

I can't disagree with him, but I convey the party line. "Colonel, Able Archer is merely a command post exercise. No actual nuclear forces are being deployed in support of the exercise. I don't know a great deal about it, but my understanding is that the exercise has been planned for some time, and it is timed to coincide with the deployment of Pershing II missiles to Germany and the new cruise missiles to the UK. I suppose that they want to exercise NATO's command and control structure, given the arrival of the new weapon systems. Don't you guys do the same thing?"

The colonel retorts, "Yes, yes. Captain, did you know that your first new, nuclear cruise missiles were delivered to Britain today? On this very day?"

This is news to me. "No sir, I was unaware."

He doesn't look surprised and continues, "Are you aware that today is the first official day of your Able Archer exercise, or have they kept you in the dark about that, too? You also should know that we have special intelligence that indicates that your President Reagan and Prime Minister Thatcher are to participate in the final phase of your exercise. The final phase of Able Archer is when your top authorities direct the release of nuclear weapons. Do you understand how dangerous this is? This is unprecedented. To our knowledge, no President and no British PM have ever personally participated in the nuclear release phase of a NATO exercise. To our leaders, this will look like the real thing. I must stress to you that this part of the exercise has created the gravest level of concern in the Kremlin."

Holy shit. If this is true . . . holy shit! No wonder they think this exercise could be disguising a real first strike. "Sir, I'm unaware of such details concerning Able Archer."

Colonel Levchenko smiles. "Yes, the operational guys don't like to share their plans with intelligence officers, do they? I know more about NATO operations than you do, and you probably know more than I do about what the Soviet forces are doing."

I nod. "Colonel, General Palumbo has authorized me to show you intelligence we have concerning unprecedented nuclear weapons activity throughout East Germany and Poland. It's important for you to understand that what we are seeing is unprecedented."

My counterpart folds his hands, stares at me with those keen eyes of his, and waits for me to continue. I retrieve a sealed envelope from my locked briefcase. I open the envelope with my tactical knife and pull out several classified images.

The colonel smiles. "Captain, that is quite a knife. Why does a staff officer at Ramstein Air Base carry a special forces knife? I think there is more to you than you have revealed."

I ignore the colonel's comment and place two images in front of him. "Colonel, this shows the nuclear weapons storage bunkers at Brand Air Base in East Germany. Do you know this base?"

"Yes, Captain, I've been there. I was stationed in East Germany for four years when I was a major. I know Brand Air Base, but these nuclear bunkers must be relatively new. I don't recall seeing them before. When were they built?"

How much should I tell this guy? "Sir, I don't know the exact dates, but I believe the nuclear bunkers were built within the last several years, to support the deployment of nuclear-capable MiG-27s at Brand."

He leans forward to get a better look. I can tell that he is intrigued.

I continue. "Colonel, if you look closely, you can see that the doors to the nuclear bunkers are open, and the tracks in front of the doors indicate vehicles have serviced the bunkers. The depth of the tracks indicates that the service vehicles were heavily loaded."

The colonel focuses on the image with great intensity. "I see. You think that the vehicles were loaded with nuclear weapons, obviously."

"Yes, sir, we do. Now, look at the second image. We sent our MLM guys to Brand to try to confirm the uploading of nuclear weapons on the MiG-27s."

The colonel takes the second photo in his hand. "Wow, this is very impressive. Your MLM guys can't get on the base at Brand, of course, so they must have taken this photo from a tree, or another elevated location off the base, and then they depressed the angle so that they could photograph the underside of the wings. This is outstanding work."

I'm gratified he recognizes professional excellence when he sees it. "Yes, sir, and those are nuclear weapons uploaded on those MiG-27s. They're standing alert at Brand. Believe me, sir, we have similar evidence from many of your airfields in the forward area. Colonel Levchenko, we are seeing preparations for nuclear war that we did not observe even during the Cuban Missile Crisis."

He studies both images carefully. "So, the first image is from one of your satellites. Impressive." He pushes his chair back, looks at me, and says, "God help us. What else do you have, Captain?"

"Colonel, I have two more images to show you, but believe me, we have hundreds more. We also have tons of signals intelligence collection that confirm our concerns. The first image is of your SS-12 missile base in East Germany. Once again, the nuclear weapons storage bunker doors are open and there are heavy tracks visible. In addition, there are tracks here and here that must be from SS-12 transporter-erector-launch vehicles (TELs). It looks like the entire SS-12 regiment has deployed from this garrison."

He looks closely at the image. "Yes, I see. Christ in Heaven."

"Sir, the second image was taken by our MLM guys. We sent MLM tours into the forests to reconnoiter your pre-surveyed, wartime launch positions. This image is of an SS-12 TEL at one of those launch sites. Look here, there are nuclear warheads fitted to the rockets—to the SS-12s."

He sighs deeply. "Your MLM is really good. So you know where our wartime launch sites are, eh? Well, taking those photos is extremely risky. Your team could have been shot." Levchenko pauses again and looks at me. "Good Christ, Captain. This whole thing can spin out of control. Quickly."

"I agree and I have more. We've seen your command-and-control units switch to wartime reserve mode communications. Taken together, this looks like preparation for nuclear war in Europe on a scale we've never observed. Beyond Europe, we both know your ICBMs are on alert, and your strategic bombers are sitting on nuclear alert at their bases."

"Yes, and yours are too, Captain. *Your* American fighter-bombers in West Germany have been sitting on nuclear alert every day since the 1950s. Who is provoking whom?"

I can't dispute that. "Colonel, that's all true. The difference is that your fighter-bombers have not maintained nuclear alert like this before. Your mobile missile forces in Germany have not deployed en masse before. You can understand why those unprecedented actions are alarming to us."

"Yes, I understand, Captain. And you haven't run an exercise quite like this year's Able Archer before! That is alarming to us!"

We both pause and stare down at the images on the table in front of us.

"Colonel, one more thing. We have indications that your ballistic missile submarines have deployed from Murmansk and Petropavlovsk to their wartime launch positions in the Arctic—under the polar icepack."

That revelation makes the colonel's head snap back. He puts his head in his hands and declares. "Good God. You mentioned the Cuban Missile Crisis a few minutes ago. That was terrifying and could've led to a holocaust." The colonel keeps staring at the conference table, his head down and still in his hands, "This situation is far worse. Both of our countries have exponentially more nuclear weapons, with far greater accuracy, than in 1962. A war today will bring on more than a holocaust."

He looks up at the ceiling. "It will be more than a holocaust. It'll be the end of the world. It will be the end of humanity. It truly will be Armageddon."

We sit in silence for a few minutes.

"Captain, you also need to know something. For the last two and a half years, both the KGB and the GRU have been directed to ferret out Western preparations for a nuclear first strike. This is the largest intelligence operation we have conducted since the Great Patriotic War. The Kremlin leadership has a voracious appetite for intelligence to substantiate their belief that the Americans will strike first. Your deployment of Pershing II and cruise missiles to Europe has convinced my leadership that you are planning a decapitating nuclear first strike. Reagan's reaction to the Korean airliner combined with your Able Archer exercise . . . have made their paranoia even worse. I'm afraid that they believe a nuclear war is imminent. You must make your leadership realize this—do you understand?"

I take in this shocking news and nod slowly.

Levchenko concludes. "We must take steps to deescalate this grave situation."

"Yes, Colonel, absolutely."

The GRU man takes out a small notebook and begins to write, while he gives me direction, "Captain, you must tell General Flannery to inform the White House that President Reagan cannot participate in the Able Archer exercise—in the final phase. The President should not go to the Pentagon on whatever day it is planned for him to go there. And the White House—maybe the National Security Advisor— should contact London and request that Mrs. Thatcher also not attend the final phase of the exercise. This is crucial. Understand?"

Good Lord. He wants us (me?) to direct President Reagan and Margaret Thatcher?

I reply, "Yes, Colonel, I understand, but I don't know if General Flannery can get the White House to agree. I personally briefed our secretary of defense after the Korean airliner shootdown, and he was convinced it was a premeditated attack by your side. I can only imagine that the secretary believes that the President's participation in Able Archer is necessary—to demonstrate resolve."

"Christ, Captain. Fuck resolve! This resolve will get all of us killed."

"Sir, General Flannery will have to get General Rogers at NATO to agree. This will take time."

"Captain, we don't have any time—I think you must realize this!"

"Sir, I understand, and I will do as you request. I suppose it would be best if both President Reagan and Mrs. Thatcher had public appearances on the day—you know the day when Able Archer is in its final phase."

"Yes, yes, Captain. That would build confidence in the Kremlin— that's a good idea."

"All right, Colonel, and on your end—what will you do?"

"You need to see de-escalation—right? It seems to me that the most important thing is to get our mobile missile units in Germany to return to their garrisons and offload their nuclear warheads. Those units cannot stay on alert in the field for long. They either have to launch their missiles or return to garrison."

"I see, Colonel. They are in a 'use it or lose it' scenario."

The colonel pauses to make sure that he understands what I'm saying. "Ah, yes, 'use it or lost it' is right. So if the mobile missiles are the most dangerous systems in the forward area, then a return to garrison is a strong step. I also will try to get our frontal aviation aircraft to stand down from nuclear alert. Those are not easy tasks, but that will be my mission when I return to Moscow."

"Colonel, my apologies, but I should leave now if I want to get back to Ramstein tonight."

He nods in agreement, "And Captain, you and I must meet here again. We must meet later this week."

"Sir, realistically, I mean given what we want to accomplish, I don't think we can meet sooner than early in the morning on Saturday—the fifth. Agreed?"

The colonel ponders the logistics of flying to Moscow and getting back to Potsdam from Moscow, factoring in the meetings he must have in the capital, and says, "Unfortunately, you are correct. It is not possible to meet before then. I will be here no later than 9:00 AM on Saturday, the fifth. Agreed?"

"Yes, Colonel. I agree."

We shake hands and Colonel Levchenko departs Potsdam House.

Jesus, what have I gotten myself into? How am I going to convince my leadership to get the President to change his plans? The whole situation is absurd. I'm afraid that I will disappoint my new Russian friend when we meet again on Saturday. I would put the probability of achieving what I just agreed to do at twenty percent.

CHAPTER SIXTEEN

POTSDAM HOUSE, REDUX

Colonel Ivan Levchenko, GRU, Soviet Air Defense Forces
Potsdam, German Democratic Republic (East Germany)

Saturday, 5 November 1983—Morning

Potsdam House is a refuge of warmth on this rainy and cold Saturday morning. I am met at the entrance by a tall, Black American Air Force NCO who greets me in excellent German and introduces himself as Chief Master Sergeant Jackson.

He escorts me to the same second-floor conference room where I met the young captain a few days ago. The Air Force sergeant pours me tea and offers me a small tray of pastries. His style is that of a cultured gentleman—one gentleman serving another as a matter of courtesy. Then he leaves me alone for a few minutes until a tough-looking Air Force colonel bursts in the room. The colonel reaches out a beefy hand and introduces himself as John LaRoche.

I rise and shake his outstretched hand, which nearly crushes mine with the force of his grip. I manage to blurt out, "I am pleased to meet you, Colonel LaRoche."

He scowls and tells me to sit down. He takes a chair opposite me, his wide shoulders blocking my view of the window behind him. I notice that he's holding a large mug of coffee in his left hand. He tilts it back and takes a big gulp.

LaRoche has blondish hair, slicked back against his scalp. He has a handsome face, but it seems to be permanently fixed in an expression of cold rage. He looks like a man who could explode with the mildest provocation.

But he speaks with a surprisingly measured tone. "Colonel Levchenko, I appreciate the delicate nature of the mission you have taken upon yourself." The American takes another gulp of coffee. "God, I wish they had decent coffee here. I need coffee to jumpstart my heart at this ungodly hour."

I note that it is just after nine in the morning, hardly an ungodly hour for most of us. This American colonel must keep interesting hours.

"Anyway, listen, Levchenko, I just called our Berlin Station, and they tell me that Major Stablinski and Captain Cattani will be here shortly. I got here so goddamn early because I wanted to meet with you before they arrive. You also need to know that General Palumbo wants me to sit in with you and the captain when you meet—I hope that's all right with you."

I'm not surprised by this request. Palumbo wants a senior officer providing oversight to the young captain. "Colonel LaRoche, I am hardly in a position to disagree. In any event, I think it makes good sense to have a senior officer present from your side, given the seriousness of the topic at hand. I take it that you are with the MLM?"

LaRoche pours himself some more coffee and responds, "Yes, this is my third tour with them. I'm the senior Air Force officer assigned here. Oh, hey, are you all right continuing in English? We can speak German or Russian if you prefer."

I appreciate his consideration. "No, Colonel, I am perfectly comfortable with English. Thank you."

"Okay, well, it looks like you and the captain established a good rapport during your first meeting—is that your view?"

That is a reasonable question. "Yes, I think we did. He's young but seems very capable. He provided me with a lot of information about what our forces are doing in the forward area and elsewhere. It was quite illuminating."

The American nods approvingly. "Since you and Cattani met, General Palumbo has briefed General Flannery and General Rogers at NATO about the nuclear alert status of your forces. I understand that he has been able to convince our military leaders in Europe of the seriousness of the situation. We're alarmed that you have missile forces in the field that essentially are ready to launch at a moment's notice—very alarmed."

No kidding. "Yes, I am alarmed as well. We are on a 'hair trigger,' if that is the correct American expression."

"Yes, it is."

"Tell me, Colonel Laroche, has General Palumbo had any luck persuading the White House to not include President Reagan in the Able Archer exercise?"

Laroche shakes his head. "I have no idea. Cattani may have an answer for you. I simply don't know."

The American gets up from his chair and tells me. "I'm going to have my men call Cattani's vehicle. They should have arrived by now. Please excuse me for a moment."

"Yes, of course, Colonel."

I eat a Saxon Prasselkuchen pastry while Laroche is out of the room. He returns about five minutes later and looks quite worried.

"Colonel, we are getting no response from the radio in Cattani's vehicle. This is very unusual. They should have cleared the Glienicke Bridge some time ago. I can't imagine that they would have been detained there, and the fact that they are not answering the radio is very troubling."

"Colonel LaRoche, do you think something has happened to them—like an accident?"

Laroche grimaces. "Well, if something has happened, it wasn't an accident. Who else from your side knew about this meeting—I mean who else in Potsdam?"

"Who else in Potsdam? Why, no one. No one else in East Germany knows about the meeting—or at least, they shouldn't have known."

Laroche muses about his next move. "All right, I think it's time to call the local hospital. Stay here and I'll be back."

Holy Christ! Call the hospital? I get up and start pacing around the room.

The American colonel has been gone for another ten minutes or so when I hear a car screech to a halt on the driveway in front of Potsdam House. I run to the window and see an East German police car. Two policemen climb out and knock on the front door. I can't see if they are admitted into the house.

Minutes pass by slowly. Suddenly, I hear the police car's doors slam. It pulls away. A moment later, Colonel LaRoche opens the door to the conference room. He looks deeply upset. "The police told me that two Americans were in an accident. They are at the local hospital."

"Good God, Colonel, is Cattani all right?"

"I don't know. The police said there were only two men in the vehicle. They also told me that the driver is dead. He's in the hospital's morgue. Major Stablinski is hurt but alive. I told Chief Jackson to take a driver and go immediately to the hospital and get Stablinski and bring him here—provided it is safe to move him. The chief is the man who escorted you to the conference room earlier. He was an Air Force PJ in Vietnam—a para-rescue jumper—and will be able to ascertain Stablinski's condition."

Jesus . . . "Colonel LaRoche, I'm sorry about your men. What of Cattani? You said there were two men in the vehicle. Where is Cattani?"

Laroche shrugs. "Well, the East German police told me that a shopkeeper called for an ambulance. By the time the ambulance arrived, there were only two men in the car. The police don't know where Cattani is, and I believe them."

"My God. Colonel, what do you think? Where could he be?"

"Colonel Levchenko, I'm thinking that the Soviets have him—your people have him. And that your guys caused the accident, and they took Cattani from the vehicle and left Stablinski and our driver for dead. That's what I think. What do you think?" He squints at me with menace. I'm reminded of Clint Eastwood's stare from his Western movies.

Goddamn it. Fucking idiots. "Sir, I can assure you that I don't know anything. No one in Potsdam was supposed to know about this meeting. Nonetheless, I think that the GRU—the local idiots—must have had suspicions about this vehicle and they took it upon themselves to ram it and take Cattani for questioning. Has anything like this happened before to your MLM men?"

LaRoche sets his jaw. "Yes, it *has* happened before. The MLM guys get harassed frequently—not every day and not every week—but frequently enough. Ramming our vehicles is a popular Soviet tactic. So is detaining our guys for questioning and beatings. The allied MLM teams in East Germany don't get the kid-glove treatment that you got when you were assigned to the Soviet MLM in Frankfurt. It's an entirely different ball game on this side of the Wall. Your friends haven't killed anyone before today, but yeah, occasionally they ram our vehicles and take our guys away and beat them. It happened to me seven years ago. But they never killed one of my men before."

What a royal fuckup! Jesus . . . this could wreck everything.

"Colonel LaRoche, I'm very sorry this has happened. I've heard stories—rumors—about rough treatment on this side of the Wall, but I honestly had no idea it was this bad. We need to get Cattani back immediately—before they do any more damage to him." I walk around the table and step right up to LaRoche's fuming face. "I don't know for certain where he is; however, I have a pretty good, goddamn idea where they took him."

Saturday, 5 November 1983—Afternoon

Shortly after noon, an Army sergeant brings me a tray with a sandwich, salad, and a can of Coca-Cola for lunch. His timing is impeccable. I'm famished.

After I eat lunch, the conference room door opens, and Colonel LaRoche rushes in with Chief Jackson beside him. LaRoche says, "Colonel Levchenko, we've made arrangements for the body of our driver to be transported back to the MLM station in Berlin. Major Stablinski is resting temporarily in one of our bedrooms here, and the chief believes he is stable, and we can move him in the next day or two. Now, I need your help. I want you to take me to where you think they are detaining Cattani. Will you do that, Colonel?"

Chief Jackson must have brought the injured Major Stablinski in through the back door of the building because I saw no one enter the front. "Yes, Colonel, I will do all that I can. I'm angry that this has happened—it's awful, especially at this fraught time."

LaRoche says, "Colonel Levchenko, let's saddle up."

Saturday, 5 November 1983—Late Afternoon

I climb into the back seat of the Americans' vehicle, behind Colonel LaRoche. Chief Jackson is driving. I direct him to drive toward the Glienicke Bridge. About one kilometer from the bridge, we arrive at a roundabout, and I direct the chief to take the second exit. There is debris from a traffic accident strewn about the road on one side of the roundabout. I see Jackson and LaRoche exchange a knowing glance in the front seat.

We drive for another three kilometers, and I tell the chief to stop in front of a drab, unmarked two-story building. I was here years ago for a covert meeting. I'm thankful that my excellent memory for direction and landmarks hasn't deserted me today.

We confer briefly. "Colonel LaRoche, I think I should go in alone.

The sudden appearance of an American colonel will cause a panic. Agree?"

"All right, Colonel Levchenko. Is it safe for you to go in alone?"

I really don't know if it is safe for any of us. "If I'm not out in fifteen minutes, you should try to gain entry. Are you armed?"

"Chief, please tell me there are weapons in the trunk. Christ, I was in such a hurry I forgot to check."

"Sir, yes, we're good."

"Thank God. Okay, Levchenko, you have fifteen minutes."

LaRoche shows me the time on his watch face, and I double-check my watch to ensure the time matches his. I climb out of the vehicle and go to the front door. I press the button on the intercom box, identify myself, and get into a protracted back-and-forth with the disembodied voice on the other end. I turn around and look at LaRoche and Jackson waiting in the car. Finally, in exasperation, I yell a direct order to open the goddamn door.

The door lock buzzes, and I push it open to find my intercom antagonist sitting at a desk—a weary-looking, disheveled warrant officer.

"I am Colonel Levchenko from the Moscow Air Defense District. Here are my credentials. You see that I am a GRU colonel, and I am now the senior officer on the scene. I believe you have detained an American officer. You have no business keeping this officer in your custody. I order you to release him to me. Get the prisoner and your commanding officer out here immediately!"

The warrant officer gives me an insolent shrug and picks up the phone. He conveys my message to whoever is on the other end of the line. He hangs up the phone and motions for me to take a seat.

"No, I will not take a seat. Get your commanding officer out here now!"

I observe that there is a video screen on the front desk on which Laroche's vehicle is visible. I point to it. "See that vehicle? There is an American MLM colonel in that car. If I don't leave here in five minutes with the prisoner in my custody, then that American and his sergeant will break down your front door. They won't be as polite as I am."

The warrant officer doesn't respond, but he picks up the phone again. He has a brief conversation in a hushed voice. A few minutes later, the inner door buzzes open and a GRU major walks through it. The major extends his hand, which I refuse.

"Major, do you have an American captain in your custody? If so, I demand his immediate release."

"Colonel, you have no authority here. If we have a prisoner, then it is none of your business. Tell me, why have you brought Americans to our facility? That is a severe security breach."

"Listen, you idiot. The captain you seized was traveling to an extremely important meeting with me at the Potsdam House. Your thugs crashed into his vehicle. You killed an American sergeant, you moron! You killed an American MLM sergeant! Do you have any idea how strained relations are with the Americans right now? Fucking moron! Get the American officer out here immediately!"

As I finish my tirade, there is a heavy pounding at the front door. I look at my watch. My fifteen minutes are up and LaRoche is at the front door.

The warrant officer and major look at each other.

The desk officer exclaims, "Comrade Major, there are two Americans at the front door, and they are armed with M16s."

I yell at the major. "Get me your fucking prisoner, you idiot, and open the door for the Americans, now!"

The warrant officer buzzes the front door open, and the two Americans rush in with weapons at the ready.

I try to calm the situation. "Colonel LaRoche, please lower your weapon. This major was just about to produce Captain Cattani for me, weren't you, Major?"

The major stumbles on his words. "But, Colonel, this is highly irregular. I have no way to simply release someone to you."

Colonel LaRoche responds for me in Russian, "Look, you idiot, get my captain out here right now. You killed one of my men, you motherfucker. You have already created one major international incident. Get my captain right now, or I will blow your fucking head off!"

In typical Soviet fashion, the major responds like a bureaucrat. "Well, this is most irregular. Someone will need to sign paperwork for me to release this American to you."

I turn to the hapless warrant officer and pick up a pad and pen from his desk. I scribble out a "hand receipt" taking responsibility for the "prisoner," sign and date it, and hand it to the major. "Here is your fucking paperwork. Now, get me the American, now!"

LaRoche takes a couple of steps forward and stands next to me. He levels his rifle at the major's midsection. The major turns and enters a code to gain entry through the inner door. He disappears behind the door, which closes with a heavy thud.

LaRoche elbows my ribs—not gently. "I'll give him five minutes to give us Cattani."

I nod. My head is nearly exploding from the tension and the rage that I'm feeling.

Suddenly, the inner door pops open. A junior enlisted soldier helps Cattani through the narrow opening. The tall, trim American has dried blood in his auburn hair. His handsome face is bruised, and he is holding one arm close to his ribs, indicating that he has a broken collarbone or ribs.

Chief Jackson steps forward and takes control of the young captain. He helps Cattani sit down and begins to perform a quick triage of his condition. The GRU major does not reappear.

I lean over the desk and command the warrant officer. "Give me the major's information. I need his full name and serial number. If you refuse, then I will have you arrested."

Alarmed, the warrant officer quickly jots down the requested information on a notepad and hands it to me.

I peruse the note and tell the warrant officer. "Tell your major that this matter is not finished. I will ensure that there is an investigation conducted from the highest levels of the GRU. Your major killed an

American MLM member, nearly killed another, and kidnapped a third. This is a catastrophe. Do you understand?"

The warrant officer nods solemnly.

"Colonel LaRoche, is Captain Cattani well enough to travel back to the Potsdam House?"

LaRoche asks Chief Jackson, "What do you think, Chief?"

Jackson, who's been crouched over Cattani, stands up to his full height and replies, "Sirs, yes, I think that he can travel. We will have to take it easy. It's pretty clear that he has a concussion and broken ribs."

LaRoche lowers his M16. "Okay, let's get the hell out of here."

Saturday, 5 November 1983—Early Evening

Once again, I'm sitting alone in the second-floor conference room at Potsdam House. Today's events are swirling in my mind. Just twelve hours ago, Chief Jackson calmly poured me a cup of tea in this very room. Now, he's tending to two injured American officers in rooms just down the hallway.

The conference room door opens, and Colonel LaRoche enters. "Colonel Levchenko, the chief thinks that Cattani is stable and that you can talk to him now if you are ready."

"Yes, Colonel LaRoche, I'm ready to talk to him. What's his condition?"

"The chief tells me that he's concussed and has several broken ribs, and he may have a broken collarbone. He has no broken bones in his face, just bad bruising. He's a lot better off than Stablinski, who has broken ribs, a broken arm, and possibly internal injuries. The chief also thinks Stablinski's left knee is probably broken. We want to move them both by ambulance to Berlin in the morning. Then we'll fly them to either Rhein-Main or Ramstein for further treatment."

"Colonel, please accept my apologies on behalf of the GRU for this outrage, especially for the death of your young sergeant."

LaRoche simply nods in acknowledgment.

We go to the bedroom where Chief Jackson has placed Cattani. The chief has rigged an IV and he has the captain's head elevated on a couple of pillows. Cattani's face is badly bruised.

I approach gingerly. "Captain Cattani, I am the GRU colonel who met you here a few days ago. Are you well enough to talk?"

The young man stirs and opens his eyes. "Hello, Colonel, yes, I can talk a bit. Need to keep it short, though."

"Yes, of course, Captain. I'll start with my most important question. Has General Palumbo convinced the White House—the national security advisor—to ask President Reagan not to participate in Able Archer?"

LaRoche leans closer to the captain to hear his answer.

"Yes, Colonel. I don't know the particulars, but General Palumbo told me before I left Ramstein that Mr. McFarlane—he's the national security advisor—convinced President Reagan to stand down. President Reagan agreed immediately. He understood how provocative his participation in Able Archer might be. The White House also asked Mrs. Thatcher to stand down from Able Archer. My understanding is that she agreed, as well. And both leaders will have public appearances on 8 November to demonstrate a 'business as usual' attitude. That is the date Able Archer reaches its climax— you know, the nuclear release phase."

I breathe a huge sigh of relief. "Captain, that is outstanding news. I'm relieved. Thank you. So, the exercise will continue to its conclusion, but without the participation of the national command authorities from the US and the UK. That is your 'bottom line'—correct?"

"Yes, Colonel, that is correct."

I lock eyes with LaRoche, who gives me a thumbs-up sign.

Cattani sits up higher on the bed. "Colonel, what news do you have? Is your leadership prepared to take units off nuclear alert?"

I wish I had better news for the Americans, especially, after today's terrible events. "Not yet, my friend. Not yet. However, I was told that if President Reagan and Mrs. Thatcher stand down, then that will be viewed as a very positive step. You see, Marshal Ogarkov himself is standing firm on our nuclear alert status. I'm not privy to such discussions, of course, but my understanding is that he has convinced Minister of Defense Ustinov and General Secretary Andropov that the alert is needed so long as Able Archer is underway."

Both Americans are silent as they take in my news, which is not what they had hoped to hear, nor what I had hoped to report. "Gentlemen, I know this is not the best news. Let me suggest the following plan: I will return to Moscow tonight. In the morning I'll report to my superiors. I will recommend the three of us meet here again on 8 November and that I remain overnight through the ninth. I hope that this will build confidence on both sides. I'll bring special radio equipment that will connect me with decisionmakers in Moscow. But you have to promise not to take my radio and exploit it for intelligence purposes."

The two Americans look at each other and smile at my last statement.

Colonel LaRoche then says, "I agree. We will have to see if Cattani is well enough to come back here that quickly. Otherwise, I think it's a good plan. Kevin, I'll go with you tomorrow. I'll need to brief General Palumbo on this plan."

The American colonel looks me hard in the eye. "Colonel Levchenko, I think you had better get going if you are flying to Moscow tonight."

I lean over Cattani so that he can hear me clearly. "Captain, I'm terribly sorry for what happened to you and your team today. Please accept my apologies."

The young man lifts his hand up to shake mine.

Chief Jackson walks back in the room, nods at me, and then at the patient. "Captain Cattani, we'll be moving you to Ramstein tomorrow. I just confirmed it. My daughter is a trauma nurse at the Landstuhl hospital, right near Ramstein. I just called her and told her that we have one of our own coming her way tomorrow. She knows what that means. I ordered her to look in on you and report back to me. She's a captain now, but her father still outranks her!"

Cattani smiles weakly. "Thank you, Chief. I'm sure I'll be in good hands."

I say my farewells to Chief Jackson and Cattani and go downstairs with LaRoche.

He shakes my hand. "Levchenko, thank you for your help today. I don't know what those clowns would have done to Cattani if you hadn't intervened. I realize you were in a tough spot, having to take us to a covert GRU site."

"Colonel, I'm very sorry about your sergeant who was killed. Today's incident will be investigated with great vigor if I have any say about it."

We exchange goodbyes and I walk to my car. On the drive to the airfield, I think of Boyka. This crisis has taken me away from her just as she was beginning to settle into her life in Moscow. I hate to leave her alone for even one day. I'll wake her up when I get home. It'll be early in the morning, but I must let her know that I need her continued patience for just a few more days. Each moment is precious with her when we may only have a few more days to live.

It's now clear that we are reaching the climax of this crisis. NATO plans to exercise its nuclear weapons release processes on the eighth and ninth of November. If we can just get through those two days without miscalculation, then the world may yet survive this insanity.

CHAPTER SEVENTEEN

YOU OWE ME
A DINNER

*Captain Kevin Cattani, United States Air Force, Landstuhl Military
Medical Center, Federal Republic of Germany
(West Germany)*

Sunday, 6 November 1983—Morning

My memory is hazy from the time I departed Potsdam House until I arrived at the medical center at Landstuhl, West Germany. In and out of consciousness, I did my best to remain still and silent during the transfers from ambulance to ambulance, and ambulance to aircraft to ambulance. Apart from excruciating periods of extreme cold, I was relatively comfortable as medical personnel moved me from one conveyance to another until I finally arrived at the hospital bed in which I now lie.

I'm half-dozing when someone enters the room. There has been a constant parade of medical people in and out of my room. I feel the blood pressure sleeve inflate on my left arm. This rouses me from my dreamy state. A nurse is checking my vitals again.

Involuntarily, I emit a long, deep sigh.

Then I hear the nurse speak. "Well, Captain Cattani, that's an impressive sigh. I guess your lungs are clear. How are your ribs feeling?"

I still have my eyes closed when I answer. "The ribs are sore. My head hurts—that's the worst thing. How is Major Stablinski? And the sergeant who drove us—I can't remember his name—how is he?"

She adjusts my bed and blankets and responds, "The major is in a room a few doors down. He has some broken bones, a bad concussion—worse than yours—and a subdural hematoma. They are monitoring his condition to determine if he needs surgery to relieve pressure on his brain."

This news wakes me up. "Jesus. What do you know about the sergeant?"

She finishes fussing with my bed. "I've heard nothing about him. I don't know—he might be in another part of the hospital. Sorry, I just don't know."

"Okay. Okay, thanks. Can you help me sit up? Can you raise the bed, please?"

I sense that she is smiling. "Sure, Captain, just say when."

My back folds as she raises the bed. "Yeah, that feels good right there. Thanks."

The nurse stands by my bed. "My father ordered me to check in on you. I can't disobey a direct order from my father."

I open my eyes to see an unexpected, familiar face. "Sandy! You're Chief Jackson's daughter? He's my hero." God, even in my state, I know that sounds idiotic.

"Yes, he's my hero, too," she laughs. "Is there anything else I can do for you, Kevin?"

"My God, Sandy, this is incredible. I can't believe it's you. I thought I'd never see you again."

"Well, I hope that it is a pleasant surprise to see me and not a scene from one of your nightmares."

I blush a deep red—I can feel the warmth crawl up my face. "It's a very pleasant surprise. I've missed you." Christ, I immediately regret saying that. She will think I am a real—a real—I don't know what.

Sandy leans down close to my face. "I'm glad that you're happy to see me. I'm happy to see you, too. Look, I have other patients to check on, but I just started my shift, so you will see me again this evening."

She leaves my room and I feel deflated. I'm surprised at the effect Sandy has on me. I don't know what to make of it, but I do remember how awful I felt that early morning at Yokota when she closed the door silently and left me alone.

Sunday, 6 November 1983—Early Afternoon

Someone is gently shaking me awake. It's Sandy.

"Kevin, I need to take your vitals again. There's an officer here from the OSI who wants to talk to you about the accident you had in Potsdam." OSI is the Office of Special Investigations—the Air Force version of the FBI.

I stir and focus my eyes on Sandy as she takes my vitals. Over her shoulder, I see a man in a civilian suit standing in the doorway. He waits while Sandy finishes her work.

The OSI officer steps to my bed. "Captain, they tell me that you are well enough for me to ask you a few questions. Are you ready to talk about the accident?"

I sit up. "Yes, but I want Captain Jackson to stay with me. I'm still very weak. I want her to monitor my condition during the interview."

The OSI man clears his throat as he shows me his credentials. "Well, that is highly irregular, Captain. I don't think that's appropriate."

I tell him in a hoarse voice. "She stays, or there's no interview."

He pulls out a notebook and pen, and nods at Sandy. "All right, all right, Captain, tell me what happened that morning."

"Sandy, can I have some water, please?"

She hands me the water cup and I take a long draw on the straw.

From his credentials, I know that the OSI man is a major. "All right, Major, we were stopped at the Soviet checkpoint on the Glienicke

Bridge. We also were stopped the first time I went across with Major Stablinski a few days ago. The same warrant officer we encountered on the first crossing questioned us about our plans for the day. Stablinski told him we were simply going to a meeting at Potsdam House. It seemed routine, but I guess it wasn't."

The OSI man interrupts. "Wait, it was the same warrant officer that stopped you both times?"

"Yes, the same guy stopped us both times. He has a huge mustache—like you see in paintings of soldiers from the Napoleonic Wars—unmistakable. Anyway, we were waved through, and everything seemed normal until we got to a roundabout. As we were beginning to exit the circle, a truck crossed into our lane and hit us head-on. The impact was mostly on the driver's side. I guess I was knocked out. I remember opening my eyes and seeing that our driver was crushed against the steering wheel in front of me. I couldn't really see Major Stablinski from where I was in the back seat. I think I passed out again, and then I felt someone grabbing my arms and shoulders. Somebody pulled me out of the car and carried me to another vehicle. I think they threw me in the back seat, but I passed out again, so I can't be certain."

The OSI major looks up from his notepad. "I see, and you don't know what happened to your driver or Major Stablinski?"

I nod. "Captain Jackson tells me that Stablinski is here at Landstuhl, but I don't know about the guy who was driving."

He clears his throat again. "Yes, well, Captain, I am sorry to have to tell you this—but your driver was killed upon impact. He's dead. The MLM retrieved his body, and it will be repatriated."

Sandy gasps.

The driver was killed. Well, that explains why Sandy didn't know his condition or whereabouts. Motherfucking Soviets.

The OSI officer continues, "Do you know who grabbed you? Can you identify them?"

"No, I don't know who took me. I was really dopey at that point."

The OSI guy is writing furiously in his notepad. "Well, where did they take you? Could you recognize landmarks?"

There's really nothing to recall. "No. If I were a regular MLM guy—you know, in the MLM—I might've recognized where we went, but maybe not, since I was so out of it."

The major ponders my response for a moment. "Okay. Once you reached your destination. What happened?"

I'm getting very tired but respond. "They took me into a room through a vault door. They put me in a chair and tied my wrists to the arms of the chair. They interrogated me about my mission."

"Captain, did they beat you? When you were in that chair?"

"They punched me in the face a few times. If that counts as a beating, then, yeah."

Pausing to make some notes, he lowers his voice to a gentler tone. "We're almost finished. I know you're tired. Did they question you in Russian? What did you tell them?"

I rub my eyes hard and yawn. "Yes, in Russian. They spoke Russian. I told them to go fuck themselves. I told them that my mission was way above their pay grades and that they were making a big mistake detaining me. I passed out a couple of times. They seemed confused— you know, like they didn't really know what they were doing."

The major stares at me. "You told them nothing. Mmm. Okay. How did you get away?"

I look up at the OSI major. "I think you must know already that Colonel LaRoche and Chief Jackson got me out. I don't know much more. I think you should interview Colonel LaRoche. He flew with me to Ramstein. Can we stop now?"

He closes his notepad. "Yes, we can stop. Thank you for your cooperation. I may need to talk to you again. Okay?"

I wave a weak goodbye to the major. He puts on his overcoat and walks out of the room.

Sandy walks to the side of the bed and leans over. "Can I get you anything, Kevin? Your story about the accident is unbelievable. I mean, I believe it, but the whole thing sounds crazy. Your driver was killed! My God. What a terrible thing you've been through."

I'm quickly falling asleep. Her voice is like warm honey to me. "Thanks, Sandy. Thank you."

Sunday, 6 November 1983—Evening

I'm supposed to be back in Potsdam tomorrow. Able Archer reaches its climax in the next few days with the weapons release protocols. Can I travel? I still feel awful.

A doctor examines me. He's satisfied with my progress and tells me that I will have to stay in the hospital for another two days or so.

"Yeah, well, that's not possible, Doctor. I have to be in Berlin tomorrow. When will you discharge me?"

The nonplussed doc responds, "Tomorrow? That is impossible. You shouldn't fly for a while anyway. You'd have to take the train, but even that is preposterous. No, you need to stay in the hospital."

I sit up. "Doctor, I appreciate all you have done for me. But if flying is so dangerous for me, then why was I flown from Berlin to Ramstein?"

He adjusts his glasses and says, "That was an emergency. We needed to get you to a qualified medical facility by the fastest possible means. It's not an emergency for you to travel to Berlin tomorrow."

I smile wanly. "Actually, it is an emergency. I need to be in Berlin tomorrow. I am asking you to help facilitate that."

The doctor is unmoved. He is used to dealing with strong-willed military officers. "Impossible. Not going to happen."

I'm about to respond when two officers walk into my room— General Flannery and General Palumbo. The Army doctor looks at them with narrow-eyed suspicion.

Flannery speaks first. "Babes, you don't look so bad for someone who just got beaten up by the Russians. How are you feeling?"

I sit up straighter in the bed. "Sir, I was just explaining to the nice doctor here that I'm much better and that I must travel tomorrow to Berlin. He doesn't agree."

The doctor, a lieutenant colonel, is not cowed. "General Flannery, good morning, sir. This man is not well enough to take such a trip. He has a bad concussion, three broken ribs, and numerous contusions. It is not medically feasible for him to go to Berlin tomorrow."

Flannery smiles and puts his arm around the doctor. "I'm sure you're right, Doctor. In most cases and under normal circumstances, I'd agree with you. However, we aren't dealing with normal circumstances. This young captain has a date tomorrow in Potsdam, and he means to keep it. Isn't that right, Kevin?"

I nod and both generals grab chairs and sit down next to my bed.

General Flannery looks up at the doctor. "Colonel, thank you for everything you are doing. General Palumbo and I need to talk to the captain, here, in private. Can you please excuse us for a few minutes?"

The doctor knows he is outgunned. "Yes, sir, but please don't get him too excited. He needs to rest."

Flannery grins at him. "You got it, Doctor."

The doctor hurries out of the room.

Flannery immediately gets serious. "Kevin, you understand the gravity of the situation, so I won't belabor it. We need the Soviets to take tangible action to stand down their nuclear forces. We need indicators this is happening—indicators we can observe with certainty. As you know, President Reagan has canceled his participation in the exercise, but we have seen no reciprocal actions on the part of the Soviets. If anything, we've seen more provocative activity in the forward area in the last couple of days. Lenny here tells me we have indications that some of their regular army units in East Germany have deployed to the field. Their troops have been issued full ammunition loads and two weeks of rations. This is alarming. Anyway, we need them to show good faith. We need some strong indication that they are standing down—especially their missile units in East Germany and Poland. You must get your GRU colonel to commit to tangible action.

This is coming directly from General Rogers and our NATO allies. The secretary of defense is not happy that the President has dropped out of the exercise. Others in Washington want General Rogers and me to step up the alert status of the nuclear forces in NATO. Lenny has convinced me that doing so might push the Soviets over the edge. General Palumbo has been the strongest voice in Europe for a nonconfrontational approach on this deal. I believe he's right, but we need the Soviets to show us something."

He pauses and looks at General Palumbo. "Lenny, did I miss anything? What else does the captain need to know?"

"Thanks, General Flannery, I think you covered it well. Kevin, let me reinforce that we need something from Moscow—some specific action or message from their senior leadership. If Levchenko brings comm gear with him to the Potsdam House, like he has planned, we need assurance that he will have a direct link to Ogarkov. I don't think anything short of that will do. Capiche?"

I take a deep breath and exhale. "Yes, General Palumbo, I understand. But there is no way for us to get a message to Colonel Levchenko in advance of our meeting. We will have to rely on him to have made those arrangements."

General Palumbo looks at Flannery. "He's right. We have no way of communicating with them in advance. This is really frustrating."

Flannery responds, "Well, what about the hotline in the White House? I know we can't communicate with Levchenko that way, but we can get a message to the Kremlin—right? The White House set up the hotline after the Cuban Missile Crisis. Why the hell aren't we using it now?"

Palumbo replies excitedly, "Because Washington and Moscow aren't talking now. At least we were talking during the Cuba thing. The Kremlin is refusing to use the hotline. No, Levchenko is our only hope. He's a smart cookie. I just hope he has the cajones to go toe-to-toe with the big shots in Moscow."

Flannery shakes his head and looks at me. "Ok, babes. You're it. You gotta make it happen."

Palumbo interjects. "I'll send Colonel LaRoche back to Potsdam with you, okay? He can be a big help. He knows how the Soviets think better than anybody I know."

I nod vigorously, which makes my head hurt like hell. "Yes, sir, and Levchenko respects him, too."

Palumbo smiles. "Levchenko is savvy. He understands the stakes and he has navigated the swamp in Moscow well so far. I think he's the best guy we could ask for on the other side to help fix this thing."

Flannery stands up. "Well, good. Kevin, you and Colonel LaRoche are a good team. I am going to call you guys our 'able archers.' What do you think of that?"

I smile—able archers! "That sounds good General—I like the name. We should include our GRU man, Colonel Levchenko—he's an 'able archer', too."

Flannery agrees. "Yep, he is integral to the team, isn't he? Well, we need to let you sleep, young man."

Sandy walks into the room and sees the two generals sitting around my bed. "Gentlemen, please. Let this man get some rest. Please."

General Flannery takes a look at Sandy, and winks at me and says, "Yes, Captain-nurse, we were just leaving. See that he is well taken care of. That's a request, not an order."

Sandy smirks. "All right, General Flannery, I have this situation under control."

Flannery puts up his palms in a pose of surrender. "Okay, ma'am, I am leaving. Just get him well enough to go to Potsdam tomorrow. He has a rendezvous with destiny there—don't you, babes? Okay, come on, Lenny, let's go see your Major Stablinski."

The generals leave me alone with Sandy.

She whispers to me. "Kevin, you need to get some rest after all that excitement. I guess you have friends in high places, eh, Captain?"

My head is pounding, and I'm very uncomfortable again, but I manage a grin. "Yes, they were very kind to visit. I don't know Palumbo well; it was nice of him to drop by. I kinda expected Flannery."

Sandy is wide-eyed. "So you *expected* the top Air Force general in Europe to visit you? You are awfully full of yourself, Captain."

I blush red again and screw up my courage. It's now or never. "Sandy, I really have missed you. I feel like seeing you again—after not expecting to ever see you again—has given me a second chance. Can I take you to dinner after this is all over? Please?"

Her face has a seriousness about it that I've never seen before. "Kevin, are you sure? I mean, you're a handsome guy, and it's obvious that you are going places in the Air Force, provided you don't blow up the planet in the next few days." She pauses. "Look at me. You could have any blue-eyed blonde you want. My father is black, and my mother is half-Ainu for Christ's sake. She's had a hard time with bigotry in Japan because of it—that's why she prefers living here in Germany. I don't fit in Japan or Germany or the States. I just don't know what to tell you."

I'm shocked by this admission. To me, Sandy is the most beautiful and exotic woman I've ever seen. She's accomplished and smart and funny. How can she see herself so differently?

I reach for her hand. "Please give me another chance. Please."

She takes my hand. "You're from southern Virginia. Aren't you supposed to be prejudiced against people like me?"

"Sandy, please?"

She squeezes my hand. "All right, Kevin. Why is it so important for you go to Potsdam? You should be in the hospital for a couple more days. What's so urgent?"

I squeeze her hand back. "You know about the KAL 007 shootdown a couple of months ago—right?"

She nods.

"Well, tensions with the Soviets have been ratcheting up since the shootdown. Their nuclear forces are on unprecedented alert status. The situation today is worse than the Cuban Missile Crisis. And I have a contact to meet in Potsdam who is trying to defuse things. Things are bad, and the next couple of days will be the most dangerous ones. I can't say more, but you get the picture."

"I had no idea. Nobody around here even knows about this. You're scaring the hell out of me."

"Not to be overly dramatic, but if the sun comes up on Wednesday morning, then you'll know we have deescalated this thing. I'm sorry to scare you, but this is really bad."

She squeezes my hand harder. "You're scaring me shitless. Just don't get yourself killed in Potsdam, or I will really be pissed off at you. You owe me a dinner, Captain."

CHAPTER EIGHTEEN

THE WHITE GAMBIT

Colonel Ivan Levchenko, GRU,
Soviet Air Defense Forces
Moscow, Russia, USSR

Sunday, 6 November 1983—Morning

I open the front door of our Moscow apartment. It's quiet. Checking the wall clock in the kitchen, I see that it is 5:10 AM—Moscow time, of course. I adjust the time on my wristwatch to match my new time zone. When I enter our bedroom, Boyka stirs and sits up in bed. Her golden hair covers the left side of her face.

I sit down on the bed beside her. "Good morning, my beautiful girl. I'm sorry to wake you so early."

She leans toward me so that I can kiss her lips. "Vanya, you must be exhausted. What time is it?" She glances at the alarm clock at the bedside. "Just after five. Did you get any sleep?"

"I dozed a little on the plane, but not much. I have to be at Air Defense headquarters at noon, so I don't have much time to rest."

She starts to untie my tie and unbutton my shirt. "Come to bed for a while. I want you. I need to hold you for a while before you go to sleep. Then you can sleep for a couple of hours—all right?"

This is exactly the homecoming I had dreamt of. "All right, my love."

I sleep afterwards. Boyka awakens me at 10:00 AM. I wash up and shave and dress in a fresh uniform. She serves tea, bread, and jam. We eat the modest breakfast together and have a refreshingly normal conversation.

Boyka is excited to inform me that she is playing her violin in a string quartet. She says that the musicians are top-notch, and they performed twice yesterday at two veterans' homes in the Moscow area. One of the homes is for men returning from the war in Afghanistan. The other is for older veterans, including many who saw service in the Great Patriotic War. The quartet plans to perform at veterans' facilities at least twice per week in the future. Boyka is especially thrilled to play for the young guys fresh from the fighting in Afghanistan. Many have terrible injuries, and many are deeply affected psychologically.

I'm happy that she's performing again, and I tell Boyka how proud I am of her for sharing her wonderful talent in such a meaningful way. As we are clearing the table after breakfast, Boyka grabs me by the arm. "Vanya tell me what's going on. How bad are things?"

I don't respond immediately, and she continues. "Should I leave Moscow and go to Kiev? Will it be safer there? I know you're involved in something very serious. You've gone to Germany how many times now?"

I stare at her beautiful eyes and contemplate what to tell her. "My love, things are not good. You know that tensions with the Americans—and all of NATO—have been growing worse since the Korean airliner was shot down. Believe me, Boyka, if I thought that going to Kiev would make you safer, I would drive you to the airport and put you on a plane this morning. But it won't. Nowhere is safe from what may come. That's why I must do what I can to help to deescalate the situation. That's what my mission is—to prevent a conflict—a war. I must return tomorrow to Potsdam for a few days. If we can get through the next few days, then we will be safe. Just a few more days, I promise."

There's a terrified look in her eyes. "I thought it must be bad, but
. . . this sounds like the end of the world. Can it be that we are so close
to the brink?"

I hug her tightly and kiss her hair. "We'll get through this. I'm
working with good people. I'll make my case today to the chief marshal
of aviation. You trust me to do everything I can to resolve this situation?"

"Vanya, of course I trust you. But I don't trust those blockheads
in the Kremlin. God knows what Reagan is capable of—but you need
to be careful. This is dangerous for you, too."

"I'll be careful. Forceful and careful—all right?"

Sunday, 6 November 1983—Noon

Marshal Konstantinov is in the waiting area of Chief Marshal
Koldunov's office when I arrive for the noon meeting. He greets me
warmly. The mistrust of a couple of months ago is gone. I'm part of
his team now and he treats me accordingly.

"Vanya, how do you like being the top dog, now that your boss
is retiring? Are you ready to take the job permanently?"

I'm shocked. Did the marshal just offer me the job as his chief
of intelligence? It's a one-star general's position. "Sir, I am honored
to serve you and the Moscow Air Defense District. If you believe
I'm ready to take this job on a permanent basis, then I will do it. I
believe I'm ready."

He smiles. "You realize this is a big promotion and must be
approved by Koldunov and the head of the GRU, but I'm confident
we can get those approvals."

What is the American expression? Ah, yes, I'm "floored" by the
marshal's statements.

A very tall, thin colonel approaches us. "Gentlemen, Chief
Marshal Koldunov will see you now."

I have not seen Chief Marshal of Aviation Koldunov since I
presented my findings on the Korean airliner shootdown back in
September. I remember vividly that he dismissed the notion that

the KAL crew may have committed a fatal navigational error. My sense of that meeting was that I failed to open his mind. How will he receive me today?

We enter Koldunov's grand office, and he rises from an easy chair to shake hands with Konstantinov. He approaches me and gives me a hug and kisses on both cheeks. Wow. What's going on?

"Colonel Levchenko, you've been a busy bee. Tell me of your discussions in Germany."

"Chief Marshal of Aviation Koldunov, it's an honor to see you again. Well, sir, the most important news I have is that the American national security advisor has convinced President Reagan *not* to participate in their exercise, Able Archer. And the White House has requested that Prime Minister Thatcher follow suit."

Koldunov looks pleased but guarded. "Gentlemen, that is very good news regarding Reagan. Nonetheless, I wonder if Mrs. Thatcher will comply? Will the 'iron lady' forgive President Reagan for invading Grenada? After all, Grenada is a member of the British Commonwealth, and the KGB in London tells me that Reagan failed to inform the British prime minister in advance that he was invading one of her countries!"

Konstantinov laughs out loud. "Maybe Reagan thought Grenada was a Hollywood movie set and not a member nation of the British Commonwealth!"

Koldunov smiles mischievously and continues. "Indeed. Mrs. Thatcher may not be in a forgiving mood. Tell me, Colonel, how will we know for certain that Reagan is not participating in the exercise?"

That is the central question, of course. "The Americans tell me that he is now departing earlier than planned on his trip to Japan on 8 November. He should be on television at Andrews Air Force Base as he departs for Tokyo. This means he can't go to the Pentagon for the final phase of Able Archer. He will *not* be at the Pentagon for the weapons release phase."

"Colonel, that's good, but you know that Air Force One is fully equipped to provide command and control of the Americans' nuclear forces and it is hardened to withstand nuclear fallout. Reagan can command the weapons release from Air Force One. He need not be in the Pentagon."

He's right, of course. I hadn't considered that eventuality. "Sir, then we need an additional signal from Reagan and Thatcher of their peaceful intent—that's your point—right?"

"Yes, Colonel. You see that Marshal Ogarkov will require a clear signal from the Americans and the British. Further, Marshal Ogarkov is unwilling to decrease our nuclear alert status. I'm sure that he'll be pleased with your news that the Americans have promised that Reagan won't participate, but he will need more than a promise. Colonel, what do you propose?"

I must think of something fast. "Chief Marshal Koldunov, as I said, we know that President Reagan will depart for Japan on 8 November. He'll board his Marine helicopter on the lawn just outside the White House. The American news agencies will cover his departure on live television. What if President Reagan were—I mean what if we were to ask—that he wear a white cowboy hat when he walks from the White House to the helicopter? This will be a public event and millions of people will watch his departure on television, especially now that the Americans have the new CNN news network. We know that he only wears a cowboy hat when he is at his ranch in California. It would be very unusual for him to do so in Washington. And Mrs. Thatcher has public appearances scheduled for the eighth. Perhaps we can ask that she wear a white suit in public. The color white will symbolize their peaceful intentions."

Both marshals look at each other. Konstantinov speaks. "That may be the craziest idea I ever have heard. A white cowboy hat - a white dress?"

I interrupt. "Sir, a dress or a suit—but most definitely white."

The two marshals exchange a glance.

Chief Marshal Koldunov says, "I agree that this idea sounds insane. But what else can we do? General Secretary Andropov won't use the 'hotline' and George Shultz won't give Minister Gromyko and Ambassador Dobrynin the time of day. There's zero communication happening at the highest levels. At least during the Cuban Crisis, Bobby Kennedy was talking to Dobrynin through a covert back-channel arrangement—at least the senior people were talking!"

Konstantinov interjects. "Do you think you can get them to agree? The Americans and the British—will they agree to this crazy idea?"

"Sir, I will do my best. Thus far, the Americans in Europe have done their part. They have been transparent and honest, as far as we know."

The chief marshal asks, "Konstantinov, what do you think? Shall we try this 'white hat' gambit?"

Konstantinov shrugs. "I can't conjure up a better plan. Let's see what Marshal Ogarkov says. Let me correct myself—let's see what Ogarkov says *after* he tells us that we are all insane!"

The chief marshal speaks again. "Colonel, you'll go with us this afternoon to brief Marshal of the Soviet Union Ogarkov. You can leave us now. Go to lunch in the general officers' mess down the hall. Meet me here again at 2:00 PM."

I'm dismissed. "Yes, Comrade Chief Marshal. I'll be here at 1400."

My head is spinning. First, Konstantinov tells me I may be promoted to one-star general. Then the chief marshal tells me to get lunch in the general officers' mess and he invites me—it was more of an order—to brief Ogarkov himself! I suppose that I'll remember this day as the day my career either soared or ended.

Sunday, 6 November 1983—Afternoon

I'm invited to ride to General Staff headquarters in the chief marshal's car. Marshal Konstantinov follows us in his staff car.

Koldunov wants to talk to me in the privacy of the back seat. "Tell me, Colonel, how old are you?"

"Sir, I am forty-four."

"I see. You will be quite young for a general if we promote you. We need to bring in new blood—younger men for this modern age.

You're well regarded at GRU headquarters, you know."

"That is gratifying to hear, sir."

"You have a reputation for hard work and taking on tough assignments without whining. Do you know that?"

"I have always thought it important to work hard, sir. I mean, what's the point if one doesn't put forth one's best effort?"

The chief marshal is quiet for a moment. "I will talk to the chief of the GRU about your promotion. But you must make this contact in Potsdam work. It has to work if we are to avoid a terrible outcome. Do you understand?"

"Sir, I do. I appreciate the gravity of this moment."

"Good. Good, Colonel, I'm sure you do. Tell me, who is your American contact?"

Oh, no. He won't react well if he knows my contact is a young captain. "Sir, my main contact is a junior officer; however, he is a confidant of General Flannery, the chief of all NATO air forces. He has Flannery's ear and was able to get the White House to keep Reagan from participating in Able Archer. I also have met with the senior Air Force officer in the American MLM. He is a very able man, too."

The chief marshal considers my response and mutters, "Well, I hope your young officer is up to the task."

We arrive at the General Staff headquarters building, characterized chiefly by its tall, square tower with large stars prominently displayed on all four sides. The three of us—all Air Defense Forces officers—gather in Marshal of the Soviet Union Ogarkov's palatial outer office. The chief of the GRU—General of the Army Pyotr Ivashutin, known to all in the intelligence service as "Peter the Great"—arrives and joins us. He shakes my hand warmly. It seems I am a pledge in an exclusive club. He asks to talk to me privately and guides me to a corner of the large anteroom. "Colonel, what do you know about an incident with the American MLM? The Americans issued a demarche, claiming that we killed one of their men and injured two more. Is this true?"

"Yes, General Ivashutin, I can confirm the story. I personally saw one of the injured men. In fact, he is my main contact on the American side regarding Able Archer. We're damn lucky the GRU station in Potsdam didn't kill him."

"Damn it! Do you know who runs our Potsdam station?"

"Yes, General, I met him when I retrieved my American contact from GRU custody. I have the Potsdam GRU officer's full name and serial number here in my pocket." I hand the handwritten note to the GRU chief. "Not only did this guy's goons ram the MLM vehicle, killing the American driver, they kidnapped my contact, took him to the covert site, beat him, and tried to get him to talk about our interactions."

The general looks at the piece of paper I just handed him. "All right, we will deal with this major in Potsdam. Fucking Christ." He is spitting mad.

When we enter the inner sanctum, Marshal Ogarkov is seated at a large desk with his back to the tall windows of his enormous office. He looks up and greets us brusquely.

Koldunov opens the conversation. "Sir, we have brought along Colonel Levchenko. He is the GRU man who has been meeting with the Americans in Potsdam."

Ogarkov looks at me and nods.

That is my cue. "Good day. I've met three times with the Americans—once in Frankfurt and twice in Potsdam at their facility. They have worked with the White House to gain President Reagan's agreement not to participate in NATO's Able Archer exercise. Further, they have requested the same of Prime Minister Thatcher."

Ogarkov looks at me blankly. "What assurances do we have? Anything beyond promises?"

"Sir, I'm told that President Reagan readily agreed to stand down, even though some of his most senior officials disagreed."

Chief Marshal Koldunov tries to help me. "Marshal Ogarkov, we understand that it would be helpful to have some kind of additional signal from the President and the prime minister. President Reagan is departing Washington on 8 November for a trip to Japan and Korea. He will be in the air when Able Archer reaches the weapons-release phase."

Ogarkov mulls over that information. "Reagan can still issue launch orders from Air Force One—that's what the plane is built to do. I'm not reassured."

The chief marshal responds, "Yes, sir, I understand. Is it possible to reopen the 'hotline' communication with the White House? It was established after the Cuban Missile Crisis for just this kind of situation—to enable the general secretary to talk directly with the American President."

Ogarkov lets Koldunov finish and says an abrupt "No. The general secretary doesn't trust the current US President. He will not communicate directly with him. You also may know that the general secretary is in hospital and his health is . . . deteriorating."

I keep my mouth shut while the elephants in the room dance with each other.

Konstantinov pipes into the conversation. "Comrades, the only viable communication link we have is through Potsdam. What assurances can we obtain from the Americans and the British that will be satisfactory to the general secretary? Levchenko here is flying back to Berlin tonight to meet again at the Potsdam House with the Americans."

Christ, I thought I was flying to Berlin tomorrow, but no matter.

Ogarkov sits back in his chair and sighs. "We're faced with a most dangerous situation. The information I am about to tell you cannot leave this room. Do you all understand?"

The four of us nod.

Ogarkov continues. "All right. Here it is. The general secretary is ill. He's restricted to the Kuntsevo Clinic. He goes to sleep each night with the 'chegget'—the device containing our nuclear launch codes— next to him in the bed. He has his senior military assistant sleeping in the hospital room with him. The general secretary may be dying, and he has the chegget on his chest at night. Do you understand what this means? Do you all get my meaning?"

Everyone in the room knows what this could mean.

"Comrades, I need to be able to give the general secretary more than assurances from the MLM. Any ideas?"

Everyone looks to me to answer the Marshal of the Soviet Union.

I clear my throat. "Marshal Ogarkov, one thought is to ask President Reagan to show us a sign of peaceful intent."

Ogarkov stares at me unblinking. "Like what? What kind of sign?"

I doubt I will get promoted to general officer after I say what I must. "Marshal, we could ask that President Reagan do something unusual—something that the television cameras will see."

"Like what?"

"Marshal, as you know, he is flying to Japan—leaving Washington on 8 November. His departure will be televised. Reagan will walk across the lawn of the White House to his US Marine Corps helicopter. He likes to stop and wave to the press. Sometimes he will take their questions. In any event, during those moments, he will be very visible."

"Colonel, I know all that. What is the sign?"

"Well, Comrade Marshal, the thought is that he would wear a white cowboy hat when he walks to the helicopter. He never wears a cowboy hat in Washington—he only wears his cowboy hat at his ranch in California."

Ogarkov looks at me like I'm crazy. "Colonel, are you serious? You are willing to bet the security of the USSR on whether the President of the United States wears a Stetson hat or not? This is insane!"

To his great credit, Koldunov doesn't let me hang alone. "Marshal Ogarkov, we can think of no other way. If the general secretary won't use the hotline, what can we do? We have no channel except through the American MLM. The Foreign Ministry isn't talking to the US State Department. Foreign Minister Gromyko has been shunned every time he tries to talk to Secretary of State Shultz. I know this tactic sounds crazy, but what else can we do?"

Ogarkov's face is red. "And what of Mrs. Thatcher, Chief Marshal? Is she to wear a white tiara on her head the entire day of 8 November?

I cannot take this crazy idea to Defense Minister Ustinov! He will have me committed to an insane asylum!"

Everyone goes silent.

Finally, Chief Marshal of Aviation Koldunov breaks the silence. "Comrade Marshal, the Americans already have told us that Reagan won't participate in Able Archer. The GRU is reporting that the American President readily agreed to stand down. It seems apparent that Reagan doesn't want to worsen the current confrontation. Surely that means something. If he wears a white hat to reassure us further, then I don't know. We could do worse."

"Marshal Koldunov, you didn't answer my question. What will Thatcher wear, or is she going to carry a white umbrella and play like Mary Poppins?"

"No, sir. A white suit. She will wear a white suit on 8 November. British women only wear white in the summer, so it will be highly unusual."

Peter the Great—my GRU boss—speaks for the first time since entering Ogarkov's office. "Marshal Ogarkov, I have additional news that everyone in this room needs to know. It is highly restricted information, for you only."

Ogarkov motions for him to continue.

"We have intelligence that Able Archer will include escalatory phases, beginning with conventional war, then proceeding to the mock use of tactical nuclear weapons in Europe. The exercise will end with a transition from nuclear war in Europe to global, strategic nuclear conflict. Further, the final phase—the strategic phase—will include the actual deployment of American Air Force B-52 nuclear bombers to Europe where they will conduct simulated cruise missile strikes on Soviet targets."

Ogarkov swears. "Jesus Christ, have they ever used actual B-52s from the United States in an Able Archer exercise in the past?"

The senior GRU man continues. "No, sir. It gets worse. Northern Fleet attack submarines yesterday detected an American ballistic missile submarine approaching our coastline. The American sub rose from its deep-ocean, covert location to its nominal launch depth, which is when our subs detected the American. The enemy sub stayed at launch depth for an unusually lengthy amount of time and opened *all* its missile tube doors—*all* its hatches—and simulated a salvo launch of its entire magazine. Just the missiles from that one American sub would cripple all of European Russia."

Everyone in the room is struck dumb. This situation with the Americans is spinning out of control.

The usually unflappable Ogarkov is visibly rattled. His eyes are on me again. "Colonel, do you think you can get the Americans and the British to agree to these sartorial choices? To these white hats and dresses?"

"Comrade Marshal, I'm confident that my contact can make it so. Yes."

Ogarkov stands up, turns his back to us, and looks out the window to a darkening Moscow sky. "I will not take our forces off full alert until I see three things. Firstly, Reagan must wear a white Stetson on the White House lawn. Secondly, Thatcher must wear a white suit on 8 November during her public appearances. Thirdly, we must get through the most dangerous period of Able Archer—I suppose it is the escalatory phase? Colonel, when is the most dangerous period of the exercise in your opinion?" Ogarkov is still looking out the window, with his back to us. It's disconcerting.

"Comrade Marshal Ogarkov, the most dangerous time is the nuclear release phase. We believe it will occur sometime between the evening of 8 November and early morning on the ninth. I will be at Potsdam House with the Americans at that time. They have agreed to this. I will bring an encrypted radio setup so that I can communicate with Moscow the entire time."

Ogarkov turns around to face me. "I see. Marshal Koldunov, you and General Ivashutin will be with me in the General Staff command bunker during that entire period—the days and nights described by the colonel. Marshal Konstantinov, you will be at the command center of the Moscow Air Defense District during the same timeframe. Understood?"

It goes without saying that everyone understands quite clearly.

"And Colonel, your radio will be tuned to communicate directly with the General Staff bunker. We will provide you with the equipment. You need to stay on the radio the entire time. You cannot sleep. Do you understand?"

"Yes, I understand."

"Colonel, you must keep me apprised of the Americans' actions through this radio. We can afford no miscalculations—no fuckups." Ogarkov sits down in his chair with an audible thud. "God help us. Thank you, comrades, you are dismissed. Now, I must go see Minister Ustinov."

Sunday, 6 November 1983—Evening

I hurry home for a couple of hours to pack my case. I had expected to depart Moscow in the morning, but the chief marshal of aviation has a plane waiting at the airfield to fly me to East Berlin's Schonefeld Airport tonight. Boyka has prepared a light dinner for us, and I have to break the bad news that I must leave tonight.

She looks profoundly worried. "When will you be home?"

"I will be home on the eleventh at the latest. If all goes well, I will try to fly home on the tenth, my love. I won't be gone long."

She is crying softly. "You won't be gone long if you can keep the planet from blowing up—do I have that right?"

I am crying now, too. "I won't let anything happen to you, my sweet girl. I will come home to you, I promise."

Christ, this better work. Cattani must be recovered from his injuries sufficiently to join me in Potsdam. This had better work . . .

CHAPTER NINETEEN

THE BRINK

Captain Kevin Cattani, United States Air Force
Potsdam House, Potsdam, German Democratic Republic
(East Germany)

Monday, 7 November 1983—Late Afternoon

The C-130 flight to West Berlin nearly breaks my will to continue the journey to Potsdam. Sick from a terrible headache, I imagine that this is how it must feel to have a brain aneurysm. I am so dizzy from my concussion during the flight that I vomit twice. My attempts at concealing my condition fail and Colonel LaRoche looks at me with alarm.

He shouts over the engine din. "Cattani, maybe this was a bad idea. Are you sure you're well enough to go to Potsdam?"

I try to smile through my agony. "Well, sir, this flight sucks. But I'll be much better once we land." I hope I am right about that.

As it happens, I do feel a lot better once we get off the plane. We stop at the MLM center in West Berlin to get a vehicle and then we are on our way toward the Glienicke Bridge and Potsdam. If I were feeling better, then I'd probably be anxious about driving through the Glienicke checkpoint. At this point, however, I just want to get to

Potsdam House and sit still long enough to regain my equilibrium.

Unsurprisingly, we are stopped once again at the Soviet checkpoint on the Glienicke bridge. Our old friend, the mustachioed warrant officer, approaches our vehicle for inspection. He takes our identification documents from the driver and walks around to Colonel LaRoche's side of the car. He tells LaRoche to roll down his window. I am curled up in a near-fetal position in the back.

"Colonel, you have three men in the car. Who is the passenger?"

"He's one of my guys. We have a meeting at Potsdam House, and I'm taking him there."

The warrant officer taps on my window, and I roll it down. A cold wind gusts through the opening.

The Soviet soldier recoils visibly when he recognizes me. "It is the young shitbird! I didn't think we'd see him here again. He looks unwell."

LaRoche sticks his head out of his window and cranes his neck up at the warrant officer. "Look, you fucker. I know you were part of the plan to ram our MLM car the other day. You killed one of my men and nearly killed the two officers who were in the car—including the guy in the back seat. If you try anything like that again today, I will kill you and anyone who fucks with us!!"

The warrant officer stands up to his full height and fingers his AKM assault rifle. "Fuck you, Colonel." He throws our documents at LaRoche. "Get the fuck off my bridge!"

LaRoche tells our driver to go quickly through the security gates. We're at Potsdam House in a matter of minutes.

Once there, LaRoche helps me get inside and gets me seated in a comfortable chair. "Kevin, just rest here until Levchenko arrives. I'll be back in a few minutes."

Colonel Levchenko arrives around 8:00 PM. This time, he is not alone. Colonel LaRoche guides the colonel and two Soviet enlisted men into the sitting room where I have been resting since our arrival.

LaRoche is not happy that Levchenko has brought the radio techs with him. "Colonel, who the hell are these guys and why are they here?"

Levchenko looks very tired, and he is taken aback by LaRoche's comment. He responds sharply, "Sir, they are communications technicians from the General Staff Headquarters—here to assist with the special radio equipment that will enable me to communicate directly with my senior leadership. I thought it prudent to have experts join me to deal with any unforeseen technical problems."

LaRoche is in a bad mood. "It would have been prudent to let me know in advance that you planned to bring people with you."

Levchenko sighs. "As you know, Colonel, communicating with your side is not easy at the moment. If I had a means of contacting you, I would have done so."

LaRoche calms down a bit. "All right, Colonel. Let's go to the conference room where we have our own radios set up. We'll install your stuff and do a comms check to make sure that everything is working."

I get up unsteadily and shake Levchenko's hand.

The GRU colonel looks me up and down. "Captain, you look better than the other day; however, you don't look well. Will you be all right?"

"Yes, Colonel, I'll be fine. I think I'll be much better after a good night's sleep. I hope I can get one tonight."

Levchenko nods, and I follow him upstairs.

The conference table is loaded with complicated-looking comms equipment. About half of it is cryptologic gear—crypto—to enable us to conduct classified discussions. Chief Jackson is monitoring the work of two US Army radio technicians who are running through a series of complex checklists.

Chief Jackson acknowledges me when I walk into the room. "Captain, you're looking better than the last time I saw you—not great—but better. Did my daughter look in on you at the hospital?"

"Yes, Chief. She's a terrific nurse and took great care of me. I don't think I could have traveled today if she hadn't prepped me so well this morning."

The chief smiles. "Yes, she is very professional. She's very opinionated, too, isn't she?"

"Yes, Chief. She is that!"

"Captain, I understand you were at Yokota for part of the time my daughter was stationed there. Did you meet her in Japan?"

Oh, boy—where is this going? "Yes, we met a few times. She's a wonderful young woman—if you don't mind me saying so."

He smiles gently. "Yes, she is, and no, I don't mind."

He turns to the radio techs. "All right, guys. Now is the moment of truth. Let's do a comms check with Ramstein."

The chief then addresses Colonel Lecvhenko in German. "Colonel, we have cleared space for you and your equipment at the far end of the table. Once we do our comms check, we will assist your men in installing your gear."

Levchenko responds in English, "Thank you, Chief Jackson. We will stand by until after your comms check."

Suddenly one of the American comms guys exclaims, "Chief, I can't get any good signal. We're getting bombarded with tons of noise. I can't raise Ramstein."

Colonel LaRoche asks, "What's the problem, Sergeant? We *must* have these comms up!"

The flustered sergeant stammers. "Colonel, sir, I don't know. We are being jammed. I haven't seen interference like this before. I can't find a way to get around it. It's blasting over a wide spectrum."

LaRoche turns to Levchenko. "Maybe your GRU major is fucking with us again. Did your people ever get around to arresting that asshole?"

Levchenko responds, "Colonel, I only just informed the GRU leadership about this reckless fool this afternoon. I doubt they have had time to act. He's probably still running the site here."

Levchenko then tells one of his radio techs to assist our Army guys who are not having any luck clearing up the jamming. A young Soviet soldier gingerly asks if he can look at the American electronics.

Colonel LaRoche translates the Russian's request to our radiomen, who move out of the way so that the Soviet tech can access their screens.

After a few minutes of investigation, the Russian tech discovers the problem. "Colonel Levchenko, I recognize this stuff—these waveforms. The GRU is jamming us! Not only is it hurting the Americans, but *we* won't be able to contact Moscow either if this keeps up."

Jesus Christ. What can happen next?

Levchenko begins to answer him when a large vehicle noisily pulls into the circular driveway in front of the house. We all hear a loud pounding on the front door.

LaRoche yells at Chief Jackson. "Chief, grab two of our guys and arm yourselves. Then go downstairs and see who the fuck is pounding down the door."

Jackson sprints from the conference room.

Moments later, Chief Jackson yells for Colonel LaRoche to come down to the lobby. LaRoche runs downstairs.

About five minutes pass, and LaRoche walks back into the conference room. "Well, Levchenko, you aren't going to fucking believe this. There is a heavily armed team of GRU Spetsnaz guys downstairs, and they want someone to guide them to the covert GRU site where we rescued Cattani. They can't find it and they finally came here out of desperation. Since Chief Jackson knows where the site is, I sent him out with your GRU team. He'll guide your guys to the site. Jesus, you just cannot make this shit up!"

Lecvhenko replies, "That team has been sent to arrest the GRU major. Colonel, Chief Jackson must get them to deal with the jamming, too! I'm certain the covert site is the source of the jamming."

"Way ahead of you, Levchenko. Chief Jackson explained the jamming to your team's commanding officer, and he understood. My guess is that we should be able to get a good signal in about thirty minutes. Jackson is on top of it. I just wish I could have gone with him, so I could see the look on the face of that motherfucker of a major when your guys arrest him."

Levchenko smiles for the first time tonight. "Me too, Colonel. Me too."

While they wait for the jamming to stop, the American comms guys help the Soviet techs set up the Russian equipment. Sometime later, they perform a comms check and get a good signal to Moscow. No jamming. Then they re-run the comms checks with Ramstein— all good. Thank God. Watching the four NCOs work together—two Americans and two Russians—I can't help but think of our respective national leaders who *aren't* talking to each other.

By the time the comms checks are completed, Chief Jackson is back in the conference room. "Gentlemen, everything went pretty smoothly at the GRU site. Our favorite major put up a fight, but his men didn't help him. I even got to wallop him in the face once, which felt really good. How are the radios?"

The senior American sergeant looks up. "Chief, we are five-by-five—all good. We have good signal to Ramstein, and I rigged one radio to connect us with EUCOM headquarters, too, in case we need it. The signal to Moscow looks good, too."

Colonel LaRoche smiles and says, "Guys, we have dinner for everybody set up in the dining room downstairs. I recommend we eat and then go to bed early. We won't be getting any sleep for a couple of days. Colonel Levchenko, you will have to bunk with your sergeants. We are tight on space. Okay?"

"Yes, Colonel LaRoche, that will be fine. I understand."

"All right, guys. Let's go eat. I hope we don't have any more excitement tonight."

Tuesday, 8 November 1983—Late Morning

I awake around 10:00 AM, after sleeping for almost twelve hours. Colonel LaRoche let me sleep in. God bless him. I feel better than I have felt in days. After getting coffee and a pastry in the kitchen, I go upstairs to the conference room.

I sense immediately that the atmosphere is extremely tense.

Colonel LaRoche sees me walk in and asks, "Kevin, how's your head this morning? On a scale of one-to-ten?"

"Colonel, if ten is the worst, then I am about a six, which is a huge improvement over yesterday."

"Great, Captain, that's great. Come with me into the hall for a minute."

We walk down the hallway to the other end of the building. "I have bad news from Levchenko. The Soviet General Staff won't stand down. They're going to maintain their highest level of alert while Able Archer is underway. Levchenko told me that he briefed Marshal Ogarkov himself. He told Ogarkov that Reagan and Thatcher won't play in the exercise, but that isn't good enough for old Ogarkov."

"Shit, Colonel, that is not good."

"Yeah, it gets worse. Levchenko wants us to get a message to the White House for Reagan to wear a white cowboy hat today when he walks across the South Lawn to board Marine One. Do you believe that shit? It gets even weirder. Levchenko promised Ogarkov we could get Margaret Thatcher to wear a white suit today at her public appearances. They want them to wear 'white' as a sign of peace or some bullshit. Christ on a crutch. I can't believe this shit. Levchenko told me about this last night after dinner—after you went to bed. I wanted you to get rest, so I didn't wake you up for this crap."

"Sir, what can we do?"

"I called General Palumbo this morning and asked him to do his magic with the White House. I just hope they can get to Mrs. Thatcher in time for her to take her summer wardrobe out of mothballs. It's November, for Christ's sake. She doesn't wear white in November!"

I can't believe this is the Soviet plan—for the leaders to wear white in public? "Well, Colonel, I guess we'll know soon enough."

"Yeah, the comm guys were able to bypass a bunch of East German and Soviet restrictions and they have rigged up a radio to the TV downstairs. We'll be able to watch BBC live on the tube. Thatcher's first public appearance today is at 11:00 AM, London time."

I check my watch. "That's less than an hour from now."

LaRoche is showing the strain. "I thought the Vietnam War was batshit crazy—what with Lyndon Johnson picking Air Force bombing targets from the Oval Office. But I think this Able Archer crap is even crazier." He pauses for effect, or simply for breath. "All right, let's get back to the conference room. Who knows what insanity has happened since we've been out here in the hallway?"

Fortunately, when we return, we learn that no new crisis has arisen since we left the conference room.

One of the Army radio techs says, "Colonel LaRoche, Ramstein has General Flannery on the line, and he wants to talk to you and Captain Cattani."

LaRoche makes an "okay" sign with his right hand. "Okay, Sergeant, put him on the speaker. Kevin, sit next to me by the mike."

The line opens, and we hear General Flannery. "Good morning, guys. What's new?"

I gulp and prepare to give him the bad news. "Sir, Moscow is telling us that they won't stand down their nuclear forces, including the SS-12s."

There is a long pause on Flannery's end. "What? The Russians won't stand down *any* of their nuke forces? How can we keep a lid on this thing if they don't meet us halfway? I mean we've already gotten the President and prime minister to stand down from Able Archer. Moscow can't show us *any* good faith?"

"General Flannery, this is Colonel LaRoche. I also have our GRU colonel—his name is Levchenko—at the table with us. He can hear everything you are saying, just so that you are aware."

Flannery doesn't skip a beat. "Hello, Colonel Levchenko. I assume you speak English. I appreciate the work you are doing with my team, but you have to get your leadership to act rationally. We need to see something from them—at the very least we need to see missile batteries in the forward area return to their garrisons—understand?"

Laroche moves the mike toward Levchenko. "Yes, General Flannery, I speak English. First, let me thank you for your great service in not escalating the crisis in Japan around the Korean airliner shootdown."

LaRoche shoots me a look as if to say, *what the fuck?*

General Flannery is back on the line. "Thanks for saying that, Colonel, but I need to see some action from Moscow—today!"

"Yes, General Flannery, I understand. The dilemma is that my leadership in Moscow believes they must keep forces on full alert until Able Archer is completed. They believe that the exercise is a thinly disguised ploy to start a preemptive nuclear war. Which leads me to my second point. In light of the view in Moscow, I think that NATO ought to drop the *live* exercise part of Able Archer—the American B-52 flights to Europe, for example. Those are viewed as very dangerous in Moscow. We also have reports that your nuclear ballistic submarines are conducting simulated fire exercises in the North Atlantic. Actions like those make the Soviet leadership believe that nuclear war may be close at hand."

There is a long pause on the Ramstein end of the line.

Finally, General Flannery continues. "Colonel, I understand that the Kremlin is paranoid. However, let me stress that the NATO leadership is equally suspicious of Soviet actions and intentions. We are in quite a pickle, and I need your help to get out of it."

Colonel Levchenko puts his hand over the mike and asks me a question. "What does pickle mean? Why is the general in a pickle? I know it is a food, but what does he mean?"

I respond, "Colonel, it means he is confronting a conundrum—a problem without an apparent solution."

Levchenko nods and uncovers the mike. "General, I understand. Let me offer this: if Prime Minister Thatcher wears white at her public appearance at the top of the hour, then I will call Moscow and tell them that this positive indicator requires a reciprocal action. I can predict Moscow's response. They will say that they must see

Reagan wear his white hat. Then we can discuss reciprocity. I believe that is what we will hear, General."

There is another long pause on the Ramstein end. "Levchenko, this is Lenny Palumbo. Look, Colonel, we need to see some positive action from your side. I know you understand that. Right? What can you do for us?"

I can see the wheels turning in Levchenko's head. "General Palumbo, I think Marshal Ogarkov will need to see a tangible change in NATO's force posture. Maybe, you could send the American B-52s home? Send them back without conducting their role in Able Archer? That may elicit a positive response. In any event, I propose that we conduct a radio call—a simultaneous radio call between Ramstein and Moscow later today. We could try for 5:00 PM Berlin time? We will need both you and General Flannery on the line."

There's a pause on the Ramstein end before Palumbo responds. "Okay, General Flannery agrees. We must let General Rogers at NATO and the Pentagon know about this proposed call, of course."

Levchenko breathes a sigh of undisguised relief. "Yes, General, of course."

Tuesday, 8 November 1983—Noon

The line goes silent, and we all hustle down the stairs to watch the BBC coverage of Prime Minister Thatcher's public appearance. We gather around the television set. The picture is grainy. We all wait on pins and needles for the prime minister to appear outside 10 Downing Street.

One of the Army sergeants yells out. "There she is sirs. There she is. All in white! How about that shit!"

Indeed, she is—dressed in white from head to toe. All of us smile at this small, yet important triumph. One leader down and one to go. President Reagan won't appear on the South Lawn of the White House until about 1:00 PM Washington time, which will be 7:00 PM

Berlin time. Moscow is two hours ahead of us, so it will be 9:00 PM there by the time Reagan strides toward Marine One.

Colonel LaRoche asks one of the Army techs, "Sergeant, how will we get TV coverage of President Reagan? The BBC won't show him leaving the White House."

"Sir, we are planning to jury rig a connection with US Armed Forces Network TV. We can't get any American-based TV here, of course. So Armed Forces TV is our only hope."

LaRoche shakes his head. "Will AFN TV even show the President live? They don't normally do that, do they?"

The sergeant replies, "That's correct, sir. But I have a buddy who produces the news for AFN, and he told me last night that they're going to get a feed that'll enable them to show the President live. If that doesn't work for some reason, AFN has a direct link with the White House Communications Service."

Tuesday, 8 November 1983—5:00 PM

Everyone reconvenes in the conference room for the 5:00 PM phone call with the leadership. The table is completely covered with radios and crypto gear. It is time for the unprecedented, simultaneous calls to Ramstein and Moscow. Our understanding from Levchenko is that Marshal of the Soviet Union Ogarkov has gathered all his military service chiefs together in his command bunker somewhere in Moscow.

General Flannery is in his command bunker at Ramstein with General Palumbo and other senior officers.

Ramstein and Moscow won't be able to talk directly to each other. Levchenko will communicate with his leadership through his radio, and we will do the same through ours. We'll have to translate each party's messages and then verbalize them through our respective radio systems. It's like a high-stakes game of telephone. The difference is that in this game, we can't afford any errors in translation or transmission.

The technicians perform a radio check and tell us that everything is good to go. General Flannery announces himself on his end. On the Soviet end, we hear a distant voice identify himself as Chief Marshal of Aviation Koldunov. It is surreal to hear the voice of the head of the Soviet Air Defense Forces. He is one of the senior officers of the USSR whom we only know through official photographs or grainy newsreels.

Colonel Levchenko speaks into his mike. "Comrade Chief Marshal Koldunov, good evening, sir. This is Colonel Levchenko speaking from Potsdam House. May I ask you to bring the microphone closer to your mouth, sir, so that we might hear you better?"

We hear some muffled fumbling on the Moscow end and then the chief marshal speaks again. "Is this better, Colonel?"

"Yes, sir, we hear you very well now. Thank you, sir. Sir, we have General Flannery of the US Air Force and NATO on the American radio. He is at Ramstein Air Base in West Germany."

There is a lengthy, silent pause. We all look at each other with the same thought. Has the line dropped? Have we lost Moscow?

Suddenly Chief Marshal Koldunov is back on the line. "Convey my greetings to General Flannery. We thank him for joining us this evening. Marshal Ogarkov sends the general his compliments. He knows the positive role that General Flannery played in the recent Korean airliner issue."

Wow. Marshal Ogarkov sends his compliments, and he knows about Flannery not shooting down the MiGs over the Tatar Strait! I almost forget to key my mike and translate the message for General Flannery.

Colonel LaRoche shoots me a stern look and I convey Koldunov's message to General Flannery.

He responds, "Kevin, please pass my compliments to Marshal of the Soviet Union Ogarkov and Chief Marshal Koldunov. Thank them for making themselves available for this important call."

Colonel Levchenko immediately translates Flannery's message.

Levchenko continues. "Comrades, I believe the Americans have a message for you regarding the current exercise."

That is my cue to ask General Flannery about the status of the B-52s that were scheduled to conduct a provocative simulated missile strike at the climax of Able Archer.

General Flannery speaks. "It took some doing, believe me, but we have succeeded in getting Strategic Air Command and NATO to cancel the simulated B-52 strike. The B-52s will remain on the ground in the UK. The plan is for them to return to their base in the United States sometime tomorrow—on the ninth. I trust this will be received as a concrete gesture of our good faith."

Levchenko translates for the Soviet leaders.

Koldunov responds after a brief pause, "Thank you, General Flannery. That is good news. The chief of the General Staff, Marshal Ogarkov, has authorized me to report that he will issue orders to the Warsaw Pact command structure this evening to stand down the SS-12 regiment that has deployed to the field. The unit will return to its garrison sometime tomorrow—the ninth. We trust that this will be received by your side as a concrete gesture of *our* good faith."

This is a very significant concession, and I translate the message as quickly as I can for the Americans in Ramstein.

Levchenko leans into my ear to tell me to clarify the intent of Moscow's message. He informs me that I have missed an important subtlety in Koldunov's statement. I make the requested clarification— the SS-12s won't return to their base until after the sun is up. It will take all night for the SS-12 units to tear down and prepare for a road march. Lastly, moving in daylight will make it easier for us to observe the SS-12 units returning to garrison.

The call wraps up with everyone agreeing to speak again later in the evening, after President Reagan departs the White House. Everyone in the conference room is relieved and smiling. The call is a success. Maybe we can pull this off, after all!

Tuesday, 8 November 1983—7:00 PM

We gather once more around the house's television set. The signal from Armed Forces Network TV is far worse than the signal we got from the BBC earlier in the day. The picture is intermittent. One of the comm techs has rigged his radio so that he can talk directly to the AFN TV studio. Even if we are unable to get a TV picture, the studio will be able to tell us what is happening in Washington.

Everyone in the room is frustrated that the TV picture transmission isn't working. We won't be able to see the President depart the White House. Colonel LaRoche tells everyone to go back upstairs to the conference room. We'll have to rely on the radio link to the AFN studio.

Back in the conference room, the mood is anxious. We wait for the Army sergeant to establish a radio link with the AFN studio. He has his headset on and gives us a thumbs-up sign to indicate the link is up. The rest of us in the room cannot hear the other end of the conversation.

At last, the radioman removes his headset and smiles. "Armed Forces Network confirms that President Reagan departed the White House wearing a white Stetson hat. The press people shouted questions at him. One asked why he is wearing his cowboy hat. Reportedly, the President responded, 'It's chilly here in Washington today. Nancy told me to wear a hat, so I wouldn't catch cold!'

The tension in the room breaks and everyone is smiling. How about that?!

Unfortunately, the break in tension is short-lived. LaRoche is handed a written message from one of the MLM NCOs. It's bad news.

LaRoche addresses all of us in the conference room and hits us with a cold dose of reality. "Well, you know that there is always one son-of-a-bitch that doesn't get the word. It appears that the SOB in this case is an SS-12 battery commander who has elevated his launcher like he is preparing to let his missile go!! We need to get the generals back on the radio ASAP!"

Colonel Levchenko looks crushed. "Yes, Colonel, but Marshal Ogarkov is traveling to the hospital to talk with General Secretary Andropov. I must ask Marshal Koldunov to have him recalled to the bunker immediately! We must ask the General Staff headquarters to get the Warsaw Pact commander to order this SS-12 unit to stand down."

We may have a nuclear war, after all.

Chief Jackson appears in the doorway. "Colonel LaRoche, the MLM team observing the SS-12 unit wants to know your orders. Should they attempt to engage the missile unit's troops to prevent them from launching?"

Can this be happening? We have an MLM team on the scene who could potentially prevent the launch of nuclear weapons. But if they move against the SS-12 unit, which has a heavily armed platoon protecting it, the MLM guys would likely all be killed. And an attack could make a nuclear launch a certainty!

Colonel LaRoche answers with characteristic bluntness. "Fuck no. They can't engage the missile unit! They'd be slaughtered, and their attack wouldn't have any positive effect. Radio the team— all the teams observing SS-12 units in the field—that under *no* circumstances are they to engage the Soviets. Clear?"

Chief Jackson nods. "Crystal clear, Colonel."

LaRoche mutters. "Jesus fucking Christ! Has everybody gone crazy? Where's the vodka?" He orders the radio techs to reopen the lines with Ramstein and Moscow.

General Flannery is the first senior officer to speak. "All right, we saw the President wear his white hat on the South Lawn. I hope that gesture reassures the General Staff in Moscow. I also passed Marshal Ogarkov's offer to stand down his SS-12 regiment to NATO and the Pentagon. I got a very positive response."

Colonel Levchenko translates Flannery's comments for those gathered in Moscow. He awaits a response for a surprisingly long time. As the silence in Moscow continues, those of us around the conference table exchange worried looks.

Finally, Chief Marshal Koldunov responds, "General Flannery, thank you for the update. Unfortunately, our intelligence people are telling us something very disturbing that occurred at the top of the hour."

I check my watch. It's 7:25 PM.

After a pregnant pause, Koldunov continues. "Yes, about twenty-five minutes ago the communications related to your Able Archer exercise became more difficult for us. It seems that NATO *changed the codes* for Able Archer communications, and now we can no longer collect anything of value. This is the worst possible signal for us. We know that a change in codes is a precursor to war! The fact that the change took place as your exercise enters its most dangerous phase is especially alarming. It seems we cannot trust NATO. Our offer to stand down a regiment of SS-12 missiles is rescinded."

I'm dumbstruck. I collect myself and translate this ominous message for General Flannery and his team. Now, there is a long silence on the Ramstein end of the line.

Finally, Flannery's voice comes through the speaker. "Marshal, we understand your concern. This is an unforeseen setback. We'll discuss this issue immediately with the NATO leadership. We remain committed to the promise we made earlier regarding the B-52s in Europe. I ask Marshal Ogarkov, respectfully, to consider the implications of not following through on his promise to stand down the SS-12 regiment. It's very dangerous for you to keep the SS-12s—especially, the SS-12s—on a hair-trigger alert. We will be available all night for further discussion. We believe it is imperative we keep open the line of communication through Potsdam House."

Colonel Levchenko translates General Flannery's message.

Chief Marshal Koldunov responds more quickly than before, "We agree to keep open the line of communication through Potsdam. We, too, will be here all night and we will stand by for further dialogue."

LaRoche speaks up in English. "Gentlemen, before we close the line, I have an important piece of information. My MLM guys have observed one SS-12 battery elevate its launcher with a nuclear-armed missile attached to it."

LaRoche doesn't wait for Levchenko to translate his remarks into Russian, but immediately repeats his statement in Russian himself and adds a comment. "I urge you to contact the appropriate authorities in your command structure and have this battery stand down immediately! Please!"

There is no audible response from Moscow and the lines with the Soviet leadership and with Ramstein go silent.

LaRoche stands up and punches the wall. "Goddamn it. What the fuck happened to the comm lines? Can you believe those motherfuckers at NATO changed the codes?! Goddamn it!! What do you do if you want to go to war for real? You change the goddamn codes! Christ on a fucking crutch!"

Levchenko stares at the equipment strewn across the surface of the conference table where the American radio techs and their Russian counterparts are frantically trying to bring up the comm lines. He sighs and says, "The Able Archer planners didn't miss any opportunity to make this exercise more realistic than any other, did they? They included live-flying fucking B-52s, they wanted the national command authorities present for the weapons release authorization, and they changed the communication codes for the authorization phase. If they intended to design an exercise to maximize the Kremlin's paranoia, then they did a fantastic job."

I can't believe this insane twist. We were so close to de-escalation. God knows how we get out of this alive. What do we do now?

Tuesday, 8 November 1983—11:00 PM

The night drags on. The radios are working again, and Levchenko has his headphones on so that he can talk privately to his leadership in Moscow.

Colonel LaRoche and I have a frantic conversation with Ramstein. We discuss different ideas that might defuse this situation. One of the general officers on Flannery's staff suggests that we just give the Soviets the new Able Archer communications codes. It is a sign of our desperation that we spend time trying to figure out how to get the codes released and sent to the Russians. Even if we received NATO's approval, it's totally impractical.

We get word from Ramstein that General Flannery is contacting NATO commander General Rogers, who's been behind closed doors with the Joint Chiefs of Staff in the Pentagon. Ironically, he is at the Pentagon to play his role in the final phase of Able Archer—and he can't be reached! As LaRoche likes to say, you can't make this shit up!

Colonel Levchenko is back on with Moscow. Suddenly, he takes off his headphones and slams them on the table. This is an uncharacteristic break in his normally unflappable demeanor.

Levchenko asks me and Colonel LaRoche to join him in a quiet corner of the conference room. "Gentlemen, you need to know something I just learned from Moscow. Our General Secretary Andropov is gravely ill and is confined to hospital. As you know already, the general secretary is deeply suspicious of NATO and the United States. He has been briefed on Able Archer."

LaRoche and I look at each other. Where is Levchenko going with this? It sounds ominous.

Levchenko continues. "I have been authorized by the highest authority to tell you that there is grave concern—concern that NATO's communications code changes portend war. Marshal Ogarkov has not yet informed the general secretary of the code change out of concern over how Andropov will react. The general secretary has the chegget with him—this is our version of your nuclear 'football.' He has the chegget with him in his hospital bed and he is gravely, perhaps fatally, ill! Senior officials are worried over the general secretary's mental state. I trust you understand what this means?"

Levchenko lets his statement sink in.

LaRoche bangs the wall again. "You mean your top guy is dying in a hospital bed and he has the nuclear button resting in his lap?! Are you fucking kidding me? He's dying, and could just decide to punch the button?"

Levchenko thinks for a moment. "You put it as delicately as ever, Colonel. But, yes, that seems to be the situation."

LaRoche issues a low whistle. "Jesus fucking Christ."

Levchenko puts his head in his hands and rubs his temples. "Unfortunately, gentlemen, it gets even worse. The General Staff has authorized me to tell you something very alarming. General Secretary Andropov has ordered a change to our master nuclear target list."

I ask, "What kind of change, Colonel?"

"He has ordered General Staff to stand by to implement a full counter-value target list."

Laroche's face turns red. "Counter-value?! What the fuck?! You're telling us that Andropov has ordered the implementation of your *city-killer* target list? He wants to kill the **entire population** of Western Europe and the United States?"

Levchenko nods, slowly. "Yes, and don't forget about Japan. He wants Japan's population eliminated, too."

The Kremlin has switched from a military target list to the list that ensures the enemy's population—our population—is annihilated!

Laroche tries to regain his composure. "Kevin, get the radio back up to Ramstein. This situation has taken a turn for the truly obscene. We need to get Flannery to inform Rogers and the Joint Chiefs. Levchenko, we need to try to get General Rogers to talk to Ogarkov via our rigged-up system here. Can you get Ogarkov on the line so that we are getting his message directly?"

"Colonel LaRoche, I'll do my best to get Marshal Ogarkov to participate. We're entering a very dangerous phase."

"Jesus fucking Christ, you are a master of understatement, my GRU friend." LaRoche pounds the wall with his fist again.

Wednesday, 9 November 1983—1:00 AM

General Flannery finally has been able to talk to General Rogers, who is ensconced with the Joint Chiefs at the Pentagon. Rogers has agreed to participate in a "call" with Ogarkov via our jury-rigged comms system. In addition, the Chairman of the Joint Chiefs has agreed to join him on the call. Our radio techs rig up a connection to the Pentagon. We will also have General Flannery linked up on a separate radio here in the MLM conference room.

The tension in our ersatz communications center is asphyxiating.

After completing a comms check with Ramstein, the Pentagon, and Moscow, we are ready to commence this momentous meeting.

Colonel LaRoche opens the call with the most senior military leadership of the Soviet Union and the United States with a simple, yet eloquent, statement. "Gentlemen, we are convened to defuse a confrontation that has reached a level of danger that requires immediate action. I believe that de-escalation can only be achieved by your intervention. We have learned alarming new information from Moscow about the health of the general secretary and his willingness to employ force, including the implementation of the Soviets' counter-value nuclear targeting list. I cannot overstate the seriousness of the situation we are facing."

LaRoche's comments are translated by Levchenko and are met with stony silence from the distant callers. I can only imagine the reaction in the Pentagon and at Ramstein to the news that the Soviet leadership is prepared to launch a city-killing nuclear war.

Finally, General Flannery breaks the silence. "Guys, what can we do on our end to tamp down these Soviet reactions to our Able Archer exercise? What advice do you have for the chairman and the NATO commander? You need to tee up specific actions for them to consider."

LaRoche looks at me for a suggestion and puts his hand over his mike to prevent anyone from hearing our conversation.

I whisper. "Colonel, General Rogers should order the Able Archer people to revert to yesterday's comms codes. Just go back to the codes they were using yesterday. This will be a gesture that Moscow will understand. What do you think, Colonel Levchenko?"

"I think you are exactly correct."

LaRoche removes his hand from the mike and conveys my proposal to the general officers gathered in the Pentagon and at Ramstein.

We anxiously await the response from the Pentagon.

General Rogers's voice comes on the line. "Gentlemen, I will so order the Able Archer team. We will revert to yesterday's crypto codes. The chairman concurs."

Levchenko immediately translates Rogers's words into Russian for Marshal Ogarkov and his General Staff officers.

We await their reaction. The wait seems interminable.

Finally, we hear Marshal Ogarkov himself speak. "We appreciate General Rogers's gesture. This will have a most salutary effect. For my part, I will reissue my order for my SS-12 regiment to return to garrison tomorrow morning. Your MLM teams will be able to observe and confirm this movement. Further, I personally will convey your actions to Minister of Defense Ustinov and General Secretary Andropov."

I am almost too nervous and excited to translate, but I manage to communicate the gist of Marshal Ogarkov's response.

`General Rogers is the first to respond from the American side. "Tell Marshal Ogarkov that we appreciate his positive response and that we hope we can bring this crisis to a rapid and mutually satisfactory resolution."

Levchenko translates this statement and the response from Moscow is calm and professional—almost placid.

And just like that—once again—it seems that the threat of imminent nuclear war is averted. We have stood on the brink of annihilation and stared into the blackness of the abyss.

The bizarre teleconference concludes. It's hard to believe that the crisis really is over. We all look at each other around the crowded conference table with numb expressions. I feel like a man who has had the gallows' rope lifted from his throat. Can this be the end of the madness?

The tension has been great, but the release is muted. We don't hug the Russians like the GIs who met the Soviet Red Army at the Elbe River at the end of the war against Nazi Germany. We sit quietly around the conference table.

Colonel LaRoche breaks the contemplative silence. "It's like a funeral home in here. Let's go downstairs and get some dinner. Chief Jackson, I hope you restocked the vodka supply in the kitchen. We're going to need it tonight."

Wednesday, 9 November 1983—8:00 AM

I am awakened from a deep sleep by Chief Jackson.

"All right, Captain, it's time to rise and shine."

Is it morning already? Why is he shouting? "Chief, can't I get a bit more sleep? Remember, I am recovering from a concussion."

The chief chuckles. "Yes, a concussion laced with a hangover. No, sir, you need to get up now."

"Okay, Chief. I'm up."

I get myself together and walk slowly to the conference room. Colonel LaRoche and Colonel Levchenko are both seated at the table, looking a bit worse for wear, given last night's vodka binge.

LaRoche looks me over. "Kid, you look like shit. I sincerely hope you don't feel as bad as you look."

Levchenko and I exchange a glance and I joke, "Colonel, I am fit and ready for a new mission. This last one was kind of a bore."

The two colonels share a laugh.

Levchenko speaks. "Captain, I will be returning to Moscow later today, provided everything goes as agreed to last night. I do want to thank you for your help in defusing this madness. I hope you recover fully from your injuries very soon."

"Thank you, Colonel. I know that all of us are glad that you were our Soviet partner. You know what General Flannery calls us? Including you, Colonel Levchenko?"

LaRoche and Levchenko look at each other and shrug.

"Well, he calls all of us the 'able archers.' That's what he calls our little team."

LaRoche smirks. "Given how fucked up this exercise was, I'm not sure I want to be part of a team that is named after it! This shit nearly got the world blown up."

Levchenko smiles and takes a different tack. "Captain, I think General Flannery has given us a fine name. The able archers. We accomplished a great deal in these last days. Of course, no one on either side will ever know about it."

Wednesday, 9 November 1983—7:00 PM

There are a few "hiccups" during the day as Able Archer 83 reaches its climax. We maintain radio contact with Moscow and Ramstein and the tense moments pass. By late afternoon, the MLM field teams confirm that the SS-12 regiment has returned to garrison. Both sides are still on high alert, but the crisis is diminishing. Able Archer 83 will wind down entirely over the next few days.

The world is ignorant of these events. It feels weird to know that. It's so unlike the Cuban Missile Crisis, which played out in such a public way.

It's 7:00 PM and Colonel Levchenko and his radio technicians are ready to depart for the airport. We shake hands and I tell the colonel that I hope to see him again under less calamitous circumstances. He laughs and pats me on the shoulder. "Something tells me that we will meet again, Captain. Good luck to you. Farewell for now."

I am anxious to get back to Ramstein. I want to see Sandy. I'll need time to put these events into perspective. Maybe she can help me do that. For the first time in what seems like a long time, I am hopeful for the future.

CLOSE TO THE EDGE

An Entry from General Levchenko's
Private Diary

A fter the perilous events of the fall of 1983, there has been a quiet, non-public reckoning in both the United States and the Soviet Union about this near-extinction episode.

General Secretary Andropov died in February of 1984 and was succeeded by Konstantin Chernenko, who himself was another elderly, transitional figure. Upon his death in March 1985, he was succeeded by Mikhail Gorbachev, who seems prepared to become Ronald Reagan's partner in addressing the looming nuclear threat. Gorbachev was a member of the Soviet Politburo during the nuclear crises of 1983 and is intimate with its nearly calamitous details.

It all started with the Korean airliner shootdown on the 1st of September, which resulted in confrontations and heightened nuclear alerts on both sides. If not for the cool thinking of the American General Doug Flannery, things would have turned out very badly.

The second major crisis was that awful night when my old friend Lieutenant Colonel Stanislav Petrov stood his ground and defused a potential calamity that the USSR kept a state secret for many years. Stas' saved the world and lost his career. The world remains ignorant of his heroic actions and the incident itself is a highly classified Soviet state secret.

The Able Archer crisis was the worst of the three. Once again, key individuals quelled the crisis. On the Soviet side, the KGB officer Oleg Gordievsky was instrumental in alerting NATO about the Kremlin's irrational concern over a surprise nuclear attack. As we know now, despite being a high-ranking KGB officer, Gordievsky was an agent of British intelligence for many years. With the able assistance of the British MI6, Gordievsky escaped from the Soviet Union this past July, with the KGB in futile, hot pursuit.

The American side and NATO benefitted greatly from General Lenny Palumbo's deep and intuitive understanding of the USSR's military posture. The world should be thankful that senior leaders were wise enough to act upon his recommendations to de-escalate the Able Archer crisis.

I know all three events have had a tremendous influence on Mikhail Gorbachev's desire to limit the potential for nuclear war. He learned a hard lesson in 1983 about the danger posed by nuclear weapons when they are kept on hair-trigger alert status. He also became aware of the importance of bi-lateral, senior-level communication.

For his part, Ronald Reagan also appears to have been shaken by the events of 1983. To his credit, President Reagan seems poised to use his second term in office to establish important curbs on nuclear arms in the United States, provided he gains the USSR's cooperation.

As for the Able Archers themselves, I have great respect for my young counterpart—Captain Kevin Cattani and his fellow "archers." I thank them (and God) that I was able to return to my wife safely after those awful events two years ago.

IVAN LEVCHENKO,
General Major, Soviet Air Defense Forces and the GRU
8 November 1985
Moscow, Russian Soviet Socialist Republic, USSR

ACKNOWLEDGMENTS

First and foremost, I must thank my wife Tracy Trencher Morra. Her contributions to *The Able Archers* are manifold: story editor, copy editor, and confidant who encouraged me every step along the journey. Tracy introduced me to her cousin, Phyllis Okon, a highly accomplished writer of children's and young adult books. Phyllis's advice has been invaluable, and she introduced me to my agent, Nick Mullendore.

I'd like to thank Nick Mullendore for his belief in me, consistent encouragement, and tireless efforts to secure a publisher. John Koehler of Koehler Books has been a great supporter and I applaud the expertise and professionalism of the entire team at Koehler Books.

When I was debating how to approach the topic, James K. Glassman encouraged me to write a fictionalized account of the nuclear war crisis of 1983. Ambassador Ken Adelman reviewed a draft of The Able Archers and helped me get the facts right. Early readers of the manuscript who gave me great feedback and encouragement include my sister Kathleen Sloan and friends Liz Rappaport and Carol Wilner. I'd like to extend my thanks to my photographer Melissa Maillett and my web designer Madeira James.

Lastly, I want to thank the team at the Secretary of Defense's Office of Pre-Publication Review. The team's professionalism and commitment to their mission is a tribute to our career federal civil service.

FACTUAL TIMELINE OF THE ABLE ARCHERS

30 April 1975: The fall of Saigon, Vietnam, and the triumph of Communist North Vietnam, ending the longest proxy war between the Communist bloc and the West.

1975–1978: The Communist Khmer Rouge regime takes control of Cambodia and conducts the worst genocide since World War II—popularly known as the "Killing Fields."

2 December 1975: The Communist Pathet Lao seize control of Laos, the final "domino" to fall in Southeast Asia, proving the utility of the much-maligned "domino theory."

March 1976: The Soviet Union deploys SS-20 nuclear missiles to bases in the western USSR, upsetting the delicate nuclear balance in Europe. The United States and NATO agree in 1979 to pursue a two-track approach with Moscow— (1) theater nuclear arms control talks and (2) the deployment of Pershing II missiles and Ground-Launched Cruise Missiles (GLCMs) to counter the SS-20 threat.

Soviet SS-20 on transporter-erector-launcher

Dec 1978–Jan 1979: A now-unified Communist Vietnam's armed forces invade Cambodia and drive the Communist Khmer Rouge from power. The surviving Khmer Rouge diehards flee to bastions in the Thai-Cambodian border region.

Feb–Mar 1979: The little-remembered Sino-Vietnamese War is waged. It begins when massive Chinese forces invade northern Vietnam (partly to punish Vietnam for ousting its Cambodian client regime—the genocidal Khmer Rouge), resulting in tens of thousands of dead on both sides. The war ends in stalemate, although both sides claim victory. The poor performance of the Chinese People's Liberation Army leads to major military reforms and eventual modernization of Beijing's armed forces.

4 November 1979: Militants supported by the Iranian Islamic government seize the US Embassy complex and imprison its staff in Tehran.

27 December 1979: Soviet KGB and GRU Special Forces occupy vital government, military, and media facilities in Kabul, Afghanistan. They kill the Afghan leader and "liberate" the capital city. The Soviets' 40th Army later occupies major cities and airfields throughout Afghanistan, kicking off one of the largest proxy wars of the Cold War between the USSR and the United States. The Soviet invasion signals the end of the period of détente between East and West that had begun earlier in the decade. The Soviet War in Afghanistan ends in February 1989, but war in Afghanistan does not. The ensuing civil war eventually brings the Taliban to power in Kabul.

May 1980: The largest Soviet intelligence program in history, Project RYaN, is launched by KGB Chairman Yuri Andropov. Project RYaN is designed to find indications of a NATO nuclear first-strike attack plan. It reflects the corrosive paranoia spreading throughout the top Soviet leadership about NATO's nuclear posture and intentions.

22 September 1980: Iraq invades Iran, initiating a war that will kill untold numbers of civilians and military troops on both sides. The war ends on 20 August 1988.

20 January 1981: Ronald Reagan is inaugurated as US President. US hostages in Iran are released and another period of détente between East and West ends. Reagan strikes a much more confrontational tone in relations with Moscow than his recent predecessors. He remains committed to the European deployment of Pershing II missiles and GLCMs, in line with the agreement made by President Carter and NATO.

American Pershing II test launch

10 November 1982: Soviet leader Leonid Brezhnev dies. He is succeeded by the far more belligerent Yuri Andropov, who had been Chairman of the KGB prior to assuming ultimate power. Operation RYaN was the brainchild of Andropov. The imminent deployment of American Pershing II missiles and GLCMs to Europe is evidence—to Andropov—that Operation RYaN needs to be amplified.

Soviet Premier Yuri Andropov

8 March 1983: President Reagan delivers his "evil empire" speech, in which he calls the Soviet Union the "focus of evil in the modern world." Reagan rejects the notion that the United States and the USSR are equally to blame for the global nuclear standoff. He asserts that the rivalry is a contest between good and evil.

23 March 1983: Ronald Reagan tells a national television audience of the existence of the Strategic Defense Initiative, a program designed to defend the US and its allies against nuclear attack. Western critics deride the program as a fanciful "Star Wars" pet project. The Soviets react with something approaching horror at the notion that the Americans could make Moscow's nuclear arsenal irrelevant. Unlike Reagan's Western critics, Moscow believes the United States can, in fact, build such a system.

US President Ronald Reagan

4 April 1983: In April 1983, the US Navy's Pacific Fleet is nearing the conclusion of a massive maritime exercise in the Sea of Okhotsk when US Navy fighter aircraft overfly Soviet military facilities in the Kurile Islands. The Soviets fail to respond to the airspace violation and many officers in the Far Eastern Air Defense Forces are purged, triggering an unprecedentedly aggressive air defense posture in the Far East that lasts through September 1983.

1 September 1983: A Soviet Air Defense Su-15 fighter shoots down Korean Air Lines flight 007, killing 269 civilians. This event precipitates a global crisis that both sides seek to use to their advantage. Tensions remain high for the rest of the fall of 1983. Normal lines of communication between Moscow and Washington break down in a torrent of acrimonious accusations. The leaders aren't talking to each other, in marked contrast to the formal and informal communications that existed during the 1962 Cuban Missile Crisis.

Soviet Air Defense Su-15 fighter

2–3 September 1983: Lieutenant General Charles Donnelly, commander of US Forces in Japan, de-escalates at least two situations that nearly cause direct air combat between the United States and the USSR. The immediate crisis passes without a shooting war, but East and West are bitterly divided over the incident and each side blames the other.

**US Air Force Lieutenant General Charles L. Donnelly, Jr.
(pictured here as a full general)**

27 September 1983: Lieutenant Colonel Stanislav Petrov helps prevent a general nuclear war amongst the Soviet Union, the United States, and NATO, by correctly assessing that a presumed American ICBM attack is actually a series of false alarms, erroneously generated by Soviet missile warning satellites. Petrov's heroics are kept secret by the Soviets and the fact of the satellite false alarms and Petrov's role in averting global existential disaster are not revealed until 1999. The United States government is unaware of the event until Petrov's former boss's memoir is translated into English shortly before the turn of the century.

**Lieutenant Colonel Stanislav Petrov
(pictured here as a major)**

23 October 1983: The US Marine barracks in Beirut, Lebanon, is bombed by Hezbollah—with Iranian and Syrian support—killing 241 US and 58 French military personnel.

25–29 October 1983: The US military invasion of Grenada overthrows the Cuba-backed Communist regime and provokes outrage in Moscow. The invasion also strains relations between Washington and London since Grenada is a British Commonwealth nation.

1–11 November 1983: The Able Archer 83 exercise is conducted by NATO—a massive nuclear war drill that Moscow assumes to be the culmination of its fears of a NATO nuclear first-strike attack—the same fears that prompted the KGB to initiate Project RYaN in 1980.

7–8 November 1983: Brigadier General Lenny Perroots convinces the NATO leadership not to respond in kind to unprecedented Soviet preparations for general nuclear war in the wake of Able Archer 83, thus de-escalating an ominous drift toward war.

**US Air Force Brigadier General Leonard Perroots
(pictured here as a Lieutenant General)**

November 1983: The first US Air Force Ground-Launched Cruise Missiles are deployed to RAF Greenham Common in England. The deployment confirms to Moscow that NATO is determined to modernize its nuclear forces in response to the perceived threat of Soviet SS-20 missiles.

9 February 1984: Soviet leader Yuri Andropov dies, and with his death, the leading proponent for Project RYaN passes from the scene. The nuclear posture of both sides gradually relaxes over the subsequent months.

Summer 1984: The Able Archer scare and Director of Central Intelligence William Casey's assessment of it have a profound effect on President Reagan's views on the potential for a nuclear war with the Soviet Union. Reagan confides to his diary that he had no idea the Soviets believed the West might launch a nuclear first strike. Many historians believe that Reagan's commitment to nuclear arms control in his second term was influenced greatly by the 1983 crisis. Reagan's new perspective leads to arms control talks later in the decade with Soviet Leader Mikhail Gorbachev. Director Casey's dire assessment of the Able Archer crisis is supported by a 1989 CIA Inspector General's report that concluded the CIA understated the danger of the events at the time they occurred.

BIOGRAPHIES OF THE FICTIONAL PROTAGONISTS OF THE ABLE ARCHERS

Current as of November 1983

Kevin Cattani, United States Air Force Intelligence

Born: Southern Virginia, USA, in 1956

Education: BA, College of William and Mary, Williamsburg, Virginia, 1977

US Air Force Training:

- Air Force Officers Training School, 1977, San Antonio, Texas
- Armed Forces Air Intelligence School, 1977–78, Denver, Colorado
- Case Officers Basic Course and Paramilitary Course, CIA, 1978, Williamsburg, Virginia

Air Force intelligence officer with a special operations
specialty code

- Special Activities unit, Tokyo, Japan, 1979–1981
- Current rank and assignment: Captain; Chief of
  Intelligence Analysis, United States Forces, Japan, Yokota
  Air Base, 1981–1983

Languages (in descending order of proficiency): English,
Russian, Japanese

Ethnicity: Mixed Italian/Luxembourgish/Irish

Marital status: Unmarried

Sports background: College track and cross-country

Ivan Levchenko, Soviet Air Defense Forces/ Military Intelligence (GRU)

Born: Crimea, Ukrainian Soviet Socialist Republic, USSR, in 1939

Education:

- English immersion school—grades 1–12, Sevastopol,
  Crimea, USSR
- BS, Kiev Higher Engineering Radio-Technical College
  of the Soviet Air Force, Kiev, Ukrainian Soviet Socialist
  Republic, USSR, 1961
- Military-Diplomatic Academy—a three-year post-graduate
  school in intelligence and foreign affairs, Moscow, Russian
  Soviet Socialist Republic, USSR, 1964.

**Air Defense Force of the USSR—Soviet Military
Intelligence (GRU)**

- Beginning in 1964, assignments as a junior and mid-level intelligence officer to units in the Western Military District of the USSR, the Group of Soviet Forces, Poland and the Group of Soviet Forces, Germany (East Germany)
- Assigned as senior Air Force officer to the Soviet Military Liaison Mission in Frankfurt, West Germany, from 1980–1983
- Current rank and assignment: Colonel; Deputy director for intelligence at the Red Banner Moscow Air Defense District, Moscow, Russian Soviet Socialist Republic, USSR

Languages (in descending order of proficiency): Russian, English, German, Polish

Ethnicity: Russian

Marital status: Married to Boyka Levchenka, a Ukrainian-born musician educated at the Tchaikovsky Conservatory, Kiev, Ukrainian Soviet Socialist Republic, USSR

Sports background: College track and cross-country

Printed in the USA
CPSIA information can be obtained
at www.ICGtesting.com
JSHW020754010224
56301JS00003B/19